LUNERSEE

BY

EDWARD G. GREGER, M. D.

Order this book online at www.trafford.com
or email orders@trafford.com

Most Trafford titles are also available at major online book retailers.

Note for Librarians: A cataloguing record for this book is available from Library and Archives Canada at www.collectionscanada.ca/amicus/index-e.html

Printed in Victoria, BC, Canada.

ISBN: 978-1-4269-0852-1 (sc)
ISBN: 978-1-4269-0853-8 (hc)

Our mission is to efficiently provide the world's finest, most comprehensive book publishing service, enabling every author to experience success. To find out how to publish your book, your way, and have it available worldwide, visit us online at www.trafford.com

Trafford rev. 2/02/2010

 www.trafford.com

North America & international
toll-free: 1 888 232 4444 (USA & Canada)
phone: 250 383 6864 ♦ fax: 812 355 4082

FOREWORD

With the exception of any allusions to the Central Intelligence Agency, all of which are fictional, much of this novel is based on historical fact, actual events and some of my personal experiences. What is true and what is fiction will be left to the imagination of the reader. This book is dedicated to several individuals, some my friends and some my enemies, who may recognize themselves as characters in this novel.

The Author

TABLE OF CONTENTS

I

A Consummation Devoutly
To Be Wished

May 1, 1990 - 9 p.m.

"You are a beautiful man," she said as she looked down on his naked body lying motionless on the bed. She stripped of the last of her clothes, tossing her bra and bikini underpants on the floor. She bent down over him, letting her long black hair flow over him as she guided her taut left breast toward his mouth inviting his kiss.

"Just close your eyes and let me do everything," she said, starting to breathe heavily as she was caught up in her own activity. She then pulled her breast back, bent over him and kissed him, her tongue darting in and out of his open mouth. She followed this with a trail of kisses on his body.

She stared at his still limp penis unbelievably for a few seconds, pulled back and sat up on the bed.

"I am sorry, M'Sieur, but I have tried my best," she said. "I am afraid that you have wasted your money."

She looked at him as she quickly dressed. He could not tell if it was a look of anger, disgust, or pity.

"I have met gay men before. You really shouldn't try to change. I've never seen one of you able to do it." She was an extremely beautiful girl in her mid 20s with coal black hair, fair skin and a perfectly shaped body. She was also a professional - a very highly priced professional. She was also proud and could not accept the fact that she could not arouse a "normal man." He just had to be a homosexual in her estimation. She finished dressing and quickly left the room without even saying goodbye.

He hated himself for trying to have sex even with such a beautiful woman such as her. He had not even asked her name. But then prostitutes never did give their real names. She was French, probably on circuit from the French Riviera. She had come to Lugano, Switzerland, one of the more affluent cities of Europe. He had met her at the bar of the Excelsior Hotel in Lugano and had brought her to his hotel room in nearby Gandria.

Gay, he muttered to himself. If anyone were not gay, it was he. He just felt as if he had tried to be unfaithful to the memory of the woman he loved. The reason he had even tried was that he thought it might help ease the pain of losing her. He had killed her with his own hand. It was also probably like a condemned man having his last wish, savoring what he had enjoyed most in life. It was just like a man who was about to be executed that ordered the finest food for his last meal. He had, in fact, visited his favorite restaurant, the Antico in Gandria. He had ordered his favorite local seafood meal but he could not enjoy it. Probably no man facing execution ever enjoyed his last meal. Even his last attempt at sex turned out to be a failure.

He was staying in Gandria in a small hotel that was built on the edge of Lake Lugano. Gandria was a small fishing village on the outskirts of the city of Lugano. He had often gone there when he wanted to get away from the busy, hectic world. He had even spent wonderful, peaceful days there with the woman that he so deeply loved. That is another one of the reasons that he had returned there. It was filled with the best of memories of her and if he were going to die, he wanted it to be where they had shared such wonderful times together. He just knew that he was going to die that night. They had spotted him two nights ago in Lugano. He recognized them because he was actually in the same profession that they were. It takes one to know one, he thought. They had probably been searching throughout western Europe for him and it was only a matter of time until they found him. He also knew why they did not take him out the night that they first saw him. It meant that the "old man" wanted to do it personally. It would take two days for him to reach Lugano so tonight had to be the night.

He expected the "old man" to come after him and he understood. He would have done the same in a like circumstance. He did not hate the "old man" and because of their special relationship - they both had loved the same woman, in different ways, of course - he actually liked him. In fact, he felt a special kinship to him. What he had done deserved his death in the eyes of the "old man". He, himself, had hated himself for what he had done. He even considered punishing himself by suicide. But his early Roman Catholic indoctrination had prevented him from doing that. If there was a life hereafter, that solution would have prevented him from joining, in death, all those whom he had loved in life. He would just have to let the "old man" do it. With self preservation instincts he wondered how he would react at the moment of truth. He had thought a lot about death in the last few days. It was something he had been oblivious to objectively in his chosen profession but subjectively was a different matter. As he stared out of his hotel room at the deep waters of Lake Lugano directly below, he thought of all his personal experiences with death. As a young boy he had cried at the lifeless body of his Irish Setter which had been run over and killed by a car right in front of his eyes. He prayed to God to return the life of the beautiful animal. The finality of death eventually set in and in tears he had to bury his beloved pet in his back yard. The deaths of his wartime comrades, his parents, and, recently of two women he loved had finally taken their toll on his reserve. He now actually began to look forward to his own demise in order to rejoin all those he loved.

The almost forgotten words kept coming back to his mind as he thought about death. "To die, to sleep. To die - to end the thousand natural shocks that flesh is heir to. To die. What dreams would come when we have shuffled off this mortal coil." The Bard had undoubtedly wondered the same as he had. He had heard of several cases of people who had been resuscitated - brought back to life from the early stages of death. They had spoken of a wonderful glow in after life - a feeling of peace and contentment. They had resented actually being brought back to life.

He wondered what it would soon be like for him. Would he soon meet those whom he had loved who had preceded him in death? He even wondered if he would see his boyhood pet that he had loved so much. He could picture Sheba running up to him as he returned, wagging her tail happily as she had always done when he arrived home from school or from wherever he had been. He would see his mother's soft, gentle smile of relief when he would arrive home. Mothers always worried when their children were out. His father, who never showed much emotion, even though he felt it, would secretly be happy to see him. And, of course, the woman who passionately loved him would rush into his arms and smother him with kisses. "To die, tis a consummation devoutly to be wished."

He dressed, putting on his best slacks and sport shirt. After all, he would not want to be found naked. There should be modesty, even in death, he thought.

He pulled a lounge chair over to the edge of the open window where he could look out at the beautiful lake below and still see the door of the room. He loaded his automatic, attached the silencer, and put it on the end table next to his chair. He doubted if he would use it in self defense but it was like a natural reflex action for him. He sat in the lounge chair and waited. He knew that they would come that night.

As he stared out at the beautiful, peaceful lake, all the names that had directly or indirectly led to his present predicament flashed before him - Bo, Max, Jackie, Susan, Shira, Sonya, Ushie, Konzett, Luckner, Mueller.

Mueller ....

II

THE FACTORY

Dachau, Germany - April 10, 1945

The early morning air was heavy with the mixture of the usual morning mist, typical of the Bavarian countryside, and the black, acrid smoke belching out of the four high smoke stacks of the "factory". The "factory", on orders of Reichsfuhrer Heinrich Himmler, himself, was on a twenty-four hour schedule, racing against time to meet the "quota" determined by the authorities in Berlin.

Oberst Ludwig Mueller, the Kommandant at the "factory" turned his swivel chair form his large oak desk and looked out the window with his field glasses at the nearby town and at the imposing castle of Wittelsbacher that overlooks the whole area. Even from his office he could see the early rising townspeople emerging from their apartments and private houses. Some opened their shops, others were on their way to nearby ammunition factories that somehow escaped the incessant, heavy allied bombing that was obliterating much of the Bavarian Hauptstadt of Munich just seventeen kilometers to the southeast.

The Kommandant's "factory" had actually been an old ammunition factory back in 1933 and had been converted by Reichsfuhrer Himmler to a Schautzstaffel (SS) run prison, complete with facilities to implement the Fuhrer's ultimate solution to rid Germany of the undesirables. They included the criminal element, mentally ill, homosexuals, and others who were deemed to be a threat to the building of a pure, healthy, Teutonic, Aryan society. This latter category proved to be a convenient one which could include all those who opposed the direction of the National Socialist Party such as communists, opposing political activists from the right or left, and in the last year of the war, Jews. All were believed by the Fuhrer to be a threat to a utopian Germany that he had visualized.

Mueller was a frustrated man. He was the perfect physical picture of a Prussian military figure. His close-cropped hair had turned from the Aryan, Nordic blond to a very prematurely gray. He had, however, been cursed with a familiar trait of nearsightedness which had kept him out of a combat command and relegated him to the SS as a prison officer. He would have been a general by now, he believed, if only his eyes had not betrayed him. But by a strange paradox, his sharp eyesight, albeit with strong eyeglasses, had been a major strength in his favorite hobby. Mueller was an ornithologist, a bird watcher. It seemed a strange interest for such a strong, athletic person, but only to those "outsiders" who do not understand the beauty of a bird in flight, the beauty of the form and colors in every species of bird and ultimately, the strength and stamina required to seek out in the woods and mountains, the rare, uncommon birds seen at the most inaccessible places. Indeed Kommandant Mueller had become one of the foremost authorities in the Reich on the color and habits of our feathered friends. Some birds are endowed with a natural camouflage to protect them from their natural predatory enemies. This knowledge of birds' colors and habits by the Kommandant had been utilized by the military in designing cover and camouflage for their equipment as well as for factories built into the hillside and forests. What a strange contribution to the war effort, he often thought, as he devoted himself to his duties at the "factory".

The "factory" was actually a death camp. The facilities, many of which the Kommandant had, himself, helped design, were a reflection of his efficient, organized mind. When the demands of his "quota" could not be met by existing facilities, Mueller had designed a much more efficient facility. The original crematorium with only one stack had been supplemented by a new permanent brick structure where the "work flow" was more organized. The subjects would first be brought into the "shower" room, many right from the train which brought them to the city of Dachau. The "shower" heads, however, were not installed to use water but rather a very quick acting, efficient gas, Zyklon (cyanide). The next room which is adjacent to the crematorium was for temporary storage of the "subjects". It was much more orderly to keep them there for the more slow process in the crematorium. Here they could be examined for gold dentures or whatever should not be wasted in the ovens. Also the "shower" could then be efficiently utilized for the next entrants. Each was given a towel and a bar of soap to convince them, as Mueller repeated the oft used axiom, that "cleanliness is next to Godliness". The crematorium was a model of efficiency. The ovens were stacked one on another, doubling their capacity in one swoop. Mueller was proud of his efficiency and, in fact, had received a special, personal commendation on it from Himmler, himself. But Mueller felt frustrated. He could have been even more efficient but the priority in the past year had gone to Oswiecim (Auschwitz) and Buchenwald where the majority of "the Jewish problem" was sent. Mueller's facility, although having its share of Jews, really was used for all enemies of the Reich. He was disgruntled that the larger facilities were the other two. He was not given, as yet, his allocated quota of Zyklon and he had to improvise. He used the carbon monoxide generated by the exhaust of his trucks. He could have handled it well if only given the support; however, it was a matter of logistics, he was told. After all, Oswiecim was in Poland, with its large Jewish population and Buchenwald was centrally located for those from the occupied countries as well as Germany itself. It was jut another one of Mueller's frustration. To increase "production, especially since there were larger shipments of Jews coming from Italy, Hungary, and Austria, Mueller decided to handle the overflow by firing squads. A ditch was dug just outside the overfilled gas chamber where the subjects could be simply shot. Just by inclining the bodies toward the ditch, the blood could be drained and they would burn much easier. Mueller was proud of his innovation and thought he might receive another commendation from Himmler. Who knows, perhaps he would even become a general if time would not run out.

Mueller, unlike some of the other operating personnel, did not take any particular personal gratification out of his work at the "factory". He was no sadist but rather a typical example of the product of the German bureaucratic system which made him and others like him oblivious to pain and suffering of others. It was the result of "insensitivity training" that was the outcome of the Germanic educational system that started in the grammar school and extended through the university level. The "Herr Professor attitude" in which authority was unquestioned carried over to all facets of German society. It was also a good indoctrination for preparing young men to serve in the military. Mueller could run his camp because "high authority" ordered him to do so. He did what had to be done.

As he glanced out the window again he was disturbed. Just the day before he was visited by an Oberst Bock from Berlin. Bock had a special secret message from Martin Bormann. The Kommandant was a long-time friend of Bormann who was one of the Fuhrer's most loyal and trusted lieutenants. In the message Bormann stated that the war was over. The Russians were already into Austria to the south and it was only a matter of time until they took Berlin where the Fuhrer had sworn to make a last ditch stand. The Americans foolishly had halted at the Elbe. They could have gone directly to Berlin with little or no opposition and their General Patton was furious at being held back. Mueller should not consider the war lost but rather just the present battle. Diehard remnants of the Elite SS were forming units that called themselves "Werewolves". Theirs, however, was just a delaying action giving those who were to carry on, time to flee the country, to the Mid-East and South America. In time, they would return and carry on their "holy war". Mueller's orders were simple. He was to join Bormann in Zurich, where there were the required documents as well as funds in the Swiss bank to get them to South America. On the way he was to hide some of the huge cache that had been accumulated from the prisoners at Dachau. It was too risky to attempt taking it into Switzerland at this time. It would be rather cumbersome and the Swiss border was heavily patrolled by security border guards. This cache had grown to a sizeable amount through the years. Mueller could not see the gold in the dental work of those gassed going to waste. With his typical efficiency he had a small room constructed adjacent to the crematorium. Those who had considerable amounts of gold bridgework were sent to this room after they had been gassed where it was extracted and then melted down into bars. Most of the unfortunate prisoners also brought all the possessions that they could carry. They were relieved of them soon after they arrived at the camp. There was a considerable amount of diamonds and other precious gems and Mueller had even managed to accumulate a king's fortune in rare stamps. This was all done with the approval of Bormann and was to serve to finance their return to power in the future.

The knock on the door interrupted his thoughts. It was Feldwebel (Sergeant) Franz Luckner, his special assistant.

"Herr Oberst, you requested that I report to you at eight o'clock."

"Yes, come in, Luckner," answered the Kommandant. "I have also asked Major Reichardt to join us, but I wanted to speak to you first."

Luckner was a young man, still not twenty years of age who had been hand-picked by Mueller soon after Luckner had graduated from the Volkschule in the Vorarlberg part of Austria. Vorarlberg is the western mountainous part of Austria that borders on a part of northern Italy to the south and on Switzerland to the south and west. Luckner was from a small village called Brand just south of Bludenz in Austria which, of course, from the time of the Anschluss, was a part of The Reich. Bludenz was a beautiful alpine town which really had not seen much of the war other than having its young men conscripted and sent off to fight for their new "fatherland".

Luckner never could understand why he had been selected to be assigned to Dachau. He certainly did not relish the thought of working in a prison, especially with the brutality that he witnessed there. However, as he was told, these prisoners were criminals and enemies of the State, and they did not have to have any personal contact with them. He preferred not even to think about it and his primary responsibility was to be an aide to the Kommandant. Selfishly he thought that perhaps he was lucky. All of his male boyhood friends and classmates from the Volkschule had been called into the Wehrmacht and most of them had been killed or were missing in action.

Mueller had taken advantage of Luckner's personal knowledge of the western Alps to go on Ausflugs (small trips) to see the rare alpine birds. He was particularly interested in the area bordering on the Swiss-Lichtenstein border which was Luckner's boyhood backyard. Luckner welcomes these Ausflugs since it gave him the opportunity to visit his aging mother and grandparents who still lived in the small village where the Luckner family had lived for generations. His father had died in an accident when Luckner was a little boy and he was raised by his mother and grandparents. His grandfather was old and Luckner never experienced the companionship that a father could offer. The visits also gave him the opportunity to bring them tins of delicacies from "the Gross Stadt" that Mueller had little difficulty in obtaining.

Actually on these trips he saw a different Mueller from the cold, authoritarian Kommandant that he saw at Dachau. On these trips, Mueller often addressed him as Sohn (son) rather than by his name or his military rank. At these times he often thought of Mueller as a surrogate father. They enjoyed visiting the high alpine Huttes (mountain huts or inns) and the Gasthauses that one could still find in the mountains and villages. For a while it was even possible to forget that there was a war on or that there was a Dachau. Mueller, at these times, seemed like a warm person who loved to talk about the rare bird that he had spotted that day, or about the rock formations they had seen. He lectured Luckner on how the mountains in that area, the northern chain of the Dolomites, were a product of the glacier age and he would point out the striations in the rock formation. Actually Mueller was a very learned man. When he realized that his eyesight could prevent him from a military career, he entered Heidelberg University and received his doctorate in the sciences. He had planned to be a university professor. It was only because of the war that he entered the military as a reservist and eventually ended up in the non-combat assignment in Dachau.

"Luckner, I want you to plan a trip for four of us to Brand," said Mueller. "We will need a truck to carry us that far but then we will need at least four mules to take us up into the mountains. You can borrow them from your friends in the area. They will be reimbursed, of course. We will return them after we use them to reach the Lunersee area. I do not want to requisition the mules from our Wehrmacht who have some in that area. I want as few people as possible to know about our trip. We will be accompanied by Major Reichardt who will be joining us soon and Oberleutnant Konzett who is coming from Berlin. We should be ready to leave two days from now in the early morning."

There was another knock on the door as Major Axel Reichardt entered. "You asked me to see you, Herr Kommandant."

"Yes, yes," replied Mueller. "Come in and be seated. I have just informed Feldwebel Luckner here that we will be traveling to Vorarlberg, and he will be making arrangements for our trip. You can go now, Luckner, and," he added, "let me know if there are any problems. We will leave at four a.m. the day after tomorrow."

As Luckner left, Mueller rose and closed the door behind him. The Kommandant suffered from a mild case of claustrophobia and normally left his door at least slightly ajar. Perhaps that is one of the reasons that he so loved the outdoors and his special hobby. Only when he discussed very sensitive material did he completely close his door.

Major Reichardt, who was Mueller's operations officer, actually ran the day-to-day operations of the facility. Mueller did not want to be concerned with details and since Reichardt loved detail and minutiae, he was ideally suited for his duties. Mueller did not actually like Reichardt; in fact, he thoroughly detested him.

Reichardt was a Jew, or at least half a Jew. He was a product of a Jewish father and a Roman Catholic mother. He denied his Jewish ancestry and at least outwardly practiced Catholicism. Mueller believed that it was, perhaps, for survival purposes and, after all, was not the late Rheinhard Heydrich also part Jewish? Mueller, although he considered himself an atheist, did not respect those who denied their birthright. In a way he admired many of the Jews who came to his facility. They were proud to be Jews and he met few who would renounce their beliefs, even in the fact of their inevitable fate.

Mueller was very clever in how he staffed his operation at Dachau. Many of the permanent personnel were Ukranians or from German-occupied lands, especially Slavic areas. They never could return to their native countries because they were considered traitors. They were not even accepted as first class citizens of the Reich and their only loyalty was to Mueller and their duties. Mueller also believed that there was a sadistic strain in all Slavs and, in fact, many of them seemed to enjoy their work. The Ukranians, especially, all seemed to hate Jews, Poles, Russians and just about everybody.

Other operating personnel at the facility were former inmates themselves. They were temporary, however, and Mueller saw to it that they joined their contemporaries in the ovens after serving a "tour" which they willingly did to survive for a while longer.

Reichardt was an athletic man about the same age as Mueller. He was a lean and muscular man who watched his diet and exercised religiously. He had dark, but graying hair, a prominent nose, and a goatee which he wore to hide his weak chin. He was an intellectual of sorts who could quote from the classics to Neitsche. He was Viennese and, as many Austrians after the Anschluss saw opportunities and took advantage of them to survive. He privately detested his work, detested Mueller even more and longed for the days when he could again, after a night at the Statsoper, enjoy a Sacher Torte and a Kaffee in his favorite coffee house in the Kartnerstrasse in his beloved Vienna.

Reichardt was also a closet homosexual. He had never made love to a woman - the thought of it nauseated him so he could not even be considered bisexual. Other than a brief adolescent encounter he had not even had sex with a male. It was a sure ticket to the gas chambers in the Reich. Reichardt felt that those in power in Germany who so vociferously condemned homosexuality were, themselves, at least latent, if not overt, homosexuals and that included the Fuhrer himself. But he was not about to test his luck by revealing his sexual orientation. At parties and at private social gatherings he had always tried to give the impression of being a "ladies man" and many times he had propositioned some young buxom fraulein. He had always done so within earshot of someone nearby, thereby insuring that he would be rejected. On the rare occasions that he was accepted, he found either a clever excuse or just privately backed out.

"Major Reichardt," said Mueller, "I asked you to see me here this morning because of a very sensitive matter that will be just between you, me, Feldwebel Luckner, and an Oberleutnant Konzett who will be joining us some time tomorrow."

Mueller repeated what was in Bormann's special message - that the present war was soon to be over and that they had been selected by Bormann himself to carry on the struggle. "I do not know what Oberleutnant Konzett's role will be with us," Mueller went on, "but I suppose that he will let us know when he arrives tomorrow. He is related to Bormann. Here is what I want you to do, Herr Major. We have accumulated a considerable amount of gold, diamonds, and other valuables in the time that we have been here. Only you and I have the combination to the vault. I want you to arrange to pack four large Kisten (containers) of what is most valuable and compact to transport to a destination that I will inform you of later. Oberleutnant Konzett will also be bringing some valuable documents and secret material. I, myself, will pack a fifth Kisten. It will all have to fit in a medium-sized truck that Feldwebel Luckner is preparing."

"We will be going out of the country and will not be returning. Fortunately, since you have no immediate family, this will not be a problem for you, but you should tell no one about it."

"Incidentally, we are receiving a new contingent of guards. Our present guards are joining a Waffen SS division on what is left of the eastern front. I want you to see to it that our present "operating personnel" take their turn in the "showers". Do that tonight. The less number there are around here who know us, the better it is. Luckner will have the transport truck ready for you."

Reichardt saluted and left the room, heading for the prisoners' compound. He would select new "trustees" from some newly arrived prisoners. They would do anything to stay alive, he thought to himself, even work the ovens. He entered the prison compound and glanced up at the arch that Mueller had constructed at the gate. It held a large sign with the words "ARBEIT MACHT FREI" (Work Makes You Free). Damn Mueller, he thought, he enjoyed these little slogans even though he knew that entrance was really meant to be a one-way street. But it probably did give hope to the incoming inmates who thought they would one day see freedom. Mueller had, indeed, coined the slogan and Himmler liked it so much that he ordered it to be at the entrance to all the "camps".

He headed over to the guard office to see the newly arrived guards and give them his latest orders. The air was still and the usual prevailing winds from the northwest were not blowing. He welcomed the winds because they helped to blow away the stench of death from the ovens. He often thought of the townspeople in the nearby town of Dachau. Even though there was strict security at the camp and no unauthorized people were allowed, surely the smell from the camp reached them and they knew what was happening. Also many of the inmates from the camp were sent on work details to the town for some of the prominent party members and for the camp military personnel who lived in the town. "I am sure that they will all deny knowing anything about the camp," he thought to himself. But then again, how could he blame them? Was he not doing even worse just staying alive in this crazy world? He would actually be happy to be leaving with Mueller. He certainly had no love for Germany and he knew quite well what his fate would be when the allies won the war. All those who had any association with the concentration camps surely would be considered war criminals. He had heard over the BBC, which he was able to pick up on his short wave radio, that the allies would convene tribunals after the war to try those accused of committing atrocities. He suspected that they would be going to Switzerland since that was a short distance away. This was one time that he appreciated Mueller's efficient mind. He knew that he would find a way to get them there.

Adjacent to the guard office was the shower room. He stopped and watched as a new group that had just been brought in from the train siding was being issued soap and towels. There was no longer any attempt at modesty and men and women as well as some children were ordered to strip naked before entering the "showers". They were even instructed to pile their clothes neatly and in their designated rows to make it easier to find when they returned. Most of them had all their remaining worldly belongings with them and apprehensively left them with their clothing. They were assured by a kindly, fatherly-looking Ukranian guard that all was safe and they did not have to worry about anyone stealing anything.

At least he was right, Reichardt thought. Mueller did not tolerate thievery. It would be a sure trip to the gas chamber for an apprehended thief. Mueller actually did have a special inventory team that would collect anything of value after the "shower".

Reichardt found himself staring at the line of people entering the shower room, especially some of the young, muscular men. They had not even been selected out for a work detail but had been brought directly from the rail yard. He felt a twinge of erotic excitement looking at a naked, well-developed teenage boy, waiting his turn to enter the building.

What a waste, he thought to himself, but it was a result of the Fuhrer's new quota program even though the end of the war was very near.

He turned and entered the guard shack and carried out Mueller's instructions. The tall chimneys belched a heavier than usual dark, acrid smoke throughout the night.

III

THE ARLBERG PASS - AUSTRIA

Early Evening - April 12, 1945

The two-truck convoy wound through the narrow, twisting Arlberg. They were approaching the small village of St. Anton. At about eighteen hundred meters elevation there was still snow off to the sides of the well-maintained road. St. Anton had been a winter ski resort at a time when there was time to enjoy sports. It served for a while as a recuperation area for wounded soldiers, mostly officers. Now it was almost deserted with only a few older townspeople still there. The Arlberg Pass is a main transportation route cutting through the Austrian Alps and is the direct connection between Bavaria and Switzerland to the west.

Oberleutnant Karl Konzett had arrived at Dachau late the previous night accompanied by two burly SS guards and two elderly scholarly-looking men. After a private, hurried meeting with Mueller, the two older companions were turned over to Reichardt and were issued towels and soap and sent to the "showers". The two SS guards left.

The two trucks had left Dachau in the early morning hours. There was a long way to go to the Swiss border and Mueller wanted to drive the first part of the journey in the dark. He deliberately avoided the most direct route to Austria to avoid traveling through Munich which was still being heavily bombed; the Americans by day, and the British by night. They drove first directly west through Furstenfeldbruck, which had been a Luftwaffe base but had been completely neutralized by Allied bombing. They then headed south past the Ammersee, through Garmisch, Partenkirchen, past the huge Zugspitze mountains and through the Fernpass into Austria. The route was heavily wooded and mountainous but it offered a certain amount of protection from Allied strafing. They carried their own petrol since it would have been impossible to find fuel anywhere along the route. There were military garrisons along the route - in Furstenfeldbruck, Garmisch and Landeck; however, they were almost deserted. There was little, if any, military capability left in Germany. Only the diehard "Werewolf" units were offering any resistance to the advancing Allies and they operated independently and certainly would not supply anyone.

Five Kisten were loaded onto the trucks just before departure. Mueller personally inspected them and then locked them, keeping the keys himself. Oberleutnant Konzett carried with him a metal briefcase with a chain that he had secured to his left wrist.

Mueller and Luckner rode in the first truck and Konzett and Reichardt in the second. In order to avoid stopping, they alternated driving and stopped only to refuel. They ate while driving.

Mueller turned to Luckner who was driving and said, "Sohn, let's stop for a short while here in St. Anton. Maybe we can find a Gasthaus that is still open."

"Ja wohl, Herr Oberst," Luckner responded. He was seeing the fatherly, kindly side of Mueller now. Whenever he called him Sohn, he knew Mueller was relaxed. All the way along the road Mueller would point out different birds that he had spotted. Here in the wooded Alps there were many and varied species and Mueller excitedly identified them and noted them in a book that he always carried. The book and the binoculars were his "trademark", the necessary tools of the birdwatcher.

On the outskirts of the town there was a Gasthaus that appeared to be open and they pulled up and stopped. There still were such places in the countryside and village people who operated them. Most were for patrons in their own village, and the people were ingeniously clever in being self sufficient. They raised their own food and even made their own wine and schnapps. Luckily this was one such place and it was a welcome stop for the four weary travelers.

The Gasthof Zur Goldene Adler was the first building in the town itself and was built, probably a hundred years previously, on the side of the mountain overlooking the town of St. Anton.

"I know this place very well," Luckner said. "The village where I live is not too far away and I used to come here to ski many times in the past."

"I know the Besitzer (owner). The business has been in the family for years. If I talk to him, I am sure he can provide us with a good meal and even rooms for the night if you wish, Herr Oberst."

"Yes, see what you can do," replied Mueller. "It is already getting late. We could leave early in the morning. Bludenz and Brand are not far."

Konzett and Reichardt readily agreed. Both were tired and welcomed the chance not to be confined in the same truck with each other. For the whole trip there was little communication between them. Both instinctively disliked the other.

Oberleutnant Karl Konzett was a typical product of the Hitler Jugend. As a nephew of Martin Bormann, he had had exposure to the Nazi hierarchy elite. As soon as he was old enough, he became a member of the Hitler Jugend and was indoctrinated at an early age on the glories of National Socialism and the inevitability of the Third Reich ruling the world. He had also been taught that Jews were an inferior race, the cause of most of Germany's ills, and must be exterminated. He was a handsome young man, just twenty years old, whose education was interrupted by the war. He had planned on becoming a lawyer with the ultimate goal of going into politics. Because of his relationship with Martin Bormann he felt he could go far himself in the Nazi party. He had the typical bearing of a young Teutonic warrior, complete with the coveted university dueling scar that ran from his left ear halfway toward the left corner of his mouth. Because of the war he had entered Heidelberg when he was only sixteen years of age and he was invited to join the sword fighting fraternity in his first year there.

He had read a dossier on all of his traveling companions before he arrived at Dachau and he, of course, knew of Reichardt's Jewish background. To him even part Jew meant full Jew. He would have rather left Reichardt at Dachau, preferably in one of the ovens. He cursed his fate at having to have a Jew as his companion on the trip.

Luckner entered the Gasthof and talked animatedly with the owner, a Herr Schmidt. "We are lucky," he said, as he rejoined the group outside. "There are no other guests and there are rooms for all of us, plus a good meal. His wife and daughter are here and he said they are excellent cooks."

They were each assigned to a room and prepared for the evening meal. It was almost difficult to believe that there was a war going on in the world around them when they entered the Speisesaal (dining room) later. A few local village people were sitting at some of the tables, several just drinking wine and talking, the others having a typical evening meal.

These country farmers obviously did not donate all their food for the war effort, Mueller thought to himself, but he was privately thankful. The Tagliche Speisekarte actually offered a selection - veal, pork, chicken and even eggs. Mueller had not seen an egg since his last Ausflug months before with Luckner to the Brand area.

Even Konzett, the super Nazi patriot, did not begrudge the country people having the food, at least not at that moment. In Berlin, where he had been for the past year, the people only dreamed of such food. He literally salivated at the thought of what he could order.

The four sat at a large table by the window where they could watch their trucks. Alpine mountain people were honest but with the war winding down and refugees and army deserters everywhere in Germany one could not be too careful. The whole country was in turmoil. Deserters were shot on the spot when apprehended by the organized diehard army troops that remained. Konzett would be the first to order their executions if he could.

"Herr Ober, Eine Flasche Wein-rot," Mueller ordered. He was the Colonel again and took it upon himself to order a red wine. Actually he knew that that was the best to order. Italy and the Sud Tyrol (South Tyrol) were not far away and some of the best red wine in the world came from there. He was somewhat of a connoisseur of wines and he knew what to order and where.

Luckner, Reichardt and Konzett all approved and agreed that he had ordered the best.

The room was warm, thanks to the ceramic oven in the corner, and with the glow of the wine having its effect, they all began to relax. It had been a very trying and strenuous day.

Again Mueller played the part of the Colonel. "Before we retire to our rooms, you three can move the Kisten to my room. Obviously we cannot leave them unguarded in the trucks."

Konzett still had the metal attache case chained to his wrist. It was always in his sight even when he was eating or, as in this case, beginning to relax. The wine began to flow freely and each ordered food. The conversation started out light. Mueller recounted what birds he had spotted during the day. Reichardt reminisced on the wonderful days he had drinking Heuriger wine in Grinzing, the wine section of Vienna where Beethoven and other great composers got their inspiration. Even the taciturn Luckner, fortified by the wine and congenial atmosphere, talked about his boyhood in the nearby mountains and valleys. Skiing and mountain climbing were his way of life. The hardships of the alpine Bauer were forgotten. Actually life was not that difficult there. There were not complexities of urban life, there was plenty to eat, and, of course, there were no horrors of the war and of the indescribable life that he was a part of at Dachau. He longed to be able to stay when he reached his village of Brand. He was not sure what Mueller had in mind for him. He knew only that the war would soon be over. American troops were no further than one hundred kilometers from where they were now. He just hoped he would get to Brand first.

Konzett, however, was not a pleasant inebriate. Alcohol, by releasing inhibitions, makes most people happy and relaxed. Others it makes mean. Konzett became talkative, but also short-tempered and abusive. His anti-Semitic indoctrination in the Hitler Jugend began to surface with each glass of wine and he could not tolerate Reichardt's conviviality as the evening wore on.

Reichardt, on the other hand, became too relaxed and alcohol served to make him believe that he was more witty than he actually was. He would say things that he had not meant and certainly would not say if he were completely sober. The usually discreet and diplomatic Reichardt began to engage in a stinging repartee with the now sullen Konzett. Reichardt thought he was being humorous. Konzett did not.

"You know, Oberleutnant," Reichardt went on (he used military rank to gain the advantage of his being a Major), "you have that case chained to your wrist all the time. How do you sleep with it? Is it some kind of bed partner for you, something new that you people in Berlin invented?"

"Queer Jew," Konzett exploded. "How dare you, a Jew talk to me like that! We should have left you in Dachau where you belong, in the ovens with other vermin of your kind. And you talk about bed partners. Have you not found any young boys to sleep with you?" he went on, his temper now completely out of control. "We know you are homosexual. You have not fooled us. It is all in your private personnel file. The Reich has had to tolerate filth like you. But you will never be a part of the Fourth Reich, if I have anything to say."

Mueller, who was at first amused by the initial repartee between the two, interceded. "That is enough," he said in a curt military tone. "We have more important things on hand than you two fighting. It is time for us to retire. We have a full day ahead of us tomorrow and we should leave at daybreak. You three carry the Kisten to my room."

IV

THE DESERTER

April 13, 1945

The two trucks pulled out of St. Anton as the sun rose over the nearby mountain peak. Daybreak arrived somewhat earlier in St. Anton because of its elevation. The villages below in the valley of the Arlberg had to wait until the sun cleared the Lechtaler alpine peaks of over three thousand meters to the north and the Ferwall peaks of more than that height to the south. The men had reloaded Mueller's truck with the five heavy metal chests. The second truck, loaded with supplies and fuel, followed with Konzett, accompanied by Reichardt.

"We should be in Bludenz in a short time, and that is not far from our destination, Brand," Mueller said to Luckner who was carefully negotiating the twists and turns of the two-lane Arlberg Pass highway. Fortunately there was no traffic. An occasional vehicle that they encountered was a military vehicle that was dispatched on whatever military missions were still being conducted. Even the farmers were staying home on their own farms to protect them from intruders roaming the countryside, most of them military deserters whose only thought was to survive and to return to their own homes wherever they were. Those whose homes were in the eastern provinces could not return home to face the rapidly advancing Russian armies. They were all forced to live off the land and some were quite desperate. There were also occasional allied prisoners of war who had escaped and were roaming free, trying to link up with any allied units. Some traveled in small bands and lived by what they stole or coerced from local farmers. With the war ending, the Prisoner of War camps were emptying since the guards were also deserting.

There were times when the two trucks lost sight of each other, at one time for about twenty minutes. Mueller thought about stopping and turning around to see if they had broken down but at about that time he saw the truck pulling closer in the rearview mirror.

At mid-morning they approached Bludenz, the town where they would have to leave the main highway and drive south up the mountains to the remote village of Brand, Luckner's home. Bludenz was a relatively large alpine valley town after which the main highway was a straight road to Bregenz, the capital of Vorarlberg and the border of Switzerland. To the south was a narrow mountain road ending in the village of Brand which was at the base of a mountain, a part of the Dolomite chain that separated Austria and Switzerland to the south. Near the peak of the mountain there was a small lake, actually the highest lake in Austria. The lake was fed by the melting snow and the Brandner glacier near the peaks. At the south end of the lake, which was called Lunersee (moon sea) because of its crescent shape, was a relatively low plain called the Schesaplana which cut through two mountain peaks and was a natural entrance to Switzerland curving around to the south.

"Pull up and stop," Mueller ordered as they reached the center of Bludenz," before we have to head into the mountains."

Luckner stopped the truck and waited for the second truck to pull up behind. Only Konzett got out. Reichardt was not to be seen.

"Where is Major Reichardt?" Mueller asked.

"Herr Oberst, I had to stop and let him out back there on the road," Konzett answered. "Major Reichardt ordered me to stop. He said that the war was over and that he wanted to return to his Vienna. I could not convince him to continue. He is like all those other deserters who we have seen. They have no loyalty and, after all, he is a Jew, even if he denies it."

Mueller did not believe the story. He could see the deceit in Konzett's eyes and he knew how violently anti-Semitic he was. But he thought to himself that it was probably for the best. Reichardt would have presented a problem in the future and Konzett was right - he was a Jew. He actually was no longer needed.

They boarded the trucks and turned south onto the narrow mountain road that led to Brand, which was about ten kilometers of continuous winding road up into the mountains.

"I hope that you can find us accommodations in Brand," Mueller said to Luckner. "I know he will," he thought to himself, since that was one of the reasons that he had recruited the young, naïve mountain boy in the first place. Mueller always planned far in advance and that was a contingency that he had had in the back of his mind from the first. And there was also the bonus of having a personal guide on his "birding" Ausflugs.

"We will stay at my family's house, of course," answered Luckner. "There is plenty of room, especially now that there are only three of us. My grandparents and mother will be happy to see us again."

They had always stayed with Luckner's family on their visits in the past and there was a warm relationship that developed between Mueller and the Luckners. They knew that he had treated young Franz as a son but they had no idea that the fatherly appearing Mueller was the Kommandant of a notorious prison and death camp. Luckner never did volunteer any information about his military assignment and his family just assumed that it was some secret duty. They never pressed him for details. They all hated the war and preferred not even to discuss it.

In less than an hour they had made their way up the narrow, twisting road and they entered the small village of Brand. Brand was really less than a village. There was the usual center of the village with a church, several small shops and two Gasthauses where the food, beer and wine were always excellent. There were a few houses in a cluster; the rest of the village was composed of spaced, individual homes all with enough land capable of providing food for the inhabitants. Many of these private houses accepted paying guests - people who, in better times, came from as far away as England to mountain climb in the summer and ski in the winter. Fremdenzimmer or Zimmer Frei signs were seen on most of these houses. There were larger farms skirting the town. Some of these farms appeared to be on the side of a mountain and the familiar cow bells from the cattle that were raised there could be heard from dawn to dusk. These farmers raised food to sell in nearby Bludenz and even in Bregenz and Feldkirch near the Swiss border to the west. This was the type of farm that Luckner came from.

As they approached Luckner's home, they were spotted by his grandfather and Luckner's pet Shaferhund (German Shepherd dog). His grandfather had been plowing in the area adjacent to the large Tyrolean house. It was mid-April and as soon as the snow melted, it was necessary to begin the heavy spring labors. In this particular area, which was out of the shadow of the mountain, the warm sun melted the snow earlier than on some of the adjacent farms, so Herr Alois Luckner always was the first of those in the area to plant his crops.

The dog ran up to his master barking happily. His grandfather dropped the handles on the flow and the reins that were attached to the huge ox and ran slowly with arms outstretched up to the approaching truck. He embraced Luckner after his grandson had alighted from the truck. "Welcome home, Franzel," he said, still calling Luckner by his boyhood name. He turned to Mueller and said, "Danke, Herr Oberst, that you bring Franzel home. Welcome to our home again. I hope that you will stay longer this time."

The dog, named Schwartzie, jumped upon Luckner and was not content until Luckner petted and hugged him. He did not even acknowledge Mueller's presence. On Mueller's previous trips to Brand with Luckner, he had tried to befriend the dog but was never successful. Shaferhunds are one-man dogs, he thought. He was secretly afraid of the dog and, like most dogs, the animal sensed it.

Luckner's mother and grandmother, hearing the commotion from inside the house, came out and also rushed to embrace Luckner and to greet Mueller. Konzett, who had driven up on the second truck, was introduced by Luckner. They all went into the house and received the typical warm welcome that the friendly alpine mountain people offered. There was the usual Schnapps, homemade wine, small cakes and endless happy conversation. Luckner was home, Mueller began to feel at home again, and even Konzett smiled once or twice. It was a happy homecoming. The war was temporarily forgotten. Schwartzie would not let Luckner out of his sight and followed him everywhere.

There was no discussion for the rest of the day and evening on the purpose of their visit. Mueller decided to wait until morning. The house was big enough for each to have his own room. Luckner, of course, had his room waiting for him just the way he had left it after his last visit. His civilian clothing was always neatly laid out waiting for his return. He looked forward to shedding his army uniform, even for a short time. Its association with his military assignment at Dachau was something he wanted for forget. From what Mueller had told him about this trip, it was probably the last time he would ever have to wear it again anyway. That turned out to be prophetically true.

When Luckner had changed his clothes he returned to the living room. Mueller and Konzett had also changed into clothing that they had brought.

They certainly look different, Luckner thought. Mueller still had his military bearing but Konzett looked more like a university student, which he probably would still be if it had not been for the war.

"Before we get too comfortable for the rest of the day, let us carry the Kisten up to my room," Mueller said. "Then we can relax. We have a very full day ahead of us again tomorrow."

After they had moved the Kisten, they returned to the speisezimmer (dining room). The schnapps, wine, and homemade liqueurs began to flow followed by serving after serving of various food and Austrian delicacies. It was a happy, warm, friendly homecoming.

Throughout it all, Konzett still kept the metal attache case chained to his left wrist.

V

THE PREPARATIONS

April 15, 1945

They were all awakened by the barnyard cock crowing at daybreak followed by the tinkling of cow bells. It was music to Luckner's ears and signaled the beginning of another day of hard country work for the farmers in the area. Only in the middle of the winter when they were isolated by the heavy alpine snow could they sleep in the morning. In fact, there was little to do at those times other than to rest and enjoy the respite provided by mother nature. They relaxed by skiing, sleigh riding, and meeting other villagers at the Gasthauses. Spring and fall were the times of the heaviest work. Spring to plow, plant and to move the cattle herds into the mountains to feed for the summer, and fall to harvest, return the cattle from the mountains, and then prepare for the hibernation type existence of winter.

You rooster. You would not last a day back in Germany, Mueller thought to himself, awakened by the crowing. With the war depleting most of the food, you would have made a delicious Backhuhn.

When he dressed and went down to the dining room, Luckner and Konzett were already there and Luckner's mother and grandmother were beginning the first round of breakfast. On most of the continent, breakfast usually consisted of coffee or tea, when available, and bread or a baked roll with marmalade or butter, again if available.

In the alpine countryside, with an arduous day in the offing, breakfasts were more substantial. With a homecoming, they were enormous. The Luckners could not stand the ersatz coffee which was about all that was available in Germany. However, that morning was a real treat. The visitors had brought real coffee that somehow came in to Germany from Africa via Turkey. In Dachau, the SS seemed to have everything.

After a more than adequate breakfast, Mueller and Luckner discussed with the older Luckner what they would be requiring for the rest of the trip. Luckner had mentioned to his grandfather that they would need four mules capable of carrying the heavy Kisten up into the mountains. There were at least four such mules left in the village that had not been confiscated by the Wehrmacht for the war. The villagers would, of course, be well paid by Mueller and the mules returned. They would also need climbing equipment and picks and shovels. "None of this will be a problem," the older Luckner said. "We can have it all ready by late this evening."

"Very good," said Mueller. "Then we should be able to leave the first thing in the morning."

The rest of the day was spent preparing for the following day and, of course, there was the continuous eating and drinking. Each of the villagers, all of whom knew Luckner since he was a child, invited them all in and offered what hospitality they could.

The Luckners began to be worried as the preparations were being made and the day went on. It looked as if Franzel would be leaving again. The grandfather, who was getting quite old, could certainly use young Luckner's help. The farm would soon pass on to him and, of course, his family worried about him when he was away and wanted him home.

The evening again was festive, but there was an air of sadness and apprehension that dampened a repeat of the previous night. Even the dog seemed subdued. When young Luckner would even walk to the other side of the room, the dog would follow him and lie at his feet. When Mueller would approach, he would quietly growl. They retired early in anticipation of what lay ahead.

VI

LUNERSEE

April 16, 1945

In the early morning, the five Kisten, supplies and personal bags were packed securely onto the four mules that had been borrowed from the villagers who refused payment since they were sure young Luckner would return them as he promised. The two trucks were to be left at the outskirts of the village and they would be going farther into the mountains by foot with the mules.

"Oberleutnant Konzett and I will say farewell to you now," Mueller said to the three Luckners who were assembled at the doorway entrance. "Your Franz will return with the mules tomorrow and then he will rejoin us to continue our trip. Be assured that I will look after his welfare and he will return to you. This war is over and we will all be able to return home soon. Thank you again for your hospitality and we will see each other again in better days."

Konzett said his farewells quickly and curtly. He had reverted to type and in spite of being in civilian clothing, as were the others, he was again the brash young officer.

As they left, Schwartzie tried to follow and, in spite of being well trained, had to be forcibly restrained by the elder Luckner.

He snarled and, at one time, lunged at Mueller. Mueller led off and headed into the direction of the mountain range directly south.

When they were out of sight of the village and alone, Mueller stopped and told Luckner and Konzett to join him. It was time to unfold his plans in detail.

"We are going to climb up to Lunersee," he said. "It is your job to get us there," he added to Luckner. "That is why we needed mules. They will be able to get us there, taking the route you showed me in our last Ausflug here.   Once we have reached the Lunersee, which should be late afternoon, we will spend the night at the Douglas Hutte next to the lake. It is deserted this time of the year and no one will be able to observe us. Then tomorrow we will bury these Kisten in an appropriate spot near the edge of the Lunersee. Only we three will know where it will be and we will not draw any maps that could be found and used by someone else. I said that we will bury it on the edge of the lake because as the rest of the snow up there melts, the lake will rise and what we will bury will be under water much of the time. That will be added security for the Kisten until we are ready to return and reclaim them for the Fatherland. They will be necessary to continue our struggle someday."

Konzett knew of the purpose of the trip; however, only Mueller, up until that time, knew where the Kisten would be buried. Luckner obviously was chosen, actually at the time of his selection by Mueller, to help find the right location.

Mueller went on. "When we have buried the Kisten, we, that is, you, Feldwebel Luckner, will return the mules. We three then will go over the Schesaplana into Switzerland. I will have the necessary passports, documentation, and funds that we will need once we are in Switzerland. There are few, if any, border guards that far up in the mountains and we should get there without being seen. When we get into Switzerland, we will go to Zurich. Oberleutnant Konzett has made arrangements through his contacts from Berlin to go on to South America."

There were no questions from Konzett and Luckner so they started the ascent up the mountain which would lead them to

Lunersee. Luckner, who was familiar with the route, led the way. Lunersee, which was approximately two thousand meters high and overshadowed by peaks three thousand meters high, was approachable by a zigzag path that worked itself up the mountain at the end of the Brandnertal (Brand Valley). It was a narrow, treacherous path in which one wrong move could be fatal, especially at this time of the year in April when there were still patches of ice and snow in the areas that did not have the direct rays of the sun. Without Luckner, they could not have made it. It seemed to take an eternity of inching up the slope because of the slow pace but was only about five hours. They reached the ledge that flattened out and served as the only entrance from Austria to the Lunersee area.

In better times under more favorable circumstances, it would be worth the climb to see this beautiful mountain lake. As they reached the top of the ledge, the three were speechless, partly because of the strenuous climb which left them breathless and partly because they were spellbound by the beauty of the area. Even the sure-footed mules, who, at times had to be pulled and pushed up the narrow path, seemed to be captivated by the beautiful sight and the accomplishment of making it to the top.

The Lunersee was a beautiful blue that appeared to be an extension of the sky and from its shore were peaks, still half covered with pure white snow stretching upward and capped by the Brandner-glacier which was a major source of water for the lake. The water itself was pure as nature could provide and was inviting to the wary climbers. All three bent down and drank directly from the lake and even the mules followed suit.

From the tip of the lake, the lower end of the crescent, a path led along the edge to a small peninsula jutting out into the lake. On this peninsula was the Douglas Hutte which served as a small overnight inn for the climbers who scaled the various mountains in the whole area. The inn was only open from May until October since the area, because of its elevation, was completely snowed in during the winter months. Mountain climbing and hiking in the summertime were popular sports in the area and were a main tourist attraction. There was a series of such Huttes or inns in the Austrian and Swiss mountains and week-long expeditions were made climbing and hiking from one to another. They were actually spaced to be a day's hiking apart.

They made their way along the edge of the lake to the Hutte. It was still too early for others to be in the area, so the three had it all to themselves.

"We will stay here for the night, and tomorrow we will find an appropriate site to bury the Kisten," said Mueller. "We had better unload them from the mules. And we should warm up this place," he added.

There was a good supply of firewood that was left over from the fall and it was not long before the visitors had a warm fire going in the ceramic space heaters. These heaters were common to Europe, especially to the alpine area and were able to heat a room or house quickly and maintain the warmth for a considerable time. Luckner also started a fire in the wood stove. After the strenuous climb, and because of the clean, invigorating air, they were all hungry.

The Hutte itself had a large dining area and several two-bed and dormitory rooms. The sleeping rooms were unheated so Mueller and Luckner decided to bring mattresses to the main dining room and spend the night there. Konzett preferred his privacy and picked out one of the small bedrooms in which to spend the night in spite of the fact that it was bitter cold at that height and at that time of the year.

The evening was relatively pleasant. They had brought the Kisten into the dining room and after Luckner had a good fire started in the wood stove, Mueller, who fancied himself as a good cook, prepared the evening meal. He had never married and was a confirmed bachelor. Being forced to cook for himself for many years, he actually cooked well. They had brought ample provisions with them including fresh veal. He prepared what turned out to be an excellent naturshcnitzel and with each drinking a bottle of good Sud Tyrol red wine that the Luckners had given them, they settled down early for the evening. In the middle of the night, Konzett, his teeth chattering, moved into the dining room dragging his mattress with him. "Verdamnt, but it's cold," he muttered as he curled up before the stove and went to sleep - with the metal attache case still chained to his wrist.

VII

The Begrabness

April 17, 1945

They slept late the next morning. The combination of the strenuous climb the previous day, the warm room, the rarified air at the high altitude, a full excellent meal prepared by Mueller, much good wine, and, most of all, no time-pressing schedule, allowed them, for the first time in a long time, to relax. Being there on top of the mountain removed them temporarily from reality - the lost war, the undesirable duty during the war, and the uncertainty of what lay ahead.

Luckner, the country boy, was the first to awake. The first sound that he heard were the familiar sounds of his boyhood, the sounds of the cowbells from the valley below that carried all the way to the Lunersee. Actually the cows would soon make their way up the mountain where they would spend the summer in the meadow on the south side of the lake. In fall, they would be brought back down into the valleys to spend the winter. Luckner's first thoughts were how he would miss this if he actually would leave the country. He thought also of how his aging family would need him. Maybe I could talk Mueller into letting me remain, he thought to himself.

Mueller and Konzett awakened to the movement of Luckner who rekindled the ceramic oven and started a fire in the stove. "What a sleep I had," Mueller said. "This mountain air is wonderful."

Konzett, too, arose, stretched and put his coat over his shoulders and went out into the cold morning air to relieve himself. The toilet facilities in the Hutte were turned off in the winter and all the pipes had been drained to prevent their freezing.

"I'll join you," said Mueller. "I've always wondered how you can shit or piss with that metal box chained to your wrist. And I want to make sure you don't contaminate the lake. That's our drinking water."

For one, the usually dour Konzett displayed a little sense of humor. "Come watch me piss on the rest of the world," he said as he walked to the edge of the ledge, unbuttoned his pants in the front, aimed his penis into space, and directed the silver stream over the edge. "That has got to be a one thousand meter piss," he said. "I wonder if it freezes into ice before it hit's the ground."

"If it does, I'm going to start an avalanche with all that wine I had last night," Mueller said as he stood along side Konzett and did the same.

They were like two young boys having a pissing contest, laughing as each tried to outdo the other.

"I wouldn't do this in front of Reichardt," Konzett said. "I didn't like the way he looked at me. He'd probably try to blow me."

They re-entered the Hutte and Luckner was preparing coffee that they had brought with them. The aroma of the boiling coffee together with the smell of burning logs from the ceramic oven again provided a pleasant "Gemutlich" atmosphere. They drank their coffee and ate black bread with real butter that they had gotten from the farm below and even had marmalade that Luckner's mother had prepared. It was that typical continental breakfast that they had known in better days. When they had finished breakfast, they packed the Kisten onto the mules.

"We will leave our personal belongings here," Mueller said. "After we have buried the Kisten, we will return here to the Hutte. You, Luckner, will return the mules to the valley. We will wait for you here to return and then we will cross over the Schesaplana together to Switzerland. We will only be able to carry a few personal things because we will have to go by foot and the terrain on the Swiss side is also difficult. We will have to avoid any possibility of being seen by Swiss border guards. There are not many in this area yet but we must be careful. Zurich is still a long way off."

"Oberleutnant Konzett, I hope that the arrangements that you made in Switzerland are completed," he added.

"There will be an automobile and a driver waiting for us in Chur," Konzett answered. "I have made arrangements for them to meet us on the evening of the eighteenth. We are exactly on schedule and we should make it easily."

Leading the mules, they headed southwest on the path along the edge of the lake. They looked at several possible locations to bury the Kisten. Since there would be no written or drawn map, it had to be a site that had definite landmarks that they could locate again by memory. The landmarks had to be permanent; they would not be moved by shifting ice or possible avalanches. It also had to be a location that would not be too obvious to passersby. In another month with the improving weather there would be the usual mountain climbers and hikers. With the war over, there would be more people with more time. Also the valley people would be here at the first opportunity.

Finally, after considering several locations they all agreed on a site about halfway around the lake. It fit all specifications and was one that they were sure they could find again. It was under a ledge, about five meters up and back from the path. The ledge, which was really a large rock face, offered protection from erosion and the elements.

All three started to dig and soon had made a shaft about two and a half meters deep at an angle under the ledge. It was wide enough to easily accommodate the five containers which measured twenty by forty by one hundred twenty centimeters each. They unpacked the heavy containers and slid them into the shaft which was dug at about a forty-five degree angle downward. After they had slid the first three into the shaft, Konzett unchained the metal case from his wrist and put it into the shaft. Then they put the last two containers into the shaft and started to fill it with soil and rocks. The rocks would keep the shaft from settling and hide any clue that there had been digging there.

Before they had finished filling the shaft, Mueller turned to Luckner and said, "I think that you should take the mules back now. It's noon now and you should be able to get them down and be back by five p.m. They are not loaded and it will be downhill. Konzett and I will finish filling the shaft and we will wait for you by the Hutte. I would like to go over the Schesaplana into Switzerland in the early evening before it is too dark but also not too light. There will be no border patrols out at that time. I will help you with the mules to the path leading down the mountain. Konzett, I will return soon. Finish filling the shaft and I think we should move some of the vegetation over the hole itself. It should be good camouflage."

Mueller, being an ornithologist, was somewhat of an authority on camouflage because of birds depending on colors and natural camouflage for survival from predators.

He walked off with Luckner leading the mules to the ledge where the path started the descent down the mountains.

"Sohn," he said as they walked back, "be sure to say goodbye to your family again for me. They are fine people and very much remind me of my family when I was young."

Mueller was the farm, fatherly type again and Luckner felt what a son would feel to his own father. Since his own father had died when he was a little boy and his grandfather was always an old man to him, he quite naturally developed this feeling toward the paternal Mueller. He felt that he could ask his advice and help and tell him what was troubling him. This feeling was reinforced by the close association of the last three days.

They reached the edge of the ledge where the path started to zigzag down the mountainside. They directed the sure-footed mules down individually. The mules seemed to have a natural homing device as they started their procession downward. Luckner was to follow.

Luckner looked off toward the valley below where his home was and avoided Mueller's eyes to that he would have the courage to say what was on his mind. "Herr Oberst, I would like to remain home. My grandfather is old and my family needs me. Would it be possible?" he asked as he turned and looked up at Mueller who was one step above him on the ledge.

Instead of looking into Mueller's eyes, he found himself looking into the barrel of Mueller's nine mm luger automatic.

"Vati, Vati," he reflexly screamed simultaneously with the loud blast that blew him over the ledge into the valley one thousand meters below.

VIII

WASHINGTON, D. C.

April 2, 1990

"Twenty first and R, driver, and take your time," said Kurt as he entered the cab at Washington National Airport. The cab sped off toward the George Washington Parkway and the Arlington Memorial Bridge, pressing the current speed limit in spite of his instructions.

Oh well, Kurt mentally shrugged, as he sat back on the cold vinyl seat trying to find a comfortable position to relax and enjoy the short ride to the "Club". The club, located near Dupont Circle in the District, had been his home away from home for years, whenever he returned to the Capital. I guess cabbies have to hustle to make a living these days, he mused to himself as he pulled out a cigarette, lit up, and gazed out the window at the old familiar landmarks whizzing by. The driver was quiet and did not carry on the usual uninteresting, pseudo-philosophical chatter that seems to be the occupational disease of many cabbies, especially those in the Washington area. Many of the District cabbies were, in fact, very bright individuals, some of them students at the several universities in the city who had to supplement their incomes to exist in the high-cost nation's capital. Many of them were foreign students and this one appeared to be an Iranian or from some other mid-east country and he had not uttered one word since Kurt entered the cab. For this, Kurt was thankful. He was in no mood for unnecessary conversation.

Kurt thought amusingly of the flight from San Francisco by way of Texas and the pretty, shapely flight attendant who had gotten on at Houston and with whom he had made tentative plans for a quiet candlelight dinner at one of his favorite Georgetown restaurants on Wisconsin Avenue. She had promised to call him at the club when she had checked out from her flight and returned to her Arlington apartment. He wondered if she would actually follow through or if this was merely the polite standard brush off for the more amorous passengers that all pretty flight attendants encountered. Nothing ventured, nothing gained, he thought. But he felt a tinge of envy at the thought of her, perhaps meeting a special beau that such a beautiful girl must have in her hometown base. What a ridiculous feeling, he thought to himself as the cab approached the Memorial Bridge.

He glanced up to the left toward Arlington Cemetery where many of his old comrades from the past war and some from the undeclared cold war now lay. He thought he could almost see the eternal light where John Kennedy was buried. Kurt thought back on that tragic day back in November 1963 when the world was shocked and sickened by the senseless murder committed by a deranged misfit. That made it even more difficult to accept. To die for no apparent cause or reason was a bitter pill. The young, handsome President had so much to offer and the entire world suffered from his loss. Kurt was often angered by some articles in the media that implied that his "company" was somehow involved in the assassination plot. My God, how ridiculous, he often thought to himself. Kurt, and almost all of those whom he knew in "The Company" loved and respected Kennedy as, perhaps, only a soldier could understand. He thought of how one day he would eventually join his comrades in Arlington. Death would be a reunion of sorts.

The cab circled the Lincoln Memorial and headed up 23rd Street in the direction of the main part of the city and Dupont Circle.

His thoughts drifted back to the girl he hardly knew. He thought again of her shapely legs and her pretty figure in the well-tailored blue flight attendant uniform, her coal black hair pertly coiffured within the limitations most airlines demand of their attendants and he hoped that she would call.

His thoughts switched to the telegram, marked urgent, that he had received only this morning to return immediately to Washington for a special briefing and assignment. Special assignment, he thought to himself. Actually all his assignments were special. This recollection he tried to shake from his mind and suddenly even his cigarette seemed to taste bad. He was, for all intents and purposes, when necessary, a professional killer - a legal executioner, he preferred to consider himself. Legal in the sense that he acted on government orders as a soldier would, he would think in self justification. He snubbed out his cigarette and opened the side window to clear the air. Even the smoke was distasteful to him and he wanted to clear the air as well as his mind. He always had the ability of instantly clearing his mind of unpleasant thoughts and memories and at least temporarily disassociating himself from his present existence. This ability he had utilized to good advantage in his assignments when, on many occasions, he had to assume a new identity and personality. I must be a potential schizophrenic, he thought to himself when he realized this ability to escape for a time from reality. But at least it keeps me from going completely overboard.

Age must be catching up on me or maybe just conscience, he thought as he seemed to find it more often necessary to try to forget the past. He had just spent a month's "recuperation" leave from his last assignment that, although not as trying as some of his previous "duties", had left him mentally and physically exhausted. This he realized was a dangerous condition in his profession, a profession which left no margin for error.

"Take a good long vacation, Kurt, and rest up," Bo McInnes had said. Bo had been his contact officer who had brought down the instructions from above and sent Kurt off to all ends of the globe.

Bo, short for Beaumont, a name that would make his blood pressure rise when he was reminded of it, was usually a congenial man, sandy-haired, freckle-faced product of a French mother and an Irish father. He and Kurt had crossed paths for years. They had met first at the Army Counter Intelligence School at Fort Holabird, Maryland as young second lieutenants. They served together in a special task force until spending more time in North Vietnam, Cambodia and Laos than in South Vietnam. Both had received the Silver Star, Purple Heart, Commendation Medal and numerous other decorations for their work which resulted ultimately in being tagged by "The Company" for work that had turned out to be a most unusual career.

"Here we are, Sir." The words broke his reverie and he glanced out the window and saw the familiar sign, Officers Service Club, as the cab pulled to the curb. I wish they would straighten the sign, he thought to himself. The sign had been slightly askew for years, probably not noticeable to others, but to the orderly, exact perfectionist mind of Kurt, quite obvious. He paid the cabbie, grabbed his valve pack and hurried up the steps into the entrance of the club.

The club was an old World War II carryover officers' club which, during the war, had been called the Club of the United Nations, but now was restricted to active and inactive reserve officers of the U.S. Armed Forces.

He stopped at the desk. The clerk glanced up and greeted him with a friendly smile. "Good afternoon, Col. Hoffman," said the clerk. "Glad to see you back. We have your reservation."

Kurt immediately thought how efficiently Bo always arranged these little conveniences, as he answered, "Glad to be back. Are there any messages?"

"Just one," answered the clerk, as he handed Kurt the call memo. "You are supposed to call this number, the man said, about five."

Kurt filled in the register - Lt. Col. Kurt Hoffman - and left the address space blank. He preferred to use his reserve military rank on occasion which, in fact, was a convenient "cover" for him at times. "Is the bar open yet?" asked Kurt as he glanced up at the clock over the switchboard which read 4:40.

"Not until five," said the clerk as he handed Kurt the key to room D6.

"Good. That gives me time to wash up." Kurt picked up his valve pack, walked past the bar and entered the familiar rotundum. His room was on the first floor and the fourth room on the left. He unlocked the room, entered, threw the valve pack on the bed and his coat over the back of the chair and opened his pack. That shower will certainly feel good, he thought as he stripped off his clothes, revealing a muscular, sinewy, six-foot frame effectively masked by his conservative clothing, and stepped into the shower stall. He lathered well and was just completing rinsing when the phone rang. He grabbed a towel, stepped over to the bed stand and picked up the phone.

"Yes," he said.

"Kurt, is that you?"

He immediately recognized the soft pleasing voice of Susan, the airline flight attendant he met on the plane. He sat down on the edge of the bed, cradled the phone on his shoulder and reached for a cigarette.

"Congratulations, you caught me in the shower," he said as he lit up his cigarette.

"Good," she laughed wickedly. "Are our plans still on for this evening or do you just flirt with all the flight attendants?"

"I have a phone call to make but I'm sure that I can wind up my business by eight. Can I call for you then?" he asked.

"Apartment 1206, Arlington Point Towers, and don't be late. I'll be starved by then," she answered as she said goodbye and hung up.

Kurt looked in the mirror and decided he needed to shave in spite of the fact that he had shaved on the flight from Houston. He still preferred a lather shave to electric razors, several of which he had received as gifts throughout the years. He lathered up with instant shave and inserted a new blade in his "antique" gold razor. It had been a gift that he had received from his father when he was old enough to shave for the first time. It was sort of his "introduction to manhood". Often when he used the razor he chuckled to himself when he thought of his father's second "gift" to him in his introduction to adult life. When he was seventeen years old, his father had taken him on a trip to Mexico. In Juarez he had taken Kurt to the most expensive brothel in town, picked out the most beautiful "hostess" in the place and turned her over to Kurt. It was probably the best way to lose my cherry, Kurt often thought. It was obviously better to start out with a real expert than some inexperienced teeny bopper in the back seat of a car. He never forgot that first one; she was a real pro, although not much older than Kurt at the time. Kids today start out too young, he often thought. As he shaved he thought he noticed a new line in his face; probably more a result of his "way of life" than from age. His dark brown hair was still free of any hints of gray that many people his age had to fight. Actually both of his parents retained their natural hair color well into their sixties. He looked youthful enough to maintain a "cover" as a student in several European universities. Age is creeping up on me, he reflected as he finished shaving.

Kurt dressed hurriedly, glanced at the blue-black 32-caliber automatic in his pack and closed the pack as he decided to leave the gun behind. The 32 was actually a Spanish-made "Star" that was a cutdown version of the standard U. S. Army 45 automatic that Kurt was most familiar with in his combat days. He had also had a silencer and a hair trigger especially made for it. Silencers are usually used on revolvers rather than automatics so he had to have his "custom" made.

He closed and locked his door and headed for the bar. "Hi, Larry. The usual," he said casually as he approached the bar.

"Sure think," the bartender answered. "Vodka martini, extra dry with a twist, Colonel."

"I don't know what I would do without you," Kurt said, as he sat down on a bar stool at the near end of the bar.

Larry, a handsome black, a long-time fixture behind the bar, was an expert on anything from martinis to any obscure middle east concoction, a curbstone authority on any subject from football to Mozart with an encyclopedic biographic knowledge of any patron who ever frequented the club. He was also a dependable "source" to Kurt for collecting information on almost anything that happened in the Washington, D. C. area. He had relatives and friends and his own private "snitches" throughout the city.

"Hold that drink for me, Larry. I'll be right back," said Kurt, glancing at his watch. "I've got to make a call."

Kurt chose the phone booth in the room adjacent to the bar to avoid going through the switchboard and dialed his number. He heard Bo's voice on the other end of the line.

"Hello, Bo," he said. "I just got in. What's up?"

"Report to the same place as last time at eight a.m. tomorrow," answered Bo. "Enjoy yourself this evening while you can because this is going to be a rough one. See you then."

Kurt returned to the bar and noticed a familiar figure sitting on his bar stool with his drink. Tapping him on the shoulder, Kurt said, "What's the matter, fellow, can't you afford to buy your own drink?"

"I wish you would drink something else, old buddy," said the familiar voice. "I can't stand vermouth. It's strictly for women and debilitated old men."

"I might have known you'd show up," said Kurt. "Are you here for business or pleasure?"

"Monkey business is more like it," he answered, laughingly. "But as you well know, that's how I get my kicks."

Maximillian Montague Mitchell III, M. D., God's gift to wine, women, and song whose benign appearance belied the existence of a mind like a steel trap.

"What are you smoking?" asked Max. "I'm fresh out."

"You're a leech," replied Kurt. "Why don't you buy your own?" as he tossed the pack on the bar.

"Shame," said Max. "What kind of a doctor do you think I am? Haven't you read the Surgeon General's report about cigarettes causing cancer, to say nothing about heart trouble, emphysema, hypertension and all kinds of other horrible diseases? Besides, if I smoke yours, I can always sue you for giving me cancer."

"How long have you been around?" Kurt asked, switching to a more serious vein.

"Just a couple of days," replied Max, "and what are you here for? Has Bo contacted you, too, for tomorrow?"

"I guess we're going to play another duet together," said Kurt. "Have you any idea what it's all about?"

"Some, not all," said Max. "I guess we'll get the sordid details tomorrow. By the way, what are you doing tonight? I can get a couple of live ones lined up, right around the corner here at the State House Apartments. Are you up to it?"

"Hell, no! I've been out with your live ones before," retorted Kurt. "The last one you conned me into going out with turned out to be a transvestite. Besides, my sister is in town and I promised to take her to see the various monuments in town and the Phillips Art Collection just down the street. The poor kid has never been to D. C. before and she wants to see the sights and I'm sure that you wouldn't be interested."

"My heart bleeds for her, old buddy," replied Max with a concerned look on his face. "I would be glad to escort the little tyke to the historical points of interest for you. It just proves what a good friend of yours I am. Are you sure that you don't want me to take your place?"

"That's a switch," said Kurt. "You probably wouldn't even know a monument if you saw one. Besides, I wouldn't know if I could trust you with my sister. She needs to be protected from perverts like you."

"Okay, if that's the way you feel about it," said Max feigning a hurt look. "I'll go and spend a lonely evening by myself. By the way, when we were in the rice paddies in Nam together, and you were pouring out your soul to me, didn't you tell me in one of your weaker moments that you no longer had any close relatives?"

"Don't believe everything you hear in rice paddies or bushes," laughed Kurt. "You, too, have been known to exaggerate a bit there, especially in the bushes."

Max laughed and walked out the front door saluting goodbye. Kurt returned to his drink.

Two drinks later and following a heated discussion regarding the merits of last year's Washington Redskins with loyal fan Larry, Kurt noticed the time and left to pick up Susan.

Susan, he thought to himself. About thirty years ago, which was about her age, must have been a banner year for naming girls Susan. He knew more girls named Susan in that age bracket than any other name. It probably reflected a popular movie star or other personality who was prominent at the time.

He noticed the flower stand was still open at the nearby corner of Connecticut and R and he impulsively purchased a gardenia for Susan. Might as well go all out, he thought.

He hailed a cab and gave directions to the Arlington address which Susan had given him.

IX

SUSAN

When he arrived at her apartment, he walked past the reception desk and entered a waiting elevator. He pressed the button for the twelfth floor. When he arrived at 1206, he pressed the buzzer for her apartment.

"Just a minute," he heard from inside. The door opened just a crack and Susan peeked out. "You're a bit early," she said. "I'm not made up yet."

"Good," he said. "I wanted to see if you are just as beautiful. Mmm, even more so," he added.

"There is more missing than just a bit of paint," she laughed. "Wait, give me a few seconds to get to the other room before you come in."

The door closed and he heard the security chain being unlatched. He waited a few seconds, opened the door and walked into the apartment.

"I have only two rooms, but make yourself comfortable - IN THERE," she called from the other room, emphasizing the last two words. "Help yourself to a drink. There's ice in the refrigerator and whatever else you need is in the cabinet."

"Thanks. Should I mix you one too?" he asked.

"Just a small scotch," she answered.

Kurt opened the refrigerator and found the ice cubes in a metal bucket which Susan had filled from the ice trays. Kurt was thankful for this. This had always been one of his pet irritations.

Man has been able to develop ultra sensitive vehicles to travel to the moon, he thought to himself, but as yet has been unable to develop a simple ice cube tray which actually works easily. He thought fleetingly of the ridiculous TV commercial he had recently viewed extolling the virtues of automatic icemakers. That would make drinking too easy, he thought amusingly. I'd probably become an alcoholic.

He put two ice cubes in a glass and added some Glen Livet scotch. She's got good taste, he mused to himself as he studied the label on the bottle. But then, she's got a lot of class and this is what I would expect her to drink. For himself he made a small vodka martini. Even the furnishings in the room, he noticed, reflected a discerning eye for quality and elegance. His thoughts fleetingly returned to the lack of an automatic icemaker. If so much was spent on such expensive furnishings, why not a little more for the convenience of not going through the ice tray routine, he mentally asked himself.

From the twelfth floor apartment, which was the top floor of the building, one could easily see the massive expanse of concrete and steel known throughout the world as the Pentagon and, beyond that, the Potomac River. From the large floor to ceiling window the entire area of downtown Washington was visible. The Lincoln Memorial, Reflecting Pool, Washington Monument and the Capitol stood out like an artist's conception of a model city. An artist must have helped design the city layout, Kurt thought. He had visited almost every major city in the world - Vienna, Tokyo, Paris, Saigon, and many others, but to Kurt, Washington was, by far, the most beautiful. He hated New York with its tall, cold skyscrapers, and most of all, the impersonal attitude of its inhabitants. Washington maintained much more of a cosmopolitan atmosphere than most American cities. After having traveled and lived so long in foreign lands, the international flavor of the nation's capital appealed to him. There were always old friends that he could count on bumping into in the various restaurants, fine shops or even walking down the street. Kurt actually looked forward to these chance encounters while in town. It's funny, he thought to himself. He had always been criticized for his remote and austere personality and had never craved companionship other than a very select group of intimate friends. In the past few months, he sensed a feeling of loneliness and he looked forward to meeting acquaintances. For his "chosen profession" this was a very unhealthy change of attitude where anonymity was a way of life - actually a necessity - to remain alive.

Washington, D.C., itself, was an interesting city that was plagued with the ills of most large urban areas in the United States. It had actually suffered from unwarranted notoriety throughout the world. It was always pictured, especially in the Communist press, as a large, black ghetto which had large unemployment statistics and a populace bordering on starvation. In actuality, it was far from this. The District of Columbia had to meet the large influx of migration from the southern states. Blacks throughout the United States had awakened to the opportunities that this great land offered and were laying claim to their rightful place in this society. In the understandable overzealousness resulting from generations of frustration, there naturally was, on occasion, over-reaction to social problems and violence resulted. Cool-headed black leaders exemplified by the late Martin Luther King fortunately emerged to lead their people in the right direction. Unfortunately, thought Kurt, an opportunistic as well as a criminal element which is inherent to every race, played on the racial issue to justify their intentions and in many cases became heroes of a sort to the misguided black population because of their opposition to any and all authority. In actuality the black population, itself, suffered the most in the crime statistics. Most of the reported murders, robberies, narcotic trafficking, and rapes were in the black inner city, not in the more secure, comfortable white suburbs in nearby Maryland or Northern Virginia. All this was reflected in the world press as typical of the ills of the country and "racism" had been blown out of proportion to its actual extent. It's funny, thought Kurt, all of a sudden I'm concerned with domestic social issues rather than foreign intrigue. He resolved to think of nothing more that was controversial for the rest of the evening and dedicate the entire evening to relaxation in the company of a beautiful woman.

Susan emerged from the bedroom and Kurt was momentarily taken back by her striking appearance. Her long black hair, no longer tied back, was parted in the middle and flowed over her bare shoulders blending with the V forming shoulder cut of a shimmering silver dress which revealed only slightly the inner part of her well-developed breasts, but only appropriately so, not cut almost to the mid section as is often seen on women desperately attempting to hold on to the last vestiges of youth. "You're beautiful," said Kurt seriously as he offered her the gardenia that he had brought and then the drink that he had prepared.

She thanked him for the flower, sat down and sipped her drink. "I love gardenias," she added. "How did you know that they are my favorite flower?"

"You look like a gardenia type to me," he said. Kurt always seemed to identify beautiful women with specific flowers.

She sipped her drink looking into Kurt's eyes. Kurt, for a moment, thought he detected a troubled look on her face. Her face, he thought, was one of the most beautiful he had ever seen. Kurt, through the years, had fancied himself as almost an authority on beautiful women from throughout the world. Her beauty was unique in that it seemed to combine features that he thought of as exclusive to women in certain parts of the world. Her coal black hair reminded him of beauties he had seen in the mid east and far east, her rather high cheek bones gave the slight impression of oriental breeding, her skin was slightly tanned and he noted that her complexion was flawless. Her full, soft lips, large, even teeth, narrow, pert nose and brown eyes combined to completely mystify Kurt in trying to classify her with any single national characteristic. Kurt had developed the ability to determine people's emotions and intentions by reading their eyes. This was one area where Susan seemed to give herself away. Right now her eyes were "smiling" as she quickly finished her drink, turned to the closet where she selected a Stone Martan shoulder wrap and handed it to Kurt. He helped her with her wrap and guided her to the door noting to himself, the soft pleasant fragrance of her Shiaparelli perfume. This girl is all class, he thought to himself, and nothing about her is inexpensive. How does she afford it on a flight attendant's salary? Could be independently wealthy, he thought. He couldn't even begin to believe that she was a "kept woman". She didn't have to be. Some flight attendants he had met in the past worked only for the adventure and travel that the job ostensibly offered. Maybe Susan is one of those, he reflected. Most, however, were soon disillusioned after a relatively short time. Many, especially those on the shorter domestic runs, found the work quite difficult and had to practically run to serve all the demanding passengers since jets had drastically cut travel time. There was a big turnover in their profession.

"If you don't have a cab waiting, let's take my car," she said as they entered the elevator. "That way I'll have you at a disadvantage." He agreed and pressed the elevator button for the garage level.

It would be better, he thought, and more private without a cabbie listening in on our conversation.

The elevator descended nonstop to the sub-ground level which was the private parking level for the huge building complex. Susan's car, a red Mercedes sports car, was parked immediately adjacent to the elevator exit which Kurt thought was quite fortunate. It did offer a certain amount of security. The parking area stretched out over the entire ground area of the building and the far reaches of the lot were rather dimly lit. The many concrete pillars providing support for the building above also provided concealment for anyone to wait and surprise some unsuspecting victim. Kurt was just naturally security conscious and apprehensive of any advantage for a potential enemy. This was actually for him a matter of survival and was a factor in his longevity up to this point. Looking around the lot he noticed the security cameras which were tied in to the building complex reception office. The cameras couldn't possibly cover the whole area, he thought to himself. A pro could easily move around without being detected.

Susan handed Kurt the car keys and he unlocked the right door, opened it and guided her arm as she slid into the right bucket seat.

These new modern sports cars are not designed for graceful entrances, Kurt noted as he couldn't help but notice Susan's long, shapely legs as she bent to adjust to the low seat causing her knees to be somewhat elevated. With the side split, long dresses currently in vogue, it proved to be even more difficult for long-legged beauties, as Susan was, to feign modesty and quite impossible to keep their knees covered. Kurt closed the door and walked around to the driver's side and opened the door which Susan had already unlocked. As he slid into the driver's seat, he thought he noticed, out of the corner of his eye, a movement in the shadows behind a pillar in the darkened parking area near the stairwell to the ground level floor. As he looked again he couldn't see anyone but it gave him a feeling of uneasiness. I guess I'm getting too jumpy, he thought. "They really ought to light up this place more," he said to Susan, "and I don't see how the surveillance cameras can see everything, especially at the bottom of those steps. If I were the insurance company for this place, I'd really raise hell."

Susan agreed and immediately changed the subject to more pleasant conversation as Kurt started the car and drove toward the exit door. The electric eye automatically opened the door and Kurt drove out, up the ramp, and onto the side street that led to the Jefferson Davis Highway.

"I hope, Colonel Hoffman," Susan said, feigning a stern voice, "that you don't think I accept dinner invitations from all my male passengers. You looked so forlorn and helpless that I felt that I had to protect you in this wicked city. There are all kinds of vicious women who would take advantage of you here. Did you know that the female to male ratio in this city is about four to one and I've also heard wild stories about all those hostesses who frequent the club that you are staying at."

"All lies," answered Kurt. "Actually they are really decent girls who are in the club. In fact, they are all screened before they are accepted as permanent hostesses. They are not even allowed to visit any of the rooms and if any do, they are thrown out of the club as well as the members. So, you see, you're worried over nothing and I was perfectly safe there."

"You mean that you aren't going to try to lure me up into your room?" Susan mocked. "I'm disappointed. All my fantasies about what went on in that place are defused. So, tell me, where are we going tonight?"

"Unless you have a special place you'd like to go, I'd like to take you to one of my favorite French restaurants in Georgetown," Kurt answered. "Do you know the St. Etienne on Wisconsin Avenue?"

"It'll be my first time there," she answered. "I'll be at your mercy, and I must admit that my one weakness is French food."

"I hope that it is not your only weakness," Kurt laughingly replied. "I've made all kinds of plans for us."

He turned off the Jefferson Davis Highway and circled around the underpass onto the George Washington Parkway. It was a circuitous route to drive to Georgetown from the direction from which he came since the direct approach to the Key Bridge had been removed. He had to take the Parkway up Spout Run, then take a U-turn down Spout Run and then up the access road to the Key Bridge which led directly to Georgetown. It would be difficult to tail somebody taking this route, he reasoned as he peered into the rear view mirror. As he looked, he thought that the car following did seem familiar. It had made the same U-turn on Spout Run and followed him up and onto the Key Bridge. He kept his eye on the car in the mirror and was relieved when he saw it turn off the bridge onto the Whitehurst Freeway. Kurt, as a result of his profession, instinctively checked to see if he was being followed, whether it was driving on a highway or even walking down the street, just as he never sat in a restaurant or any public room with his back to the entrance, or established a behavior pattern such as taking the same route every day to work when he was on a job or assignment for any length of time. That was probably why he was still alive.

He turned right on M Street at the end of the Key Bridge and drove up several blocks to Wisconsin Avenue. The St. Etienne was a short distance up Wisconsin Avenue on the corner on the left. The restaurant, as most of the business establishments in Georgetown, had no private parking lot and Kurt had to park on the dark side street near the restaurant.

Georgetown was a unique section of the District of Columbia which had experienced the transition from an exclusive part of Washington in the capital city's early history to a slum and then back in recent years again to an exclusive fashionable area. Following the depression years and the mass influx of military officers and high government officials in the war years, Georgetown was resurrected from a decaying haven for poverty-stricken migrants from the south. Because of its proximity to the government offices it was a convenient location where a member of Congress could drive to Capitol Hill in a matter of minutes or a stateside ambassador could reach his E Street office in a very short time. It became chic to boast of a Georgetown address and the area probably reached its pinnacle during the Kennedy Camelot era.

Along with the restoration of the residential areas came the fashionable shops and exclusive restaurants which catered to the wealthy residents, embassy personnel, and the tourists who flocked to the Nation's Capital. The St. Etienne, which was Kurt's favorite, was one of the restaurants that survived the test of the discerning Washingtonians who demanded the best, albeit for a price, and got it. Many of the new restaurants, hoping to capitalize on a gullible public, folded, usually in the first year, because of the intense competition.

Kurt and Susan were greeted at the front door by the maitre-d' who Kurt did not recognize. Actually Kurt preferred not to be recognized. His only concern was that the quality of the food remain the same. Too often the quality varies with the personnel who, unfortunately in the restaurant business, are usually transient. In Europe, in contrast, such restaurants are usually family affairs which, for generations, can be depended upon for excellence of service and cuisine. The St. Etienne, Kurt hoped, would be consistent.

Kurt requested and they were given a candlelit table in an alcove toward the rear of the restaurant and away from the door to the kitchen. Kurt had learned from past experience to be as far from the kitchen as possible. French chefs are an emotional lot and their ravings and rantings when everything is not to perfection can often carry out to the dining room itself. Kurt wanted a nice, quiet, restful evening with a beautiful woman with light, pleasant conversation and with no problems.

"I love it here," Susan said. "I'm glad you brought me. The many times I've been in Georgetown I've never been here before."

"The men you date are too cheap or have no class," Kurt humorously responded. "Would you like to order a drink first?"

"I'd prefer some red wine," she answered. "Somehow it seems more appropriate in a French restaurant."

"You're absolutely right," Kurt said. "You know, I have never been able to get a good American martini in any place but an American bar or restaurant. In Paris, you have to go to Harry's Bar to get a decent American drink. If you order a martini anywhere on the Continent, you usually get just Martini & Rossi vermouth. If they ever try to mix a drink, it is invariably too much dry vermouth. Let me order a good Bordeaux red wine."

Kurt called the waiter and ordered a St. Emilion. Much to the consternation and over the mild objection of the French waiter, he ordered it slightly chilled. "That's one concession he'll have to make for an American," Kurt said. "Bordeaux is a heavier wine and cooling it slightly seems to lighten it a bit without sacrificing any of its aroma and making it taste like a burgundy. I actually prefer a burgundy during the day but a bordeaux in the evening, especially in the company of a beautiful woman like you."

"You're saying all the right things," Susan answered. "Do go on. You are good for my ego and I must admit, I like St. Emilion and I also prefer it chilled."

The waiter brought a bottle of wine in an ice bucket, swirled it several times, uncorked it, and served a bit to Kurt to taste.

"Perfect," Kurt said. The waiter almost reluctantly filled Susan's glass and then Kurt's. When he left he hurriedly took the ice bucket with him before Kurt would have the opportunity to ask for it.

"Well, at least it proves he's an authentic Frenchman," Kurt said. "It's a good sign that the food will be authentic also."

It was a very pleasant and relaxing evening. The food was excellent. Each ordered a different appetizer, entrée, and dessert and, like a typical married couple, would exchange portions of each when the waiter was out of sight.

The conversation was light as each sought to learn more about the other's likes and dislikes. Topics ranged from trivia, which both enjoyed matching each other, to food, to contemporary music, to financial interests.

"What do you do for a living?" Susan asked. "For all I know so far," she said, "I may be dining with a Brink's robber or a serial killer. Although you do stay at the Officers Club, I don't see you as a gung-ho military type. For one thing, your hairstyle gives you away. I never really could stand those close-cut military haircuts. I was an army brat, my dad was a regular Army general, and that's all I saw most of my life."

"You're very observant," Kurt answered. "I'm a reserve officer and that's why I stay at the club. I like it there and I meet many of my old Army buddies there. It feels like home. I suppose that's the same reason why there are so many veteran's organizations. When you've served in the military, especially when you've been in hairy situations, you develop a close camaraderie with people you served with and you transfer that feeling toward the military as a whole. There's the old saying, 'You can take the man out of the Army, but you can never take the Army out of the man'."

"Actually," he went on, "I am a stock market consultant specializing in international issues. I consult to most of the major firms and am on a retainer for each one. You're going to be sorry you asked," he added. "I love the work and usually end up giving a lecture on international economics when people listen."

"No, do go on," she replied. "It's fascinating. Maybe you can even give me some tips. I must admit my meager investments aren't making me independently wealthy. My father gave me a stock portfolio when I graduated from college, but I let a broker handle it and he hasn't been too successful lately, but then the whole market isn't too good."

"I don't advise on day-to-day transactions," Kurt said. "What I do primarily is look for potential foreign investors for U.S. firms, especially when there are merger or take-over possibilities. With some governments such as France becoming more socialistic, many Europeans want to pull out and invest in U. S. companies. The Germans and the British also are looking to get into the U. S. market. This is still the land of opportunity. The Japanese are investing heavily in U. S. businesses and frankly, that worries me. They are benefiting by our advanced technology and eventually may control it. Right now, they are investing heavily in U. S. genetic engineering firms and drug firms. In the long run it will be more profitable for them than electronics has been in the past. Look what has happened to our automobile industry and radio and television industry in this country. See, I told you I'd lecture you if given the chance," he added. "Suffice to say, I enjoy the work I am doing because it does give me a chance to travel, something that's in my blood."

Kurt was convincing, almost to the point of convincing himself, because much of what he was telling Susan was true. Part of his "cover" was being a business consultant on international affairs. It gave him special entrée to many foreign businesses and political leaders throughout the world. U. S. intelligence, under the pressure of the U. S. media and overly liberal interpretations of the first amendment by U. S. courts, was being forced to use such "non-official" covers. Actually, Kurt preferred it that way although there was a greater risk when not under official cover.

"Now for the big question," Susan said, "and it's a devil of a time to ask while you're wining and dining me, but are you married?"

"I was," answered Kurt. He was no longer talkative. The inevitable question brought back painful memories. "Someday I'll tell you all about it," he said, a tactic to avoid the subject.

X

JACKIE

Kurt had, indeed, been married. Because of his early indoctrination in Catholicism he sometimes felt he was still married to Jackie. Jacqueline Ann Prescott, the high school and college beauty queen and the most beautiful girl on campus marrying the most popular athlete and school leader. It was a marriage social columns love to describe. It was sure to have a "they lived happily ever after" ending, but that's not the way it turned out. Kurt often had thought that he should have gone to work for Jackie's father as she had begged him. PRESCOTT, YOUNG and HALSTEAD was one of the most prestigious Wall Street firms and Kurt would have "had it made" as he was often told. He actually did try it for a year, as an apprentice stock broker and that is where he acquired the background for his present cover. They, with the older Prescott's help, bought a beautiful Connecticut ranch style home, in New Canaan, an hour's commuter distance from Kurt's Wall Street office. They became the typical suburbanites. He was almost relieved, however, when the war intervened and took him away from it all. As a reserve Army officer he was one of the first called and he was in South Vietnam in record time. What should have been a one-year tour overseas eventually turned out to be a career after Kurt had been tapped by "The Company".

63

The absences were not what makes young marriages work. The first was a six-month separation on his first tour in Vietnam. They met in Hawaii for his mid tour leave. It was like another honeymoon, he often thought. They were still very much in love and within minutes of their first reunion - he had arranged to meet her at a suite at the Hilton Hawaiian Village rather than in an impersonal airport - they made love, almost violently. It was almost a premonition, he later thought, as if they were trying to combine a lifetime of lovemaking into a short two-week leave period.

They were separated again for another six months when he returned to his combat intelligence unit in Pleiku. On his return to America he told her he had been recruited by "The Company" and it was from that point that the marriage began to die, at least for Jackie.

The early training and indoctrination courses and the initial assignment to Washington headquarters resulted in more separations. Since Kurt anticipated an overseas assignment, he decided to have Jackie stay in Connecticut. She actually preferred that too, hoping at first he would tire of "playing spy" as she described it, and go back to her father's firm in New York. He would come home for a weekend, at most once a month. Of course, there were the nightly phone calls. He would call her and she would return the call the next day. Eventually she did not religiously return his call every time and on increasing occasions she was not at home in the evening when he called.

In the sixth month, the bomb burst and Kurt's world almost fell apart. He came home for his weekend visit early. The course he was attending ended early and he was able to leave Washington on Thursday evening rather than the usual Friday evening. He thought he'd surprise Jackie with flowers, French champagne and an extra night with her. He would graduate from his course the next month and they could start making plans to go overseas together. He had heard that it would possibly be Vienna, Austria and he was excited about that possibility.

He had taken the shuttle to New York and the commuter train to New Canaan. It was only a short walk from the train station to his house but he almost ran in anticipation of his surprise homecoming.

The house was dark except for a night light in the living room, a light that Jackie usually left burning when they expected to be out late. He let himself into the house but Jackie was not home even though her car was in the garage. It was already ten p.m. and he wondered where she was. He didn't want to call any of her friends; perhaps she was playing bridge at the club, but bridge was on Wednesday night, not Thursday night, he mentally corrected himself. He mixed himself a drink, turned on the TV and tried to get interested in a western. The western ended, the late news came on, eventually a late night movie which Kurt could not even remember the name of, and still no Jackie. He thought about calling the police or, perhaps, her parents' apartment in Manhattan but he kept waiting.

About four a.m. he heard an auto drive up in front of the house, a car door slam and the car drive off. He could hear a woman's walk coming up to the house, the key turning in the lock and the door opening.

Jackie walked in alone and was momentarily shocked to see Kurt standing there in the hallway waiting for her. Kurt did not really have to ask; he knew that their world together was over. It was suddenly a stranger he was talking to with a barrier between them that was permanent.

Jackie had been a virgin when they had first made love, admittedly before they have been married, and from that first time Kurt had never had another woman. The opportunities in Vietnam and in Washington, D.C. were too numerous to mention but he would never be untrue to Jackie. He had even been accused by an overly amorous female whom he had met at a Washington party of being "gay" because he did not seem interested in other women. With Jackie he felt that they were almost one person. He felt that they owned all of each other and as a result they were completely without inhibitions with each other. He could not imagine anybody else making love to Jackie and much worse, he could not imagine her responding to another man.

She admitted to Kurt that evening that she was having an affair. She was lonely and she was alone too much. Her lover, who was a bachelor lawyer in town, even proposed marriage to her. Kurt felt betrayed. His reaction was first shock, then hurt, then anger; he wanted to strike out at anyone but even in anger he could not strike Jackie.

In the nightmare that followed, his marriage disintegrated. He blamed himself for neglecting her, he blamed her for being weak, he blamed any man who would seduce another man's wife, he blamed the Army, "The Company", friends who he later found suspected Jackie's infidelity. On the brief occasions that they attempted a reconciliation, he found that he could not even make love to Jackie anymore. When he would see her lying naked before him, he thought of her lying naked before her lover. When he would fondle her beautiful breasts he would visualize another man doing the same. When he was able to have an erection he was not able to maintain it to climax. He felt he had become impotent and was no longer a full man. It was not until he met Sonya almost a year later that he found it was not true.

They were soon legally separated and after a decent interval they were officially divorced. Even after the several years that had passed, Kurt would wake up in the middle of the night and wonder if it had all been a bad dream. Through the years he managed fairly well to forget the painful experience but the question from Susan made it all come back; the same, he supposed as a drowning man reliving his whole life in a few seconds.

XI

SAYING GOODNIGHT

"Hello, are you still there?" Susan asked, bringing him back to reality.

She could see the pain in his eyes and quickly changed the subject to light talk.

"I've been doing all the talking," Kurt said. That was true and uncharacteristic of him but it was necessary to establish his cover story in the beginning of a relationship, and he hoped that his relationship with Susan would be more than a one-time event. "Now you tell me about yourself," Kurt added.

"Well, my name is Susan Smith, that much you know," she answered. "With a name like Smith, naturally I attended Smith College. As I mentioned before, I was an Army brat. Dad was a major general. He's retired now and he and Mother are living in San Antonio where all "old soldiers" seem to end up. That's one of the reasons that I asked for a Texas run on the airline. Now I have a chance to visit my parents more often. I've been a flight attendant about two years. It gives me an opportunity to travel around the world since my airline has international flights. I'll do it another year at most and then, perhaps, go to grad school. I think I'll eventually try fashion merchandising since I love new clothes. I'll try to find a grad school with a program in Paris. No, I am not married and you can relax. I am not out to trap you. I was engaged once," she went on. "The day before my wedding, I panicked and ran off. Dad was furious, especially after he lost the deposits on the wedding gown, the orchestra, the country club, and who knows what else."

"I guess that having been an Army brat and never having had a permanent home, the thought of settling down permanently terrified me. Jeff, my fiancé, was a doctor, an internist, and what he needed was a typical doctor's wife who stays home, has several children, plays the country club scene and eventually becomes a bored, American housewife. There, I've told you the story of my life. Just don't ask me my age," she added. "I don't want to tell you my first lie."

The rest of the evening was idyllic. The conversation was light and interesting. Soon it was time to leave the restaurant.

"Would you like to stop somewhere else here in Georgetown for a drink?" asked Kurt.

"I'd prefer if you would just take me home," answered Susan. "We can have a nightcap there. It's getting late and I do have to check in with the airline tomorrow. I may have a flight out tomorrow afternoon."

It was after midnight and Kurt remembered his eight a.m. meeting with Bo. He was scheduled for a full day of briefings and he liked to be awake and alert for them.

"That's probably for the best," said Kurt. "I hope that we have many evenings together like this."

Kurt paid the bill and generously tipped the waiter for the fine food and excellent service. The waiter thanked him profusely as only a well-tipped French waiter can do. Kurt even felt that the waiter forgave him for the sacrilege of the chilled bordeaux - well, maybe not entirely.

They left the restaurant and, like two young college sweethearts, walked hand in hand, laughing and chattering back to their parked car on the dark Georgetown side street.

The glow of the pleasant evening and the warm companionship of Susan desensitized Kurt and made him oblivious to the rest of the world, so much so that uncharacteristic of him, he did not notice the movement in the shadows across the street from their car.

Kurt opened the door for Susan, helped her in, closed and locked the door and then walked around to the driver's side and opened the door that Susan had unlocked from the inside. It was an automatic precautionary procedure that Kurt did reflexly and apparently Susan also did. He started the engine, did a U-turn on the side street, drove up to and then down Wisconsin Avenue in the direction of Susan's apartment. At a distance, another car pulled out of the same side street and drove in the same direction. It was late in the evening and traffic was light so if a car was following it would not have to follow close. This time Kurt did notice it in the magnified side view mirror of Susan's car. It looked to him like the same car that he had seen earlier in the evening on the way to Georgetown.

Kurt retraced his route to the Arlington Point where Susan lived. He entered the ramp leading down to the lower level parking area, opened the automatic garage door with the remote control provided to every resident and parked Susan's car in the assigned parking slot. They parked and instead of immediately leaving the car, Kurt leaned over and lightly kissed Susan. What began as a light kiss turned out to be a lingering kiss increasing in intensity to the point of being passionate. Her lips parted and he could feel the tip of her tongue exploring his lips, forcing his lips apart. Not a word was spoken as he slipped his arms around her and pulled her as close to him as possible in the bucket type seats of her sports car. He could feel her arms circling him and reciprocating as he noticed her deepening breathing. With their lips pressed together they breathed as one person, an experience which, at that time, was more emotional than physical. Kurt, who had been holding her tightly and pressing her closely to him, relaxed his told. He then bent over and kissed her.

"I think it's time to go upstairs now, Colonel Hoffman," she said. "I feel like a high school girl parking after a date."

"Yes," Kurt answered. "Let's go upstairs. A sports car is hardly the appropriate place for me to whisper sweet nothings to you."

Kurt, who at this time was physically as well as emotionally aroused, was anxious to go up to the privacy and intimacy of Susan's apartment.

They locked the car and entered the elevator which was at the ground floor level.

"I'll bet we were on closed circuit TV," Kurt said, "although with the poor lighting, I'm sure that most was left to the imagination of the building guard in the security office."

"I haven't parked in a car in years," Susan said. "I must admit for a moment I felt like a young girl again." She reached up and lightly kissed Kurt again. "At least there are no cameras here in the elevator," she added.

"And I hope that there aren't any in your apartment," Kurt said.

The elevator reached the twelfth floor and stopped. They stepped out, hand in hand like two young sweethearts. Susan squeezed his hand as they reached her apartment. She handed Kurt the key, he unlocked the door, and they entered the apartment.

As he offered to help her with her fur wrap, she turned and kissed him quickly on the lips. "I think we should skip the nightcap. It's time we said good night," she said nervously looking around.

"It's not exactly what I had in mind," Kurt answered but he could see that she was serious and not just teasing. He did not want to jeopardize their relationship.

"But, I warn you," he continued. "You haven't seen the last of me. I'll call you as soon as I can after my meeting today. Okay?"

She looked up into his eyes, hesitated for a moment, and answered, "I hope you do."

He left and he could hear the door being closed and locked behind him. "That was rather strange," he said to himself. "She seemed really excited in the car but she really cooled quickly in her apartment." I hope that she's not expecting someone else, he thought with a feeling of jealousy overcoming him. After Jackie, Kurt had learned to control his emotions. He swore to himself that he would never let himself get into another position of feeling jealousy over any woman, and he had not, not even over Sonya.

With Susan this feeling started to surface and he did not like it. My God, I've only known her for one day, he thought. Why should I feel this way?

XII

THE RIDE HOME

He took the elevator to the lobby and asked the desk clerk to call a cab for him.

"It's not necessary, sir," replied the clerk, not even getting up from his desk which was behind the reception desk. It was adjacent to closed circuit TV cameras which gave him the opportunity at a glance of seeing all the major exits and hallways and also the parking area under the building.

He was a small, gray-haired man, probably one of many retired military men or government workers who took these jobs to supplement their retirement pensions.

"Because we are so near the airport, there are cabs that drive by in the front of the building every few minutes, even at this time of the day," he added. He looked at Kurt with a sly, knowing smile on his face.

The dirty old bastard, thought Kurt to himself. Probably was training his eyes at the TV camera from the garage.

"Thanks," he said as he walked out the front door which opened as the desk clerk pressed the release button for the automatic door.

He looked down the street and there was a cab parked at the nearby corner. He waved to it and was relieved to see the lights turn on and the cab drive up to him and stop.

Kurt opened the door and jumped in, telling the driver to drive him to the club at Twenty First and R in the District. The driver grunted in acknowledgement and drove off in the direction of the Parkway. Kurt did not even see the driver's face. The driver had on a Greek fisherman's hat which was popular with aging, hippie types that were still in Washington and frequented the DuPont Circle area. The hat was pulled down to just over his eyes and it was obvious that he had not visited his barber in months.

Kurt leaned back and rested his head on the back of the seat and tried to recapitulate in his mind the events of the day and night. He truly enjoyed meeting Susan. It was a feeling that you experience seldom in life but when it happens you know that it is something unique and special. From the first time he saw Susan in the plane as he boarded it in Houston, he was attracted to her. When their eyes first met he could feel that there was a special communication between them. Perhaps it was some extrasensory phenomenon but he knew that something would develop between them. When, in the course of the flight, he finally asked her to have dinner with him that evening, he somehow knew she would accept, almost as if it were predestined. His mind drifted as he thought of the all too brief romantic episode in the car. Damn it, I sure would like to have spent the night with her, he thought, but that, too, will come. I just know it.

Thinking about Susan he did not even notice that the cab drove off the Parkway into one of the deserted parking areas that overlook the Potomac River. The cab suddenly stopped and the driver turned around, pointing a 38 revolver directly at Kurt. In that split second Kurt noticed that the driver was wearing a rubber Halloween mask with long hair.

Instead of bolting for the door, Kurt reflexly kicked the front seat simultaneously with the first shot which he could almost feel as it whizzed by his ear and hit the back seat. He rolled forward and at the same time grabbed for the door handle. The door opened as Kurt continued to roll and tumble head first out the door onto the asphalt parking area. The second shot was wild and even farther off target; the driver was off balance as a result of Kurt's kicking the seat. Fortunately for Kurt there was a wooded area at the edge of the parking lot where the cab had stopped, the cabbie apparently thinking it would be good cover and a place where he would not be observed by anyone on the nearby parkway. Kurt quickly ran into the woods and out of sight of the cab. He had left his automatic in his hotel room and was in no position to make a fight out of it.

From the woods he heard the cab start up and quickly drive off onto the parkway. Watching the cab speed away, Kurt walked back up to the parkway. Several cars sped by as he walked along the road in the direction of the Key Bridge, but none stopped. In the high crime area of Washington, especially at this time of night, Kurt did not really expect anyone to stop. He also hoped that no park police car would drive by. He did not want to have to give any explanation to the police of why he was walking alone on the parkway in the middle of the night. He would, of course, have to report the incident to "Security" as soon as possible.

The half mile walk to Key Bridge took only a few minutes and Kurt walked up the hill from the parkway to the large Marriott Hotel at the southwest end of the bridge. There were several cabs waiting. He picked one and again gave directions to Twenty First and R.

After he reached the club he decided to wait until morning to report the incident. If I call Security now, he thought, I would be up the rest of the night answering questions.

He did call Bo at his unlisted home number and reported it to him before he retired for the night. Bo told him that he would pass it on and they would talk about it the next morning at the briefing.

XIII

THE BRIEFING

April 3, 1990

Kurt had left a wake-up call for six-thirty a.m. and as usual the desk clerk was efficient and called exactly at that time. It gave Kurt enough time to shower and shave and have a quick breakfast at the all-night restaurant on Connecticut Avenue, just a block from the club. He then hailed a cab on the corner of Connecticut and R Streets and gave directions to the cabbie to a location which would take him about one block from the "safehouse" where he was to meet Bo and where the briefing would take place. This time he paid a little more attention to the cabbie after his experience of the previous evening.

The "safehouse" was in a high-rise residential building not far from George Washington University. It was in a rather congested part of the city where the comings and goings of many people of different nationalities were commonplace and did not seem unusual. It was the same location in which Kurt had had his last briefing about six months earlier, before his last mission.

Kurt paid the cabbie and walked the one black to the apartment building and took the elevator to the tenth floor, the top floor of the building, where the apartment was. Safehouses were almost invariably on the top floor of such buildings. It provided a little more security than other floors since it was less vulnerable to audio surveillance from a floor above. The KGB and other intelligence services did the same so in a sense this practice was actually a vulnerability.

Kurt's elevator reached the tenth floor simultaneously with a parallel elevator carrying Max.

"Can I bum a cigarette from you, buddy?" were words of greeting from Max even before Kurt had the opportunity to say good morning.

"Sorry, buddy," Kurt answered, emphasizing the word 'buddy'. "Sis lectured me half the evening on the hazards of smoking and made me promise to kick the evil habit. I've smoked my last cigarette so you'll have to bum them from someone else from now on."

"Your sister would have had a better time with me last night," Max said. "I went the culture route and took in Rostropovich at the Kennedy Center. How did your evening go?" he asked.

"Nothing eventful," Kurt replied. "Just a quiet family affair."

"I'll bet it was an affair," Max said as they reached the apartment at the end of the hall, knocked on the door and were admitted by a young crew-cut security man. I wish these ambitious young security types wouldn't have military-type haircuts and be so conservatively dressed, Kurt thought to himself, especially here in the university area. They either look like cops or what they really are.

Kurt and Max walked into what was a darkened living room with a slide projector, screen, and briefing boards set up. They were the last to arrive and the room seemed half full with serious looking analyst types who were to brief them on their upcoming mission.

Bo approached Kurt first, took him aside and said quietly to him so the others would not hear, "The police found a cabbie early this morning shot in the back of the head with a 38 and dumped off the George Washington Parkway. They found his cab a couple of hours ago on a side street here in the District. There was a rubber Halloween mask similar to the one you described to me last night. I've a feeling that what happened to you last night was more than a robbery attempt. I hope it wasn't related to what you'll hear today. The project security officer wants to talk to you later today about it."

After brief introductions of first names, Kurt and Max each chose a soft cushioned chair, sat down and made themselves comfortable for what they were sure would be a seemingly endless series of briefings.

The chief of the briefing team, a white-haired man, probably in his mid fifties, who was called Walter, led off. "Kurt," he started out using only first names, "you and Max were specifically selected for this mission for several reasons. One, you two work well together, especially in dangerous situations and believe me, this will be a dangerous situation. Two, there probably will be 'terminations' necessary and you two are our experts at this, Max, especially, when it has to look natural. Three, the locale will be in Austria and the German part of Switzerland, and, of course, you, Kurt, are our specialist in that area. And fourth, and probably most important," he added, "Willi Gross is involved and I'm sure I don't have to elaborate on that, do I, Kurt?"

Willi Gross - Doctor Wilhelm Gross, Kurt thought to himself. How that brings back memories, some good and some very unpleasant, some painful.

Kurt had met Willi years ago when he was first assigned to Vienna, Austria and not long after his breakup with Jackie. Willi was a doctor who was a resident physician in Gmunden, in the Salzkammergut Lake district of Austria. Willi, who was a prominent figure in the beautiful, picturesque city built on the edge of a lake, was also an agent of "The Company" and Kurt was assigned to work with him on his first case in Austria. They became very close friends and Willi and his family, a wife named Lisa and three children, made Kurt almost one of the family.

Willi had been a military doctor in World War II and served with Rommel in the Afrika Korps in North Africa. He was captured at Tobruk and was sent as a POW to Canada. There was a severe shortage of physicians in Canada during World War II, especially in the western lumber area. Willi, who had never been a Nazi and who spoke excellent English, was given the opportunity to work, as a doctor, in a north woods town. As a prisoner of war he had complete freedom and actually lived as a Canadian. He rewarded the trust with excellent service and became a loved and respected member of the province. In a three-year period he is reported to have delivered over two hundred babies, performed countless operations and saved many lives. He was offered Canadian citizenship after the war but he chose to return to his beloved Austria where he descended from nobility. He returned to Austria, married, had three children (two sons and a daughter) and had a very successful practice as a "Praktische Arzt".

But Willi had had his taste of adventure and could not resist an overture from "The Company" to work as a deep cover agent in addition to practicing medicine. Because of his performance in Canada, he was highly recommended by Canadian Intelligence to "The Company". He was an excellent agent and had actually helped train Kurt in specialized operations. He and his family knew about Jackie and Willi secretly hoped that his daughter, Ursula, who was then a teenager, and Kurt would eventually end up together. Ursula, or Ushie as she was called, actually had a school girl crush on Kurt. She told her parents and friends that she would one day marry Kurt, she just knew it. Kurt jokingly kept telling her that he was waiting for her to grow up.

Everybody does make at least one big mistake in his life and Willi made his. At the pleading of the daughter of a prominent Austrian political leader, he performed an abortion on her. She had made a mistake in having an affair with a married man and had become pregnant. Her parents were unaware of this problem and she begged Willi to help her. He thought of his own daughter, Ushie being in the same predicament and he could not refuse. The one in a thousand odds came up and Willi lost. In spite of doing a very expert professional procedure, complications set in and the poor girl died. A police investigation pointed directly to Willi and in Catholic Austria, where abortions were illegal at that time, Willi faced disgrace and certain imprisonment. The only countries where there were no extradition laws for criminal cases were in Communist eastern countries. Willi fled with his family to East Germany confessing his association with "The Company" and claiming that he had seen the error in his ways. The last Kurt had heard of Willi he was practicing medicine in Dresden, East Germany (DDR).

The second briefer, who was introduced only as George, looked like a true operational agent. Kurt thought he detected a slight accent, probably German, in the man who was possibly in his late fifties. He began his briefing recounting in minute detail, events that had begun in Dachau in April 1945.

"We have," he said, "reconstructed what we believe is an accurate account of a series of events that can have a profound impact on our national security. From files on individuals that we confiscated in Berlin immediately at the end of the war, the Nazis kept a very complete dossier on everybody living in Germany or occupied countries and we were fortunate to get those files before the Russians. We were able to identify a top secret military project that the Nazis had hoped would win them the war."

He went on. "Adolf Hitler had promised that the Reich would develop a secret weapon that would win the war for Germany. With our preoccupation at that time with missiles, the U-2, and with nuclear weapons which we, in America, were developing, we assumed that the Nazis were also trying to make a nuclear bomb. Through our Alsos Mission under Colonel Boris Pash we learned that this was not the case. Their nuclear program was far behind ours and that always seemed inconsistent to our intelligence of Germany fighting with their backs to the wall. They were too good as scientists to fall that far behind unless their priority went to another type of weapon. Well, we found out what it was, and Hitler was not just making idle threats. The Nazis had developed a charged particle beam weapon, that is, a death ray. It could literally wipe out any living creature in its path for miles. With proper calibration it could knock out any plane in the air, destroy any standing structure or anything in its path. The beautiful thing about it was that it didn't require a huge, expensive, cumbersome program like our Manhattan Project which developed our first atom bomb. It could be done relatively easily in an unsophisticated facility, as long as one had the plans and specifications. The Nazis actually did get to the production stage but by the grace of God or by just plain asshole luck," he turned and apologized to the one woman briefer present for the expletive, "the factory that produced it was accidentally destroyed. Some of you old enough to remember might recall an incident near the end of the war when a U. S. flyer who had been on a bombing mission over Linz, Austria was hit and bailed out by a nearby city called Attnang. As he landed he was pitchforked to death by some farmers. Word about it got back to our Air Corps and on any bombing mission that was even remotely in the general area, the planes would detour and make a final run over Attnang. There was a motto at the time, "Save one for Attnang". Anyway, the production facility for the weapon happened to be in the woods near Attnang. The Germans thought it had good concealment. Well, to make a long story short, the whole area eventually looked like a moon landscape. Everything was destroyed, including their prototype weapons that could have wiped us out. All they had left were the plans and specifications. They were last seen in the hands of Martin Bormann and his nephew, a man by the name of Konzett, Karl Konzett. Later we will have a briefer from Scientific Intelligence explain what a charge particle beam weapon is. It would be good for you to know about it and it will hopefully impress you about the importance and urgency of this mission that you're going on." George continued his lengthy briefing. He related the story beginning in April 1945 in Dachau concerning Mueller, Reichardt, Luckner, and Konzett and their trip from Dachau to Vorarlberg. The story was a result of painstaking research and fitting together of bits and pieces of related events. He first gave a brief biographical sketch of all the characters involved. "Axel Reichardt," the briefer continued, "survived the trip from Dachau. Konzett, who was Bormann's nephew, and who was driving one of the two trucks, stopped by the side of the road and shot Reichardt. However, Reichardt was only superficially wounded but pretended to be dead. He managed to find his way back to Vienna and somehow survived the Russians who took the city. He went underground and during the occupation he lived under a new identity. However, in

1950 he was uncovered by Mossad agents and was carted off to Israel as a war criminal. The Nuremberg Trials were over so the Israelis decided to try him themselves, just as they did Eichmann later on. Before he was brought to trial, however, he did the first honorable thing he had done in years and hanged himself but fortunately not before he told as much as he could about Mueller, Konzett, and Luckner. He was able to provide us with the one key element to this whole puzzle. The two gray-haired types that Konzett brought to Dachau with him from Berlin, turned out, according to Reichardt's description, to be the two scientists who developed the death ray weapon. Reichardt, who had been a stickler for detail, did learn their names before he arranged to "send them up the chimney" at Dachau. We were able to cross check their names with the Nazi files we confiscated in Berlin."

"Feldwebel, or Sergeant Franz Luckner was another story. You almost had to feel sorry for the guy. He was at Dachau so you couldn't just give him a clean slate." The briefer continued to unfold the long, detailed events that had occurred over thirty five years previously. "Most of the rest we got from Luckner, himself," he said. "Luckner was shot by Colonel Mueller. Somehow, through some miracle, he survived being shot and rolling down the whole mountainside. It was probably because he was unconscious at the time. He was found by his own pet German Shepherd dog who was able to alert his family. He was nursed back to health by his family but because he was on the "faculty" at Dachau, he was eventually arrested, tried in a war criminal court and sentenced to hang at Landsberg. And guess who he met at Landsberg? Willi Gross. Willi was a physician who was assigned at that time to examine all those prisoners and to surreptitiously interrogate them for "The Company". Before he was hanged, Luckner confided to Willi about all the gold and other valuables buried up in Lunersee. He made Willi promise that if he would find it he would split it with Luckner's family in Brand. Whether Willi would ever have done that, your guess is as good as mine."

"Hoffman," the briefer went on, for the first time calling Kurt by other than his first name, "do you remember when Willi asked you to borrow a mine detector from the U. S. Army in Germany? He had apparently tried for several years to find the buried gold and other valuables by just following Luckner's description and he always failed. I suppose it became an obsession with him just like "The Lost Dutchman" mine in Arizona has been in this country for so many years. Even with the detector that you provided for him he was unable to locate it. First, mine detectors at that time only detected metal a few inches below the ground and second, all the original landmarks were changed. For that I will let our next briefer, Michael, explain to you what happened. I'll then return."

He sat down and the next speaker, a scholarly-looking young man, probably in his late twenties, placed a slide in the projector and showed it on the screen.

"In the early 1950s," he began, "there was a need to provide electrical power for industry in the German Ruhr that was being restored. Germany, in collaboration with Austria, decided to build a hydroelectro facility at Lunersee, south of Bludenz. Because of melting snow from the glacier in the higher peaks, there is a constant source of water for the lake. A dam was built which raised the water level of the lake by over seventy five feet at the highest point at certain times of the year. What is especially unique," he went on, "is that the lowest level is in the spring and the highest level is in the fall. You would expect that it would be highest in the spring as the snow melts but that is not true. The German government arranged with the Austrians to use the hydroelectro plant to handle increased demands for power at peak periods. The greatest need is, therefore, in the winter and spring when there is a larger need for electricity. In the summer and fall, especially since they don't have much air conditioning over there, there is less demand for electricity and the lake is at its highest."

"Willi Gross, and whoever else might be looking for anything buried there, usually looked in the summer and fall thinking that would be the lowest level. Actually what was buried there according to Luckner's original description to Willi is probably about thirty meters or one hundred feet under water most of the year. Therefore we feel that it is probably still there after all these years."

Michael then pointed to the screen where he had projected an engineer's map of the Lunersee area and a drawing of the dam in relationship to the mountain.

He was obviously an engineer and he went into great detail on the dam, its construction, and its operational capabilities.

"There is another point I would like to stress," he added. "As I mentioned before, all the original landmarks were moved when the dam was constructed. The Douglas Hutte, which is a mountain lodge, was moved to a higher elevation. The original site, which was a peninsula extending out into the lake, is now under water. The other landmarks, two large rock formations, have also been moved. By comparing maps and pictures from the 1940s we feel we can pinpoint exactly where the "goodies" were buried. With current sophisticated electronic gear it should be quite easy to pinpoint the site once the water level is down. The water level at the end of this month should be low enough that the site will be out of water completely, by about ten meters, I would estimate." Michael then turned the briefing back to the second speaker, George, after several questions from Kurt and Max.

George then brought back the subject of Dr. Wilhelm Gross. "Willi," he said, "can never come back to the West but he would like a better life for his family, especially his daughter, Ursula, or Ushie, as you know her, Kurt."

"He has been able to get word back to us that he will tell us approximately where the buried containers should be. The time element is very important so we can't afford to spend a lot of time finding it. What I mean is that you two," he said, pointing to Kurt and Max, "will have no more than ten or twelve hours to find it, dig it out, and secure it somewhere. The water level, which is controlled at the Krafthaus at the base of the mountain, will be at its lowest level for only about twelve hours at a time sometime later this month. The Austrian government, which doesn't know anything about all this, made a public announcement of their intention to lower the water level to test the Krafthaus and make minor repairs. We will find out the exact date and time soon and get word to you. You should be in Austria and be ready to move at a moment's notice."

"You have probably surmised by now," he continued, "that we are not just interested in digging up gold and diamonds. We are really interested in that metal attache case that Karl Konzett buried along with the other containers. That, we are sure, contains the plans and specifications for the Nazi charged particle beam weapon. Not that you two can keep the gold and other valuables. Incidentally, according to Willi it includes, and I quote 'Edelsteinen, Goldmunzen und Goldbarren'. That, you'll have to turn in to us."

Max leaned over to Kurt and whispered in his ear, "If we find it, we had better make sure they give us a receipt. I don't trust these headquarters bastards. They've all become a bunch of fucking bureaucrats."

"There are, of course, some complications to all of this," the briefer continued. "Naturally, nothing comes easy and that is why we selected you two. As I mentioned before, Willi has promised to get an exact description of where the containers are buried. He won't write out or draw a map but will get the word to us through his daughter, Ursula. She will be in Vienna this month. She has become an accomplished musician and is the number one cellist in the Dresden Symphony Orchestra. It will perform at the Vienna Stats Oper, fortuitously this month. She will only talk to Kurt, no one else. We have promised Willi that we will help his daughter defect after she has told Kurt the location at Lunersee. When she arrives she will contact us by telephone at a number we have given her. You will also have this telephone contact, Kurt. Naturally we do not want you to come even near our station in Vienna or any of our safehouses. There, unfortunately, may have been a leak and we don't want to take a chance in the event any of our locations have been blown. Nobody must know of your assignment. Before I go on," he said, "I'll let our next briefer, Julian, from Counter Intelligence, fill you in on the complications and possible leaks."

Julian, a rotund, balding, middle-aged man, stood up, put several slides in the projector and began to speak. "Willi, as you know," he said, "has two sons, one is an engineer, Josef, and the other, Willi Junior, is a military officer in the East German Army. Junior is no Communist, but he is ambitious. He knows just vague details about the gold and the old man, in spite of prodding, won't tell him anything more. Through our intercepts we know that Junior has passed the word on to the KGB. The KGB knows that there is more than just gold involved. They are smart enough to put two and two together and they know what those two scientists who ended up in Dachau did. Rather than sweat it out of Willi, and possibly blow the whole operation, we believe that they will let Ursula out, under close surveillance and let us lead them to it. So you two will have the KGB to deal with," he said, speaking directly to Kurt and Max.

"Don't think that you are going to be able to get off that easy," he added. "We believe that the Dachau Kommandant, Mueller, and Karl Konzett eventually ended up in Paraguay, South America after first going to the Mideast. There are a lot of ex-Nazis down there and they are collaborating with some of the more radical Arab elements. A lot of these Arab terrorists, individuals such as Carlos and others who are violently anti-Semitic and would like to see the Nazis return, have been working closely with these Nazis in South America. They need more money to finance their operations, especially if efforts to force Qaddafi in Libya to withdraw his support are successful. They could use the gold and other valuables and you can just guess how much they would like to have a death ray capability. They all know that the Lunersee is going to be lowered. It was even in the newspapers. That's one of the reasons we believe that Mueller and Konzett never did come back and dig it out before. By the time they got to South America and would have a chance to sneak back, the dam was built and it would have been technically impossible to retrieve it. They know that they will have only this one chance."

"Thirdly, before you relax too much, " he continued, "you are going to have Mossad to deal with. We know that the Israelis have penetrated the KGB Operations Directorate as well as some of the Arab terrorist groups, so they probably have an idea of what's going on. They have the reports on Reichardt before he did himself in. Reichardt never did get to Lunersee but had an idea that it was where Mueller was taking them. And, of course, the Israelis know about the water level at Lunersee. So, gentlemen," he finally said, "you will not be alone and lonesome on this mission."

Before he sat down, Julian quickly flashed pictures of all the individuals who Kurt and Max might encounter. It included old pictures of Mueller and Konzett, pictures of Willi and Ursula, and pictures of possible Israeli agents, Arab terrorists, and KGB agents who had been reported to be in Austria or said to be heading to Austria.

Kurt was taken back by the pictures of Ushie. He had not seen or even communicated with her father or her for several years. She was no longer an awkward young teenage but a beautiful, mature woman. He looked forward to seeing her again.

The briefing team chief, Walter, then introduced the next speaker, the only woman briefer present, whose name was Barbara. She was an articulate and obviously very bright engineer who was in her mid thirties and from the Company's Scientific Intelligence section. First, she gave a short presentation on the status of research on charged particle beam weapons. "As far as the Soviets and we are concerned," she said, "the operational use of such weapons is several years off at best. It is amazing that the Nazis had developed it back in 1945."

She then opened a small suitcase that she had brought and explained some of the items that she carefully placed on the table in the front of the room.

"This is some operational equipment that you two will need," she said. She described and demonstrated a small walkie-talkie the size and shape of a wristwatch that her section had developed. She also showed them a small apparatus, the size of a cigarette pack, that was a remote sort of EKG. It had the capability, using low level microwaves, to determine heart rates and respiration up to a distance of forty feet. "With this capability," she said, "you can not only detect an individual's presence within this distance , and that is even through walls, but it can be used as a remote polygraph - a lie detector."

The third and last item she demonstrated was a lightweight, highly sensitive, compact metal detector that she, herself, had helped construct. "This apparatus," she proudly said, "operates on the principal of an electromagnetic field either produced or detected by the instrument. It can detect ferrous and non-ferrous metals to a depth of thirty feet. I hope you gentlemen don't have to dig that deep," she said in conclusion.

Walter and then George, the first two briefers, made concluding remarks and the briefing was over.

XIV

THE REVELATION

It had been a lengthy, thorough, and exhausting briefing. It had started in the morning, did not even break for lunch (sandwiches and coffee had been brought in), and the briefing continued on until about five p.m. They had even had a briefing from a security man who had come and gone. He had brought Kurt up to date on what they knew from the cabbie murder the night before. There was nothing new. The briefers left one by one in intervals of about ten minutes until only Bo, Kurt and Max remained.

Kurt went into the kitchen and found a bottle of scotch whiskey in the pantry. Such safehouses were usually well stocked and could support several people for days, if necessary, with food and drinks. Furniture, however, was usually sparse and provided only basic needs such as beds, chairs and kitchen appliances. Since such places were leased for relatively short periods, to lessen being identified, there usually was no permanent carpeting, unless furnished by the owners. Electrical appliances were always provided by the Company to lessen their possibly being bugged or facilitating audio-surveillance by the opposition.

"Pour me a scotch, too," Max said to Kurt. "I'm really beat. All these briefings are too much."

Kurt half-filled two drinking glasses with scotch, went to the refrigerator, struggled with an uncooperative ice cube tray, finally put two ice cubes in each drink, and handed one to Max.

"Those cheap bastards from Logistics," he said to Bo who was assembling his notes and putting them in his attache case. "Why don't they invest a little more in refrigerators and get ice makers? They're always trying to save money on those things so you can always tell it's a safehouse."

He started to drink the scotch and suddenly he stopped and stared at Bo. He put down the drink quickly, turned, picked up the telephone and dialed a number. He listened, as the color began to drain from his face. He then leafed through a Virginia telephone book that was on the desk by the phone, found and dialed another number.

"Arlington Point Towers?" he asked in the telephone. "Is this the front desk? Would you please connect me with 1206? Are you sure?" he asked. "The apartment has been empty for over a month?" He put down the phone quietly and looked at Bo.

When Kurt was very angry he did not exhibit his temper. He had always been cool and collected in such situations but his voice betrayed his anger by lowering a pitch.

"You had better have a good explanation for this, Bo," he said in this voice. "I don't have to explain to you why I'm pissed off, do I?"

Bo looked uneasy and started to stammer but Kurt continued on. "Chance encounter on the plane, top floor, the fucking cheap refrigerator, a lot of personal questions. You even know that I get turned on by black-haired women. What in the hell is really her name?" Kurt was not only angry, he was hurt and ever since Jackie he did not like the feeling of being hurt. Susan, or whatever the hell her name is, really got to me, he thought to himself.

"What in the hell is the matter, Bo?" he asked. "Am I under a cloud? Doesn't the Company trust me anymore? Haven't I given up my whole life? My marriage? Everything?" he went on.

"Don't take it personal," Bo sheepishly replied. "It's just routine these days before sensitive assignments and there is Sonya," he added.

Kurt stared at him and the whole room was deathly quiet. Even Max, who had taken it all in, did not utter a word.

"If I weren't so deeply involved in this mission, I'd tell the Company to go and fuck themselves," Kurt replied. "But I'll remember this, I promise you," he added. He gulped the drink down and filled his glass again.

.

XV

"Wien"

Vienna, Austria - April 5, 1990

The trip to Austria was uneventful. To tourists, Kurt thought, visiting Vienna, one of the most beautiful cities in the world, is a remarkable experience, very often a once in a lifetime event and one that a person who loves music, art, and old world atmosphere will remember the rest of his life. Although this was a "business trip", Kurt still loved to see the city and each time he arrived there he experienced the feelings of a first time tourist. The city brought back many memories, some, but not all, pleasant ones. It was the first assignment for him after his breakup with Jackie. In any other city the pain and loneliness that he felt would have been almost unbearable. Vienna helped him survive through that trying period.

He had left Washington on Saturday, the day after the briefing. He had once again tried to call Susan hoping that he could get some kind of plausible explanation. There was no number listed for her. No one had even heard of a Susan Smith. He had even visited the Arlington Point where she had lived. He was told that apartment 1206 was unoccupied. He demanded to see the apartment and the assistant manager reluctantly showed it to him. It was indeed empty, even the refrigerator that he had struggled with was gone. In its place was a modern, standard apartment refrigerator that was usually furnished in such an apartment in the Washington area. This one even had an ice-maker. He looked for the "dirty old man" desk clerk that he had met previously but since it was a weekend he was not in nor expected to be in until the following Monday. The Company has been very efficient, Kurt thought.

He met Bo briefly on Saturday and then took a mid-afternoon flight from Washington National Airport to Kennedy Airport in New York. From there he boarded a Swissair flight to Zurich, Switzerland and connected there with Austrian Airlines to Vienna.

Kurt had made his own travel and hotel arrangements, much to the consternation of the Company, which was developing, more and more through the years, into an old line bureaucracy and became involved in making even these minor decisions under the guise of economy. "Company" bureaucrats insisted on their people traveling on U.S. carriers. This, Kurt always thought, presented an additional security problem. It made KGB's counter-intelligence work much easier by just checking manifests of U.S. airlines and having a man at the international airports. Because of the ultra-sensitivity of his assignments, Kurt thus far was given the authority and the budget to act independently of Headquarters but with each new empire builder stationed in Washington, he knew that eventually it would be more difficult for him to continue doing so and it worried him. He did not travel with Max and each had made his own arrangements. They would reach each other in Vienna through the telephone contact that Bo had given them. Kurt felt that this provided an additional element of security for them both. Kurt had checked into the Astoria Hotel this time. It was actually his favorite but just one of several that he stayed in while in Vienna. He did not want to establish a pattern and frequent the same hotel while in the city.

Knowledgeable Austrians would choose a first class Viennese hotel such as the Astoria. Most of the Americans would stay at the luxury class Hotel Bristol or Hotel Sacher which were near the Opera House on the Ring. The Ring was a street that could be compared with what is usually known as an inner city belt-way found in many American cities. The Ring started at the Danube River and circled around the First Bezirk (or precinct). Along the Ring and within it were most of the important points of interest such as the Vienna State Opera, Hofburg Palace, St. Stephan's Cathedral and countless museums, churches, theatres and historical buildings.

The Astoria was located at the corner of the world famous Kartner Strasse with the main entrance on Furichgasse, a side street. It was located only two blocks from the beautiful Vienna State Opera House and a block from the well-known Hotel Sacher, a luxury class hotel whose reputation Kurt thought was greatly overrated. The Sacher had, at one time, been one of the great hotels in Europe like the Claridge Hotels in Paris and London, the Vierjahrzeiten in Munich, the Danieli-Excelsior in Venice and others. It had, for over a century, reflected the typical "Gemutlich" charm of old Vienna but unfortunately fell victim to publicity and rich tourists in recent years. Its one great claim to fame, at least as far as Kurt was concerned, was its famous Sacher Torte, a chocolate cake topped with whipped cream that no one else could duplicate and one that Kurt could not resist whenever he was in Vienna.

The coffee shop in the front of the Sacher Hotel was Kurt's first stop after he had checked into his hotel, bathed and changed his clothes. He entered the coffee shop, asked for and was seated next to the window where he could look out and see the back of the mammoth Opera House. Looking at it brought back fond memories of his first assignment in Vienna. His cover at that time was as a student studying at the University of Vienna. One of the fringe benefits of students was getting student tickets for all the cultural events in this culture-loaded city. As a student he was qualified for a "Stehplatz Karte" at the Opera House. It meant a reduced price ticket only for students where one would have a ticket to stand at the rear of the theatre at the various levels. Once the event for the evening had begun, the students were permitted to move into an empty seat in the house. Since there were seldom many such empty seats, it was usually a race to find one. Kurt laughed to himself as he remembered how he and his Austrian school mates would conspire to get those prize seats. At that time, with the favorable currency exchange in the 1970s, Kurt actually could well afford to buy the best seats but in establishing his student cover, he assumed the role to the hilt. He thought back to those days when those tickets cost him four Austrian Schillings or about sixteen cents in U. S. money. For that he had seen the best operas, concerts, and ballets in the world. He missed those days; he never seemed to have time any-more for those cultural events that he had learned to love.

"Einmal Sacher Torte mit Schlag und eine gross Expresso," he told the waitress who took his order. As she scurried off to fill his order, Kurt walked to the public telephone that was near the entrance of the shop. He dialed the number that he had re-ceived from Bo in Washington. In calling his contact number, he always called from a public phone and never the same one twice. He never did call from his hotel room. After just one ring, a woman's voice answered. Speaking German, Kurt and the German voice exchanged pre-arranged greetings establishing each other's identity. Kurt mentioned that he was staying at the Astoria and he arranged a code for "the voice" when he called. A particular name or event would be mentioned at the beginning of each call. He would call in twice daily at irregular times to accept any incoming messages or instructions. His East German contact, Ursula Gross, would call the same number when she arrived in Vienna and it was through this mechanism that they would arrange for a personal meeting. Kurt also learned that Max had not yet arrived in Vienna. When he did, he would be given Kurt's hotel in order to establish contact.

Kurt finished his call and walked back to his table where his Sacher Torte and his coffee with whipped cream awaited him. As usual, it was delicious and Kurt savored every morsel. In Vienna such events are an occasion and not to be rushed and Kurt did just that. He finished his cake slowly and after one hour and one more cup of coffee, he paid his bill, leaving the appropriate "Trinkgeld". American tourists could always be identified by the exorbitant tips that they left not knowing that such service was always written into the bill. Kurt, passing as a typical Austrian, left the small change from his bill to his appreciative waitress.

He walked out of the shop and passed the entrance to the Hotel Sacher where the doorman was helping some wealthy, obese woman from her Mercedes. He continued to the corner which was Kartner Strasse and walked in the direction of The Graben and St. Stephan's Cathedral, a landmark in the center of the city. Kartner Strasse, like some of the centrally located streets in some European cities, was made into a promenade and no vehicular traffic was permitted. Kurt liked that. When many of these cities were built, sometimes centuries ago, there was no thought of heavy automobile and truck traffic with its resultant pollution problems. With growing prosperity after World War II, traffic problems increased in direct proportion to the standard of living. The beautiful, picturesque streets and sections of the cities, some dating back to medieval days, became congested, noise nightmares. To preserve their historical heritage and to prevent the inhabitants' flight from the cities as happened in United States cities, far-sighted city planners in such cities as Munich, Salzburg, Lugano, and Vienna closed off some of these streets, planted trees and flowers, installed park benches and made the areas into promenades complete with sidewalk cafes, "soap boxes", and stands where amateur and, sometimes, professional entertainers could perform. In Vienna, it became a place where a businessman could, on his lunch time break, sit in his favorite outside café and watch the world walk by, or where the wealthy lady, usually with her well-groomed French poodle or dachshund, could window shop or make purchases in the exclusive shops fronting on the promenade. In the evening the street was alive with people strolling up and down the way, listening to whatever entertainment there was, visiting the many shops that stayed open late, or just enjoying a drink and conversation at the cafes.

Kurt continued his leisurely stroll toward the Graben. It was a warm and balmy day for April and the spring weather brought not only the early tourists for the year, but many Viennese who wanted to enjoy the new cultural attraction of the promenade. The favorite pastime on such a Sunday afternoon for the city inhabitants was a "Spaziergang", or afternoon stroll. There were so many places in Vienna to stroll; the Vienna Woods, immortalized by Johann Strauss; Schonbrunn Palace with its beautiful gardens and its rich history of the Hapsburg Dynasty; the Prater, a park noted for its huge ferris wheel and made famous by the post-war movie, "The Third Man"; Grinzing, the wine district and the home of Beethoven; and now the promenade in the center of the city. The attractions in the city were endless and one could spend a lifetime and not seem them all.

Vienna did have one other distinction. It probably had the greatest concentration of spies per capita than any other city in the world. Vienna is the city where East meets the West. It had become a window for Western spies into the Communist Bloc and for Eastern European and Soviet spies into the West. Many had speculated that the only reason that the Soviets had agreed to end their occupation of eastern Austria, which encircled and included part of Vienna, was to create that window. As a window to the West, it also served as an excellent route to channel agents. With the mass emigration of Russian Jews through Vienna to Israel and to other Western countries, many agents came who had assumed Jewish identities and could be very easily concealed in the large number of people seeking the freedom of a non-Communist country. It served also as an economic port and became a trade center. The country of Austria, itself, claimed to be neutral in the continuing struggle between East and West but it was difficult to find any Austrian who sided with the Russians. It was to the benefit of all sides, however, for Austria to effectively maintain that role.

Vienna had probably the largest Soviet KGB and G.R.U. (comparable to the American CIA and Military Intelligence) contingents outside of Moscow. It did, in fact, serve as a training base outside the Soviet Union for new aspiring agents "to get their feet wet". The Western powers, especially in the early postwar years and, to a certain extent, to the present day, did the same. Thrown into this cauldron of espionage and intrigue was also the violent world of international terrorism which also found Vienna to be a convenient center for activities. Not only was it a "combat area" for Mossad and Hammas, the militant branch of the Palestine Liberation Army (PLO), but also for the various factions within the Arab world. The kidnapping of the entire OPEC hierarchy at their meeting in Vienna by Carlos and his mostly Arab accomplices was such an example. The presence of the headquarters of the International Atomic Energy Agency and the site of the ongoing multinational disarmament conferences in Vienna only added spice to this whole scenario.

Kurt looked at the displays in some of the exclusive shops. Vienna had become an expensive city, quite opposite of what it was when he first had come to the city. Combined with the devaluation of the U.S. dollar and of the prosperity that Austria was now enjoying, prices by U.S. standards were very high. He paused for awhile to listen to three young musicians who were performing on their guitars. They would switch from Austrian folk music to modern music and on to American country music. They're quite good, he thought as he dropped a five Schilling coin into a hat that was on the walk in front of them.

He continued to deftly avoid "changing his luck" with a quick side step. He chuckled to himself as he remembered his first exposure to that phrase during his student days. The Europeans and, especially Austrians, and most of all, Viennese all loved dogs, everything from Shaferhunds (German Shepherds) to French poodles to dachshunds. In fact, it was often said that they loved their pets more than they did their children. Even in the most exclusive shops or restaurants, it was not unusual to see people leading their dogs on a leash. Of course, they also took their dogs on these daily "Spaziergangs" and, of course, the telltale evidence one could very easily find if one did not watch where one was walking. To make light of this unpleasant but inevitable event, the Austrians claimed that "it would change your luck". I'll bet there is not an American tourist who ever visited Europe who didn't have his luck changed at least once, Kurt laughed to himself.

Kurt reached the corner of Kartner Strasse and the Graben which was an even wider short street with several sidewalk cafes. You really can't call them sidewalks anymore, Kurt reflected, since the whole street is now a sidewalk. He decided that he would sit at one of the tables and order a drink. He was beginning to experience jet lag from his long trip from America and he was a bit tired. He had only slept about one hour on the flight from New York but when he had finally arrived in Vienna, he just could not go right to bed. The city was too exhilarating for him and he had to see some of it first. The last three or four days had been rather hectic for him. He had left California, met a beautiful woman, been deceived by the same woman, had survived an assassination attempt, had undergone a very extensive briefing, and had flown all the way to Vienna. His adrenaline had been up for all this time and now he was beginning to unwind. It will probably be a week or so, he thought, before I meet my East German contact. So he decided to relax and try to enjoy himself. Maybe I'll even take in a concern or ballet, he said to himself.

"Eine einheimische Bier, Herr Ober," he told the waiter who came to the table to take his order.

"Leider, Wir haben nur Export Bier, Mein Herr," answered the waiter.

"Also gut, ein grosse Export Bier," Kurt reluctantly said. He had ordered a domestic local beer but this café, like all the others in the promenade, offered only what they called premium beer or export beer. Actually it was exactly the same as was made for local consumption but by adding a fancier label and calling it export, that is, made to export out of Austria, the price could be almost doubled. One had to visit the Gasthauses that the local inhabitants patronized to avoid paying the premium price.

The waiter quickly returned with his drink. On a Sunday afternoon with many people walking up and down the promenade, the waiters hoped to have as much turnover at the tables as possible. When a patron's drink was low they would hover in the vicinity to take another order or to present the bill. Kurt was a little annoyed at this. In the old days here in Vienna, he thought to himself, life was more leisurely. You could sit at a sidewalk café and enjoy a coffee or a drink and not be hustled. I guess that's the price we pay for progress.

Kurt was not about to be hurried, however. He had bought a copy of the international edition of the *New York Herald Tribune* at one of the newsstands on Kartner Strasse. He filled his glass from the bottle of beer, took a sip, unfolded the paper and started to read.

He really enjoyed reading the *Herald Tribune*. It had, at one time, been owned by the now defunct *New York Herald Tribune* but had always been published in Paris. It was now partly owned by the *Washington Post* and published in Zurich, Switzerland. It had all the important news and the syndicated columnists from the *Post*, and covered much more European news. Because it had comparatively little advertising, it was, of course, more expensive than its American counterparts but Kurt thought it was well worth it.

He was halfway through a humorous Buchwald column in the paper when he heard a commotion off to his side. Since Art Buchwald was at his best and was one of Kurt's favorite columnists, he tried to ignore the growling of two dachshunds practically at his feet. It was inevitable with so many people strolling on the promenade with their pet dogs on leashes that eventually there would be a clash. The pets were not quite so enamored with the cultural delights of the area as were their owners. One little dark brown dachshund had pulled loose from its owner and had caught up with a larger, fat, black dachshund held on a leash by a large fat man. Kurt would have ignored the whole incident except for the fact that the growling and snarling, and the shouts and screams of the owners were getting close to him. "Steh, Dachsie, Steh," he heard a feminine voice shout.

He looked up and saw a shapely, dark haired woman running toward the dogs, which were now almost under Kurt's table. He instinctively grabbed at the loose leash of the small, aggressive brown dog and caught the loop at the end. The fat dachshund with its fat master went scurrying off, the dog whimpering and the owner muttering obscenities at all untrained dogs. Kurt, holding the leash of the straining brown dog, turned to hand the leash to the owner and looked up into the surprised eyes of the owner - Sonya!

XVI

SONYA

Sonya Krymko. When Kurt would think of Vienna, his first thoughts were of Sonya Krymko. It was here in Vienna, ironically no more than a block from where he now was, that he had first met her. In some ways it was like just yesterday, and in other ways it was like a century ago.

It was during Kurt's first assignment to Vienna. He had been there almost a year, the year after his breakup with Jackie. Kurt was a real "spook", the name coined by The Company for those under deep cover and being a "spook", the last thing Kurt wanted was to be detailed to escort Company VIPs around Vienna. If nothing else, it posed the possibility of "blowing his cover". The Company was going through a transition and according to the real pros, not for the better. It was becoming more of a political pawn and where formerly the higher echelon was always composed of professional intelligence people, it was now being handed over to the politicians. The occupant in the White House wanted "his men" running The Company and, as a result, with each change of the Administration came a change of the top management of The Company. This new management, in order to make their presence known, always made changes - changes based on political expediency or merely for the sake of change. Political cronies were brought in from the outside and switches were made of chair borne professionals inside The Company. These professionals were probably the worst, at least as far as those out in the field were concerned. They had worked their way up into the higher echelons by never leaving Headquarters and by surviving the various in-house "purges" that took place. The way to survive an in-house purge was to never have done anything controversial and never to have made a decision of importance. Those really dedicated professionals who had built the reputation of The Company were those who had been out in the field and who had been involved in operations that were usually successful, but unfortunately not always. One mistake would usually negatively affect the career of these truly dedicated professionals. The survivors, those who had never made such mistakes, usually ended up in the top echelon of management. They and their political counterparts, whom they had so impressed, would, at the first opportunity, go out to "inspect" the operations in the field. It afforded them, at Government expense, to inspect such hardship spots as London, Paris, Rome, Athens, Tokyo, Bangkok, Munich during Oktoberfest, and, of course, Vienna during the opera season. It would also give them the opportunity in the cocktail circuit in Washington to impress everybody on their overseas exploits.

To Kurt eventually fell the obligation to help entertain a group of these visiting dignitaries from Headquarters. It soon became obvious that the group was less interested in Company operations (and for that Kurt was thankful) but more in the night life of the city. Kurt, in his capacity as a student, did not have much opportunity to frequent the many night clubs that the city offered but he was familiar, at least by name, with two of the most famous - the Opium Hohle and he Casanova Club. Both were on side streets off the Graben near Kartner Strasse, they were expensive, but then there was a generous expense account for operational entertainment, and both were probably infested by rich tourists and intelligence agents from all over the world also entertaining their VIPs.

The Opium Hohle was the first stop for Kurt and his four guests. It was first built as an air raid shelter in World War II and was converted to the night club complete with the usual contingent of "hostesses" willing to help make patrons drink expensive champagne. It was actually four flights down and indeed was what one would picture as an opium den. After about an hour there, Kurt left with two of those on his guided tour, the other two remained to further sample the vintage wines and cultural aspects of the establishment. The next stop was on the next street where one walked up one flight to the Casanova Club. Since the headwaiter assumed that they were rich American tourists, or high American government officials on fat expense accounts, they were given the best table in the club, complete with three extremely beautiful hostesses. One of them was Sonya Krymko.

Sonya, according to her story, was a Polish refugee from the Polish Ukraine. She had come to Vienna on a government-sponsored tour, had slipped away from the group, and had asked for political asylum in Austria. She said that she was enrolled as a student at the University of Vienna studying physiology and hoped one day to emigrate to the United States. She supplemented her Austrian government scholarship by working as a hostess in the Casanova Club. She told Kurt that her job also gave her the opportunity to practice her English on patrons. She was also very impressed by Kurt's fluency in German and they played a guessing game on what dialect he had. Actually, Kurt could switch from his Sudeten father's German to his Banater mother's German, to his university polished classic German.

Sonya was a strikingly beautiful woman, at that time about twenty one or twenty two years of age. She had coal-black hair, high cheekbones characteristic of her Slavic background, and a figure which could only be described as stunning. From the first instant that he looked into her beautiful green eyes, Kurt felt a stirring within himself that he had not felt since Jackie. He knew from that first moment that something would happen between the two of them - it would not end there that night in the club. Sonya seemed to react the same. Neither were aware of the existence of their companions who were carrying on the usual B-girl/patron chatter. They were in a world of their own, drinking wine, dancing, talking as if they had known each other for years. What seemed like minutes was actually hours and eventually theirs was the only table occupied. The other two hostesses, after an evening of drinking expensive champagne with Kurt's two companions, predictably disappeared and it was time to leave. Kurt offered to take Sonya home and she appreciatively accepted. They just did not want the evening to ever end. Kurt just knew he had to make love to her that night. He had not wanted to make love to any woman for over a year.

At the entrance to the club, Kurt hailed a taxi for his two companions who, after several bottles of champagne and the companionship of young, beautiful women, did not want to call it a night. Anticipating their desires he directed the taxi driver to take them to Maxim's on the Ring Strasse. Maxim's was and still is a syndicated night club and brothel in Vienna. It had branches in all the major cities of Austria but the most beautiful women were found in Vienna. Kurt knew his companions would have fond memories of "Old Vienna".

Sonya lived about a half hour's drive from the center of the city, even in the deserted streets at four a.m. She sat close to Kurt in the car and he could feel her warm body pressed up close to his. He welcomed the several stop signs that he came to because it gave him the opportunity to bend down and kiss her full inviting lips. Other than the directions that she gave him, there was little said, but there seemed to be an extrasensory communication between the two of them.

They finally reached her apartment house and Kurt parked the car near the corner under a street light. He noticed from the sign on the corner street post that they were in the 10th Bezirk which was the less desirable, blue collar area of Vienna. He was hoping she would invite him in and she did. She had told him that she lived alone and from the looks of the apartment, it looked as if she did. She locked the door from the inside and then took out the key and hung it from a hook next to the door.

She opened the door-like window to let in the warm early summer air. These old Viennese apartment houses, and hers was obviously a pre-war one, were old and musty when there was no circulation. She walked into her bedroom and opened that window too. It was a first floor apartment but high enough off the ground to prevent anyone from looking in.

In an instant they were in each other's arms and without a word she walked over to the bed and lay down, not removing her clothes but motioning with her hands for him to come next to her. He walked over to the bed, sat next to her and softly kissed her at the same time starting to unbutton her rositta blouse that came up around her neck. As he kissed her, he could feel her hand touching the back of his head, holding him closer to her. She whispered to him that she wanted him to make love to her. He could also hear another unusual noise.

It was the sound of a key being inserted into the front door lock which was in the next room. He could hear the key turn and the lock unclick. From the side of his eye he could see the door at first slowly open and then quickly, as two dark, huge figures burst into the front room, hesitate and then head toward the bedroom. He instinctively pulled loose from Sonya, ran toward the open window, and dove headfirst out the window feeling a hand grasp at his leg as he flew out into space. Kurt, who had been an excellent athlete in college, and who had had training as a paratrooper in the Army and in The Company, easily managed the one floor jump, and in a perfect tumble, rolled and landed upright on his feet running toward his car. By the time the two dark figures had run back out the front of the apartment, Kurt was in his car racing down the deserted street back toward the center of town. It had obviously been a set-up and many times afterward he thanked God that it was only the first floor and he still had his clothes on.

Sonya did not show up at the Casanova Club the next day nor did she ever show up there again. A check with records at The Company office in Vienna did not reveal any information about her. If she were a Soviet KGB or G.R.U. agent, it was speculated that she as new, under deep cover, and probably in Vienna for "on the job training". To reinforce this theory was the fact that only a novice would try to do what she and her accomplices had done. Old pros from both sides just do not do each other in unless there is an unavoidable operational clash. The Soviets have a fairly good idea who The Company agents are. They do not need an expose' by an Agee-type traitor. That serves only to inform "kooks" and terrorists. By the same token, The Company has a fairly good idea of who all the Soviet agents are. The Soviet Embassy in Washington and the U. N. in New York are infested with them. When the FBI in the United States did catch one of them with "his finger in the pie", the Soviets in Moscow would simply pick up one of The Company people and there would be a quiet exchange. Actually the old pros on each side, who are really in the same business and do have a measure of professional pride, do not dislike each other personally, and they do not want to be involved in an underground war against each other. So it was believed that Sonya must have been new to the business and an extensive analysis at Company headquarters eventually verified that.

It turned out to be a family affair. An exhaustive search of files revealed that the Deputy Director of KGB Foreign Operations, Bohdan Krymko, had a daughter, the age and description of Sonya. It was later learned that "Father" sternly lectured his daughter on attempting what turned out to be an unauthorized attempt against a suspected Company man.

It was a couple of months before all the pieces were fitted together and Kurt had always wondered what it would have been like if he had taken Sonya to his apartment rather than hers. He fantasized many times how it would have been to make love to her. She was undoubtedly one of the most exciting women he had ever met. He did find out, in Rome six months after their original meeting. She was everything he had dreamed she was.

Their paths crossed several times in the next few years. In Athens, Istanbul, Bangkok, Singapore, London, Paris, and even once in New York, and between them, there developed a love and actual trust toward each other. He, of course, reported each meeting. He would have done so even if he did not have to undergo a polygraph examination periodically as all Company agents do. She reported the meetings to her superiors also. It was condoned because each side believed that their person would recruit the other. They both actually tried to the point that it had

become almost amusing to each of them. Their respective organizations would even foot the bill for the trysts. The only thing
that worried each of them was that they might really fall in love
with each other. What had really surprised Kurt was that until
their first meeting in Rome, Sonya had been a virgin.

XVII

LIKE OLD TIMES

"Sonya!" "Kurt!" they both almost shouted each other's names simultaneously. "Of all people to catch my Dachsie," she said, still breathless after the chase of the brown dachshund. The little dog knew his mistress was angry with him and he apprehensively lowered his head and looked up at her with his tail between his legs.

Sonya and Kurt quickly embraced and kissed each other momentarily forgetting about the dog.

"It's been months," Sonya said. "I've missed you so. I was hoping we would meet again soon."

"God, I've really missed you too, Sonya," Kurt replied. "When was the last time? Ten months ago in Paris? Here, here, have a seat next to me," he said as he pulled out a chair and held it for her.

She sat down and hooked the loop of the leash of the now docile little dog on the arm of the metal chair.

The waiter was over to the table to take her order almost before she was seated.

"Eine Expresso, bitte," she said to the eager waiter.

"Noch eine," Kurt added, pointing to his empty beer bottle.

"How long have you been in Vienna? How long will you be here?" she excitedly asked.

"I just arrived today and I'll only be here for a few days at most," he answered. "How about you?"

"I've been here for about three months and I hope that I can stay here for a year or two," she replied. "I have a flat nearby, directly on the Schubertring, next to the park. It's within walking distance."

Considering the profession that they were in and on opposite sides, it seemed like an unusual conversation. It was entirely a personal thing between the two of them and neither suspected any ulterior motive in the questions. They were like two lovers who had met again after a long separation. And that actually was what they were.

The waiter served the small black expresso coffee and the beer along with a small computer printout too.

"God, even Vienna is being computerized," he said reaching for his wallet to pay the bill.

"Why are we even sitting here? I have coffee and drinks in my apartment," she said. "We're wasting our time here and we have so much time to make up for."

"Zahlen bitte, Herr Ober," Kurt said before the waiter could walk off to another table. He paid the waiter and reverting to a bad American habit, gave the waiter a large tip. It was probably because he was so excited at seeing Sonya and also because he did not want to have to wait for change from his one hundred Schilling note.

Kurt and Sonya, holding hands, and the little dachshund on the leash, no longer worried at being punished by his mistress for his earlier misdeeds, hurriedly walked down the Graben and up Kartner Strasse toward the Ring and Sonya's apartment.

By the time they had reached her apartment they were almost running. Although it was only a few seconds, it seemed like an interminable time for the elevator to arrive to take them to her top floor apartment in the ten-floor apartment house. Kurt kissed her on the neck in the elevator going up, on her cheek walking down the hall to her apartment, and on her ear as she was unlocking her door.

They entered the apartment and she closed the door and double-bolted the lock. Without a word being said she headed directly toward the bedroom leaving her shoes by the entrance door and a trail of clothing in the route to the bedroom. By the time she had reached the bed, she was completely undressed. Not even bothering to pull back the bedspread she lay down on her back looking up at Kurt who was close behind breaking every record in taking off his clothes. Usually this was not the way they made love together. Foreplay with words of love and endearment was usually a prerequisite. Making love for them was an experience that was not only pure sex but one of deep love and warmth. They experienced fulfillment only by knowing the other was completely fulfilled and satisfied. They had no inhibitions with each other.

"Moy Yebuik," she whispered into his ear, lightly kissing the lobe of his ear.

"Moya Yebushka," Kurt responded.

If Kurt had one inhibition it was profanity with women. It was probably a result of his strict Catholic family indoctrination where his mother had always lectured him on not exposing women to vulgarity. In the proper setting such as in the Army or even on a night out "with the boys", he could handle profanity like a pro. However, around women he could not utter a four letter word if he tried. On many occasions in public or at parties which inevitably some man would over imbibe and start using profanity in the company of women, Kurt would always intercede. What especially "turned him off" would be for a woman to use such profanity. On one occasion when he was in the midst of making love to a woman, she, in the heat of passion, started shouting, "Fuck me, fuck me!" He suddenly lost all interest and embarrassingly dressed and left. He was even accused of being chauvinistic by some so-called liberated women who insisted on their prerogative of using obscenities. Somehow in Russian, coming from Sonya, it did not seem that way; in fact, if anything, it seemed to arouse him more. She even taught him Russian words to call her, words he could never utter near her in English. Their relationship was trilingual. When they made love they would speak Russian, and in regular conversation they would alternate between German and English. He would even correct her English, not with the intention of belittling her but only of perfecting it. He was probably helping her to be a better agent.

There was one creature, however, that was not at all amused by all the activity and that was Dachsie. His protective instincts toward his mistress finally overcame him. All during the initial activity on the bed he growled but was completely ignored. When the activity died down he jumped up on the bed growling at Kurt and burrowed himself between the two of them.

"We're going to have to do something about him," Kurt laughed.

"Poor Dachsie," she said consoling the little dog. "He's never seen me in bed with anyone before."

She sat up, picked up Dachsie in her arms and carried him into the other room where she put him down, ran back into the room, closed the door, and got into bed again with Kurt.

With Dachsie howling and scratching on the bedroom door they made love again, and again, and again.

Kurt awoke with the early morning sun streaming through the wide open window in his eyes. He could hear Sonya puttering around in the kitchen and he could smell the distinctive odor of strong expresso coffee being brewed.

It's difficult to get used to American coffee after drinking this European coffee, he thought to himself. You really can get the taste of all the coffee this way, when the oil is steamed out of the coffee beans which are usually freshly ground just before preparing it.

Sonya appeared carrying a tray with a pot of coffee and two cups and a dish with semmelen with butter and marmalade.

"Breakfast in bed for Moy Yebuik," she announced as she sat next to him in bed holding the tray in her lap.

She had on a high neck flannel nightgown with buttons down the front that she had apparently put on sometime during the night.

"You look beautiful, even the morning after," Kurt said.

"We never did have dinner last night," she said. "Come now, let's have breakfast. I do have to go to work today, you know. I am a working girl. I can't very well call my office and say that I am entertaining an Ami spy."

Kurt sat up in bed as Sonya poured him a large cup of the thick black coffee. She put in a cube of sugar and added a little fresh cream, just enough to make it a dark brown. "See, I even remember how you like it," she said.

Kurt was hungry. The little food he had on his flight from America the day before and the "pause" he had at the Sacher hardly could sustain him much longer. The evening before, the last thing he could think about was food. Seeing Sonya after so many months made him forget everything else, even the real purpose of his coming to Vienna. He was sure that she had no idea of what his mission was, at least he hoped not. The KGB did know about Willi Gross but since their bureaucracy is even slower than The Company's, he believed that they would not be able to connect it with Kurt. At any rate, Sonya had been assigned to Vienna long before Kurt was ever involved with his present mission.

They ate breakfast in bed. Kurt loved fresh semmelen, the hard rolls that are baked in the middle of the night and delivered fresh to the door of those who could afford this special service. Sonya had them delivered along with a bottle of milk every other day. This was a service that one could still get in most cities in Europe; in France, it was croissants. In America, it was a thing of the past with the monopoly on the food market by the large supermarket chains. It would probably eventually happen in Vienna also. There were chains of supermarkets starting in most large European cities. My God, Kurt had thought yesterday when he first walked down Kartner Strasse, there's even a McDonald's restaurant there, three blocks from the Opera House.

Sonya quickly finished her breakfast, jumped out of bed and hurried into the bathroom. Kurt could hear the bath water running as Sonya was starting what, for most women, is the long ritual of dressing for the day.

He poured himself a second cup of coffee and looked out the wide open window at the awakening city of Vienna below. Vienna was not a city of skyscrapers and the tenth floor apartment house that Sonya lived in looked over most of the city. He could see the spires of St. Stephan's Cathedral in the middle of the First Bezirk and since Sonya had a corner apartment, he could look off to the right and see the beautiful Stadt Park with its concert hall and small lake. From this vantage point, he could even hear the ducks and swans in the lake below starting their busy day by calling out to each other.

It was April and still a bit cool. Kurt, who was still completely nude, draped a blanket around his shoulders as he sat up and studied the beautiful city. Because of the temperate climate there were few insects in Austria and the buildings did not require screens. To take advantage of as much sun as possible, buildings in Europe had double door-like windows that, when fully opened, as Sonya's were now, let in as much sunshine as possible. Looking out, Kurt had almost a panoramic view of the most interesting part of the city.

Kurt began to dress as Sonya hurried out of the bathroom already half dressed. She went to the Schrank, which was the European counterpart of a closet, and selected a conservative dress.

"I hate to hurry, but I do have to be in my office by eight o'clock," she said as she sat on the edge of the bed and put on a pair of mid-heel shoes. Her long black hair was pulled back in a ponytail accentuating her high cheekbones and revealing her small half heart shaped ears each adorned with a small platinum earring in her pierced lobes. Kurt finished dressing, thinking he would return to his hotel to bathe, shave, and change clothes. He had to check in with his telephone contact and he hoped to be able to reach Max who should have arrived in Vienna by now. Max had arranged to have the metal detector and other necessary operational equipment shipped through diplomatic channels and Kurt wanted to check on that also. The past day had been like a day in a dream but now it was time to think about his assignment.

Sonya was like a whirlwind rushing around the apartment. She quickly, with Kurt's help, made up the bed and hung up her clothing from the previous day. She took the breakfast tray and dishes into the kitchen, rinsed them, and put them into the dishwasher. Soon it was time to leave and before they opened the door, she quickly kissed Kurt on his cheek and turned her cheek to him to kiss.

"You are taking me to dinner tonight," she said. It was just assumed by both of them that they would see as much of each other as possible. There was really no question about it. "I'll be ready by seven," she added.

She closed the door behind them as they left the apartment and locked it, and put the key into her purse.

"What about the dog?" Kurt asked.

"Our 'gopher', as you Americans say, comes by during the day and takes him for a walk," she replied. "Of course I'll have to report that I have seen you. I assume that you will do the same."

"Of course," he matter-of-factly replied.

They took the elevator to the ground floor and out the main entrance.

She walked off in one direction to her KGB office and he in the other direction to his hotel and Company assignment.

XVIII

THE TAIL

Kurt briskly walked the few blocks to the Astoria. He was still basking in the afterglow of his evening with Sonya and was already looking forward to seeing her that evening. He thought he would take her to a very elegant restaurant. There were so many in Vienna and he wanted to take the most beautiful woman in Vienna to one of the most beautiful places. Suddenly he felt like a young man again wanting to impress his best girl.

He walked into the hotel lobby and headed directly toward the elevator, not even bothering to check at the reception desk. He always carried his hotel key with him and never deposited it at the desk. He did not want to announce to anyone that he was not in the hotel. He took the elevator to the third floor and then walked up to the fourth floor where his room was. It was just an automatic thing to do. He did not think that he was under surveillance at the time but if he were, he did not want to reveal to anyone watching the floor indicator on the ground level, on which floor he exited. He entered his room, locked the door, stripped and went into the bathroom and started the water running in the tub. Like most Austrian hotels, his room with a bath meant a room with a bathtub. It usually included a handle shower which Kurt could never quite figure out how to use properly. It was actually used more to rinse with than to take a shower. Like most American men, he preferred to take a shower. It just felt cleaner and probably was. The tub was quickly filled and he stepped in and very slowly submerged himself up to his neck. It was initially a little too warm but his body quickly adjusted to it and it felt very relaxing. He almost dozed off lying there thinking pleasant thought of the previous evening.

His reverie was interrupted by the ring of the telephone in the other room. He first thought he would ignore it because no one was supposed to call him. All calls were supposed to be by public telephones. As it continued to ring, he grudgingly got out of the warm, comfortable water and, dripping wet, walked into the other room and answered the phone.

"Moy Lyubov Kurt. I just wanted to say that I miss you already," Sonya said on the other line. "I can hardly wait to see you again tonight. I love you," she added and hung up before he could even answer.

She's really a good case officer, Kurt chuckled to himself. I don't even remember telling her I was staying at the Astoria. Oh well, maybe I did. You don't remember everything you say when you're making love.

He climbed back into the tub, soaped and rinsed himself and got out. He shaved and then leisurely dressed.

At about ten o'clock he left his room and took the elevator down to the ground floor. He walked out the front door and turned left, walked to the first corner to the Mozart Restaurant. He remembered that there was a public phone just on the inside of the restaurant.

He called his contact number and this time a male voice answered. After going through the usual identification verification routine, Kurt was told that Max had arrived and wanted to meet him. Max would call back to the number at noon and a message could be passed on to him. "Tell him to meet me at the Augustiner Keller at two p.m.," Kurt said. "He knows where it is."

The Augustiner Keller was actually directly across from the Mozart Restaurant. It was a cavernous-like restaurant that was attached to a Catholic church sponsored by the Augustinian

Monks. In the olden days, all the religious orders had their own restaurants and breweries that served as an excellent source of revenue. The Augustiner Keller was now owned by a wealthy Austrian family named Bitzinger and was a famous stopping place for travel groups, students, and for the Viennese themselves. It was always busy enough so that no single person or group would stand out. It was an ideal place for a clandestine meeting, a rendezvous with a lover, or for someone in the "spy business."

Kurt learned one other thing from his telephone contact. Ushie Gross was not due in Vienna until the twelfth. He had almost a week to enjoy himself before she came.

Kurt finished his call and headed back toward the Astoria. He stopped to look into a store window and in the mirror reflection of the window, he noticed that he had picked up a "tail".

He still had some time before he was to meet Max and he did not want to lead his follower to that meeting. Max had never been assigned to Vienna other than TDYs (temporary duty) and he was not at all known by the other intelligence agencies as Kurt probably was after a tour here. He wondered who it was. It would be several, although he thought he had been clever in traveling to the city. It could be Austrian security which has a fairly good idea of who comes and goes in Austria. He doubted if it could be the KGB. Even if Sonya had alerted them, there had not been time to set up a surveillance. He had been briefed on expecting Israeli, PLO and Nazi problems. Whatever it was, Kurt had to lose the tail.

He reached the corner of Kartner Strasse and turned left toward the Graben and St. Stephan's Cathedral. He looked at the opposite corner to see if it was a double surveillance. When two people follow someone, it is customary to have the second person walking on a parallel route with the first. At the street corners the first changes direction while the second crosses and picks up the subject. It is simply textbook technique and all professionals use it. It take a real pro to detect another pro.

Kurt could quickly see that there was no second follower so it made it easier for him to lose this one. He had the perfect solution. Having been assigned to Vienna in the past, he had always had contingency plans for just such an occasion. He had time to kill before he met Max, but he did not want to cut it too close. It was only about eleven o'clock so he decided to take advantage of the sunny spring morning and read a newspaper and have a cup of his favorite expresso. It was a Monday and there was no *Herald Tribune* on Mondays so he bought a copy of *Wiener Kurier*, the local Viennese paper. He walked down to the Graben and went to the same outside café that he had visited yesterday where he had met Sonya. His "tail", after first going through the pretense of window shopping at the adjacent stores, eventually sat down several tables away but behind Kurt and close to the door of the café.

Kurt ordered his coffee and started reading his paper as if he were oblivious of his follower. He was quickly served and he immediately paid, leaving no "trinkgeld". The waiter quickly walked off, not going through the bowing, thank you ritual, that Austrian waiters do when they receive a good tip. Kurt noticed that his "tail" ordered a drink also. He, too, was quickly served but he did not pay when he was served.

Seeing this, Kurt quickly downed his coffee and walked off in the direction of Kartner Strasse. His "tail", watching Kurt leave, got up and started to follow but was stopped by the waiter shouting at him that he had not paid. By the time he had paid, Kurt was around the corner heading for the entrance of St. Stephan's Cathedral, which he quickly entered. There were tour groups walking around and at one of the side altars there was a Mass in progress. Only when there was a Mass going on were confessions being heard so Kurt went to the third altar on the right and slipped into one of the booths. He chose the priests' booth because it had a louver window on the door which the priest could normally look through but could not, himself, be seen.

Kurt watched through the slits in the door and eventually saw his "tail" rush into the front entrance and worriedly look around the church.

His "tail" was not a young man. He was medium sized with busy gray hair. Kurt guessed that he had to be in his fifties or sixties and he was not a real pro. A real pro, at that age, Kurt thought, would never have been suckered into the sidewalk café incident.

The gray-haired man slowly walked through the huge cathedral with its many pillars, alcoves, and sub-altars. The large main altar was at the opposite end of the church and was elevated so that during the main Mass, everybody could have a good view. At one time he walked within two feet of where Kurt was sitting. At just about that time Kurt could see a young college age girl step into the confessional to his side. He could not ignore her presence in the opposite booth without possibly revealing his hiding place.

He slid open the small door between the booth which was screened so neither could see the other.

The young girl, who was probably an English tourist on holiday in Austria, started her confession in halting German.

The gray-haired "tail", standing outside the booth, hearing what should be private conversation, discreetly walked away and out toward the main entrance where he stood, still surveying the activity in the church.

"You can speak English with me if you wish, my child," Kurt said, feigning a German accent. He felt guilty about going through with the confession but he could see the "tail" still standing at the entrance.

"Bless me, Father, for I have sinned," the voice started in the confessional as she recited her time since her last confession and what sins she wanted to confess.

Boy, I'm glad that I'm not in that next booth, Kurt said to himself. I can't even remember when I went to confession the last time.

Kurt actually had, at one time, been very religious and in his own way he still believed he was. He had gone to a Catholic school as a boy, had been an altar boy, and had even considered, as did many young Catholic boys at that time, being a priest. But then he reached the age when he noticed girls and that possible vocation never again entered his mind. Kurt was also disturbed by the direction he thought the Church had taken. He was a traditionalist by nature and preferred the Latin Mass and the ritual that the Catholic Church had had for centuries. When he would travel throughout the world as he did, he felt he could always go into any Catholic church and understand everything in the one common language, Latin. Vatican II, in hopes of luring back Protestant religions, sacrificed all this. Concessions brought very few Protestants "back into the fold" and, Kurt believed, weakened the Church.

Compared to what I would have to confess, this girl's a saint, Kurt thought. I'll give her a small penance. He sent her off with two Hail Mary's two Our Father's, and an Act of Contrition.

Fortunately no one else entered the confessionals on either side and a few minutes after the gray-haired man left the church, Kurt left his hiding place, walked to the far end of the cathedral and out one of the back exits.

Kurt had used St. Stephan's in the past for the same purpose. It had six exits and offered the best odds in escaping surveillance. He took the back streets and worked his way through Kohlmarkt, a market place, to Augustiner Strasse to the Augustiner Keller. He had forty five minutes to spare before Max was due to arrive.

Max never late; he was usually early for an appointment and this time was no exception. Kurt had just been served a glass of Gumpoldskirchner white wine when Max arrived.

The Augustiner Keller, although it was on the round floor or the first floor as Americans counted, looked like a basement room. It was a long, large room with many alcoves separating it into many semi-private sections. The walls between the sections were thick, affording not only privacy but sound proofing. One could not actually hear conversation in the next section. It was probably the best location in Vienna for private meetings of the sort that Kurt and Max were having.

Kurt had taken a seat in the farthest section from the front. There was less traffic that far back. Max eventually found him after walking and looking into each section as he walked.

"That's one thing I like about you, Max," Kurt said. "You're never late." Kurt, in fact, was always very annoyed when someone would be late for an appointment. Some of his Arab friends, who were, by nature, late, used to infuriate him. When meeting them, he would always schedule a meeting an hour or so before he actually intended to be there, and still more often than not he would be kept waiting.

"Give me one of your cigarettes," were the first words out of Max's mouth.

"One of the reasons I quit was so I could say no to you," Kurt responded. "Here, have a seat.   How about a drink before we get down to business?"

Max ordered a glass of red wine and asked the waiter to bring him a pack of Austrian cigarettes too. The waiter quickly returned with the wine and a pack of "Osterreichische II Filter" cigarettes.

"He didn't even try to stick me with their phony export cigarettes," Max said as he opened the pack, took out a cigarette and lit up. He blew the smoke in Kurt's face and then offered him one.

"You are a fucking sadist," Kurt said, "but you can't tempt me with those Austrian weeds."

The Austrian cigarettes were much stronger than American ones and contained a high amount of aromatic Turkish tobacco, the kind that Kurt always detested. Actually, Kurt was not having too much difficulty quitting smoking. It was a habit and really only that. He did not feel that he was addicted to nicotine.

"The detector arrived and I'll pick it up with the other equipment tomorrow," Max said. "I've already rented a car, with a large trunk, I might add, and we should be ready to roll as soon as your little Kraut Fraulein arrives.

"I've gotten the word that she will be here in Vienna in about a week," Kurt replied. "Her orchestra is scheduled to perform ten days from now and they usually try to be here two or three days before. I'll try to see her a week from today if I can."

"Incidentally," he went on, "I've met Sonya. She's assigned here in Vienna, has been for the past three months, so I don't think there is any connection with us. Since I have nothing to do for a few days, I'm going to try to get her to take a few days off and we'll head for the mountains. It's sort of an uncomfortable feeling meeting her here in Vienna. I'm not paranoid but I get the feeling that there's a KGB-type watching me wherever I go. In fact, I picked up a tail already this morning but I lost him. I have no idea who he was. At any rate, I'll let you know if I do take off and, of course, I'll call in every day so you can reach me if necessary."

"Just be careful," Max answered. "I can see why Sonya turned you on, but no piece of ass is worth getting your throat cut."

Kurt winced at the reference to Sonya but he knew that Max's admonition was well intended.

"Incidentally, I almost forgot," Max said. "The Company is sending someone named Shira to join us to go to Lunersee. I got the word just before I came here."

"Who the hell is Shira?" Kurt asked. "We don't need anyone else. The equipment isn't too complicated so we don't need a tech specialist. Besides, three people attract more attention than two. I wish those bastards back in Headquarters wouldn't interfere. What in the hell do they know about climbing mountains? Well, I hope whoever he is, he has a strong back and knows how to dig. Oh, by the way, before I forget. We're going to need some good mountain climbing shoes and warm clothing. It's still pretty cool up there in the mountains and the terrain is pretty rugged. But don't get any here in Vienna. If you do pick up a tail, we shouldn't tip anyone off that we're going to do any mountain climbing. We'll pick up all we need on the trip, probably in Innsbruck. We can get some picks and shovels there also, the collapsible kind we can pack in a backpack and won't arouse anyone's curiosity. One last thing. While I'm gone, have our I.D. people make up an American press identification for me. I'll need it to get to Ushie."

They each finished their drink and started to leave. "I'll go first," Kurt said. "We'd better not leave together. You can take care of the bill, old buddy," he added, relishing the thought of sticking Max with the bill before Max could stick him with it. "See you around," he said as he waved goodbye to Max and headed out the entrance and in the direction of his hotel.

He crossed Augustiner Strasse and walked down Fuhrichgasse. When he reached the entrance of the Astoria Hotel, he noticed his "tail" standing across the street reading a newspaper. Now why do all these characters pretend they're reading a paper? If anything, it makes them look more conspicuous, he thought to himself. But that's the way they do it in the movies so I guess that's why these people do it. He went up to his room. He still had about three hours before he was to meet Sonya. The combination of jet lag, which he was still experiencing, and the activity of the previous evening was catching up with him. If I don't want to fall asleep on Sonya tonight, I'd better catch up on a little sleep, he said to himself. He called down to the front desk for a wake up call in two hours. That would give him plenty of time to take a short nap, dress, and be on time to meet Sonya.

He had gotten his wake up call exactly at six p.m., took a bath, shaved and dressed, then slipped out of the back of the hotel and arrived at Sonya's apartment at exactly seven p.m. Punctuality was something one could always count on with Kurt. It was almost a compulsion, and, in fact, from a vulnerability standpoint could be detrimental in that it helped establish a predictable pattern. Kurt knew this and he would sometimes force himself to be a little early or a little late but that bothered him. Must have been something in my childhood, he often thought.

Kurt's knock on her door was first answered by Dachsie's bark followed soon by the sound of the security lock on the inside being turned. Sonya opened the door.

"I didn't even have to look through the peephole. I know that you are always exactly on time," she said as she turned her cheek up for Kurt to kiss. "I'll get my wrap and be right with you."

She quickly darted back into her apartment and returned with a white ermine wrap. She handed it to Kurt and he held it for her as she put it on. She quickly closed the door before the little dachshund could get out. "Sei brav, Dachsie," she called to the dog as she locked the door.

"Do you always speak German to him?" Kurt asked. "How is he going to understand anything when you take him back to Moscow?"

"Well, dachshunds are German dogs," she laughingly responded.

Kurt took one step backward to take a good look at Sonya. She looked absolutely stunning this evening. She certainly did not resemble what one would picture a Soviet career woman to look like. It was obvious she had been exposed to the best that Western fashion could provide.

Her black knee length dress could only have been Givenchy. The dress, form-fit around a figure that Aphrodite would envy, revealed only a proper bit of cleavage protected by a gold cross on a gold chain, certainly not indicative of an atheistic background. Her extra high Italian black pumps helped accentuate her long, perfectly formed legs. Her long black hair, swept back and atop her head, revealed her swan-like neck. Her high cheekbones helped emphasize her rich Slavic heritage and her dark green eyes added to the mystery of determining her whole heritage. All this, complemented by her full soft lips and beautiful white teeth, presented a picture that artists would fight to try to duplicate.

For a moment, Kurt was speechless. To think that this woman was his, at least for the moment, overwhelmed him. "You are lovely," was all he could utter.

They took the elevator to the ground floor and walked out the main entrance to the Schubertring Strasse. It was only a short distance to where Kurt had made dinner reservations for the evening but he wanted her to arrive there as if in a royal carriage rather than walk. He hailed a taxi that was cruising nearby and directed it to the Drei Husaren Restaurant. He had noticed, on leaving the apartment house, that his gray-haired "tail" was waiting in the front. There was no second taxi in the vicinity so Kurt could see his "tail's" frustration again as their taxi drove off.

Sonya noticed Kurt looking out the back window. "Is something wrong, Kurt?" she asked.

"We are being followed, or at least we were being followed," Kurt answered. "Is he one of yours?"

"No, I have no idea who it could be. I swear it," she replied.

"Nothing is going to spoil this evening," Kurt said as he grabbed her hand and squeezed it. He just wanted to touch her, to hold her. He felt almost euphoric being with her and her nearness and the soft scent of her French perfume made him forget, at least for a moment, the outside world. It was almost a feeling like being in love again. Maybe I am, he thought to himself.

It was only a few minutes until the taxi pulled up near the Drei Husaren. It was on a side street off Kartner Strasse. Everything of interest to Kurt seemed to be near Kartner Strasse. The taxi was able to drive right to the restaurant but no farther since beyond that it became the promenade.

The Drei Husaren was one of the most elegant and the most expensive restaurants in Vienna. Its specialty was Balkan-Slavic but the kind that one would associate with the days of the Czar rather than of the present. They were greeted by a maitre'd in tie and tails and escorted to a quiet table in a cubicle off to the side, exactly where Kurt had requested in making the reservation. It one wanted to describe a romantic atmosphere, complete with a violin, accordion, and balalaika trio and candlelight, one would describe the Drei Husaren. Everything was perfect - the atmosphere, the music, the drinks, the food, and the company, Kurt was thinking. In everyone's life there must be two or three occasions which one would always remember. Certainly this evening would be one of them.

They started out with the usual Limonnaya vodka - to sip, not to down as most Americans do, caviar, borscht, Balkan red wine, a lamb shahlik with a sour cream side dish, and, of course, baklava with strong Turkish coffee. Both Kurt and Sonya were in a mellow, romantic world and neither would let even the existence of an outside world interfere with the moments that they were savoring.

"I have almost a whole week before I have an assignment," Kurt said as they were finishing their dessert. "Why don't you and I just drive into the countryside for a few days and get away from the city? I want you all to myself and here in Vienna that is impossible."

"That sounds wonderful," she sighed. "I do have some vacation time coming. I will, of course, have to tell my superiors that I'm going away for a few days with an American agent. They do sort of frown on such activities, you know."

"Just tell them that you have me on the verge of being recruited," Kurt said. "Tell them that your father would approve. They are all afraid of your father."

"I'll try," she said. "I'll call you tomorrow morning to let you know."

"Great. We'll leave in the early afternoon and we won't tell anyone where we're going."

"Not even Nicholai," she responded.

"Who?" Kurt asked.

"I'll explain all that tomorrow," she answered.

They decided to walk back to Sonya's apartment. It was only about four or five short blocks, but it was a beautiful, warm April evening and they were together. It was not like the previous evening when, after having not seen each other for over ten months, they had almost raced to get to bed and make love. They knew that would come later.

They walked hand in hand, looking into several store windows, comparing what they saw with stores in different countries they had recently visited.

"I have to admit that our stores in the Soviet Union don't have all this merchandise," she said. She quickly changed that subject because it always gave Kurt the opportunity to needle her on the failure of communism, or really of a socialist society to provide not only luxuries but even consumer goods for their people. Kurt knew that the Soviets were always concerned about exposing their people like Sonya to the Western world. Just walking through a Western city like Vienna very poignantly illustrated the vast difference between the fruits of a capitalist-oriented society and a socialist society. After over sixty years of socialism the people in the Soviet Union still must wait in long lines to purchase even the basic necessities of life. Kurt did not pursue the subject since he did not want to get involved in anything controversial with Sonya. She was an opinionated, headstrong woman who was not reluctant to express her viewpoint on any subject. That was one of the many things that Kurt admired in her.

They passed some antique shops and admired some of the displays in the now-closed shops. Sonya was quite an authority on antiques and gave Kurt the history of several of the items that they saw.

Eventually they reached Sonya's apartment house on Schubertring and Kurt waved to the gray-haired man who had stationed himself across the street from the entrance. He noticed a second figure, a man younger and taller than the first, standing on the entrance side of the street a few meters from the entrance. Sonya noticed him also. "He's also not one of ours," she said.

"I wonder if they are together," said Kurt. "They could save themselves a lot of paperwork by just comparing notes if they're not."

They were greeted at the apartment door by a happy, tail-wagging Dachsie. The dachshund even seemed to welcome Kurt this time.

"See, even Dachsie loves you," Sonya said, petting the little dog who had refused to rub up against them until both had petted him. Sonya kicked off her high heeled shoes, went to a cabinet and selected a bottle of French Pinot Noir wine and two glasses. "Dorogoy, there is a corkscrew in the kitchen. Would you get it?" she asked walking to the bedroom with the bottle and glasses.

Saying darling in Russian is a good omen, Kurt thought as he rushed into the kitchen, rifled through the utensil drawer and found the corkscrew.

Sonya was lying on the bed, completely nude as Kurt walked into the room. The lights were out but the moonlight, streaming through the wide open window illuminated her entire body creating moon shadows that accentuated the contour of her well-developed curvaceous breasts and thighs.

Kurt stared down at her, momentarily stunned into indecision on whether to struggle with opening the wine bottle or quickly stripping and making love to her.

"Pour me some wine," she ordered, making the decision. "And take off your clothes."

It did not take Kurt long to do either. He filled two glasses of the dark red wine, handed one to Sonya and sat next to her on the bed.

Between short naps they made love the rest of the night. The next morning was a repeat of the previous morning, kissing goodbye and each going off to their respective assignment.

"I'll call you as soon as I know if I can go with you today, probably around ten," she added as she waved goodbye to Kurt and walked off in the direction of Stubenring where her office was.

Kurt walked in the opposite direction toward his hotel, noticing that both "observers" from the previous night were gone.

I guess even they have to get some sleep, he thought, although I sure haven't been getting much sleep myself. He walked back to his hotel, bathed, shaved, and awaited Sonya's call.

XIX

A Trip to Paradise

The telephone rang at exactly ten a.m. Sonya's voice on the other end of the line sounded happy and excited. "Kurt, I'll be able to go," she said, "and I can be ready by noon."

"Great," Kurt answered. "I've already arranged to rent a car."

"Oh, one thing, though," she said. "Pick me up at the main entrance of the air terminal here in town. I'll explain it later," she added and hung up.

Kurt immediately called the front desk and notified them he would be checking out but would return on Sunday, five days later. He verified his car reservation and asked that it be waiting for him at the hotel entrance. He dressed in casual clothes, slacks and a turtleneck sport shirt and unpacked a London Fog windbreaker from his valve pack. He packed the rest of his clothes, first checking his "bible" that he carried in his three-suited Samsonite bag. The "bible" actually looked like the Bible. It was a hollowed-out book with a cover made of a lightweight metal with the same properties of lead making it impenetrable to x-ray inspections at airport checkpoints. In it he kept his 32-caliber star automatic, a silencer, and an ample supply of ammunition. Everything looked in order so he packed the bible in the side pocked of his valve pack where it would be more readily available if needed.

He decided not to call into his phone contact from the hotel or from a phone in the vicinity but rather to stop at a public telephone on some street corner on his drive out of town. His "tail" was probably in the front again and he did not want to have to lose him once more to make a phone call. Whoever it was out in front probably knew that he used public phones in the vicinity so there was a possibility of a telephone surveillance. He did not know the sophistication of his tail's organization, whatever it was. The Company's tech people had developed a gadget for listening in on phone calls from a distance, if it were in line of sight. He was sure that the KGB also could do it so he had to be cautious.

At eleven thirty, he checked out of the hotel and, as had been promised, his car, a Mercedes 380 SL, was waiting on Fuhrichgasse at the entrance to the hotel. He quickly put his Samsonite bag and valve pack in the trunk of the car and drove off. Fuhrichgasse was really a dead end street, as far as automobile traffic was concerned; that is, dead-ending into the Kartner Strasse promenade. It would be difficult to exit the street without being seen so he anticipated being followed if his tail had an automobile. He did. Fuhrichgasse was a short street, no longer than one hundred yards long. By the time the tail had gotten into his car, Kurt was already at the street corner where he made a left turn and drove in the direction of the Ring. At the next corner was a traffic light which was about to turn red. For once, luck was in Kurt's favor because there was an Austrian traffic police car parked at the corner. Kurt was through the intersection just as the light changed. The gray-haired man, seeing the police car, decided not to tempt fate and drive through the red light. It was a three-way light and by the time it changed, Kurt was halfway to the air terminal several blocks away. Before driving to the terminal which was on the opposite side of the Stardtpark from Sonya's apartment house, Kurt drove several blocks beyond and circled around to make sure he was not being followed. Fortunately he was not and exactly at twelve noon, Kurt drove up to the front entrance of the air terminal and Sonya quickly walked out of the building entrance and up to Kurt's

Mercedes. She was followed by an old, gray-haired "Trager", an Austrian porter, carrying two bags, one obviously Sonya's overnight bag and the other a pet travel box containing a barking Dachsie. In less than a minute, Kurt kissed Sonya and opened the door for her, put her overnight bag in the trunk, put Dachsie's travel box with the still barking Dachsie in the storage area inside the two seated Mercedes sports car, paid the Trager, and was driving off on Landstrasser Hauptstrasse in the direction of the Autobahn, which would take them out of Vienna into the Austrian countryside.

"Decadent capitalist," Sonya jokingly said. "I might have known that you would drive such an expensive automobile."

"It's really just a good cover for you, Moya Lyubov," Kurt replied. "Who would be looking for a dedicated Bolshevik like you in a car like this? I see you brought your bodyguard along also."

"Poor Dachsie. He just insisted on coming along and I knew you would miss him if I didn't bring him," she said.

Actually, Kurt did not mind at all. He was getting used to the little dog and, after all, it was because of the dog that they accidentally met in the promenade. Besides, Dachsie was becoming attached to Kurt and Kurt did not discourage it by surreptitiously feeding him snacks and even pouring samples of wine and beer for him. "That dog is going to become an alcoholic if he hangs around me," Kurt laughed.

Kurt drove down Landstrasser until eventually he reached the Gurtel, which corresponds to the outer beltways in U. S. cities. Before he reached the Gurtel which would take him to the autobahn heading west, he pulled over to a telephone booth on the street corner. He called his contact number, mentioned that he was leaving the city, but would be in daily telephone contact, and asked that the message be passed on to Max. "Something big has come up," Kurt said, "so I have to take care of it in the next few days." He was told that Shira had arrived. Kurt assured the voice, this time a man, that Max would be perfectly capable of meeting Shira, whoever that was. He would be back Sunday afternoon at the latest.

Kurt got back in the car and they were soon on the autobahn heading west in the direction of Graz.

"Ami spy, where are you taking me?" Sonya asked playfully poking Kurt in the side. "You really have me at your mercy. I neglected to tell my superiors that I was going out of town with you. They might have said no. When our driver dropped me off at the air terminal, I am sure that they assumed that I was going on a business trip. Actually, I think that they welcomed the idea that I was going out of town knowing that you were in Vienna," she added, turning serious. "And I'd rather keep it from Nicholai if I can."

"Who in the devil is Nicholai?" Kurt asked. "You mentioned that you would explain him to me."

Sitting up straight in the bucket seat of the car, Sonya, now very serious, looked out the side window at the countryside whizzing by and answered, "Nicholai is my fiancé. I have to be realistic, Kurt. I really don't believe that you are going to come over to our side and, as you say in America, I am not getting any younger. Nicholai would be good for me and my father likes him very much. In fact, he is a protégé of my father. It's sort of like keeping it in the family. And he really loves me."

"What's his last name?" Kurt asked.

"I'd rather not say," she answered, "and I am sure that your computers can tell you that."

"Do you love him?" Kurt, now very serious, asked.

She turned to him with tears welling in her eyes. "You are the only man I love. I've never loved any other man and I don't think I ever will." She leaned over and rested her head on his shoulder. He put his right arm around her shoulder and held her.

For the next hour, neither said another word; even Dachsie was quiet, as the Mercedes sped down the autobahn, which ended just beyond Wiener-Neustadt. It was still under construction and would eventually run all the way to Graz, Klagenfurt and the Italian border at Tarvisio.

The long silence was eventually broken by Sonya. "You never did tell me where we are going."

"We're going to Velden on Worthersee," Kurt said. "It's beautiful there and quiet this time of the year. I think you'll like it. I've made reservations at Schloss Velden."

"I've never been there," she said, "but I've heard a lot about it. Isn't that where all the rich Austrians and Germans go - the so-called Austrian Riviera?"

"I didn't think that there was a chance of meeting any of your people there," Kurt said. "Also it's the off season and some of the hotels are just opening up and getting ready for the summer season. There's even a casino in Velden. We could try our luck there."

"Wonderful," Sonya said. "I love to gamble."

Without even saying it, they both vowed not to get into any more serious discussions. They sensed that this might be the last time that they would be together and they did not want anything to spoil it. With the exception of one emergency countryside stop for Dachsie, they drove on continuously, arriving in Velden on the western end of Worthersee in the early evening.

Worthersee is a narrow mountain lake about fifteen miles in length lying between the cities of Villach and Klagendurt in the Austrian province of Karnten. On the very western end of the lake is the resort of Velden, a beautiful village with many hotels, shops, restaurants and a casino, which, like other casinos in Austria, is State controlled. On the hill on the edge of the lake is Schloss Velden, an old castle that had been converted into a luxury class hotel, with beautiful grounds maintained to perfection. It reflected the privileges of nobility in the past. Its restaurant and adjacent outdoor patio fronted on the calm crystal blue lake noted for its graceful, beautiful swans that made it their natural habitat. The village and the picturesque castle hotel were a picture of tranquility as they arrived. Kurt drove off the main road into the courtyard, parked the car and went directly to the reception desk. The reception clerk, expecting their arrival, assigned them a room on the second floor overlooking the lake. Since the castle was built on the side of a hill, the second floor was actually at a third floor level. The room, which was large and spacious, was in one of the four round corner turrets that identified the

structure as a castle. The four windows of the room gave a panoramic view of the village on one side, the lake and the gardens
on the other side. A picture postcard could not do it justice in
terms of pure beauty and atmosphere.

"Oh Kurt, it's lovely," Sonya sighed, taken in by the luxury and
sheer beauty of it all. "I wish we could stay here forever, just the
two of us. Well, the three of us," she corrected herself as Dachsie,
standing on his hind legs with his front paws on the window sill,
happily surveyed the lake outside.

The houseman brought in the luggage from the car and Kurt
generously tipped him. It's always a good idea to make friends
with the houseman, Kurt thought. They can always give you
good tips on the best restaurants and sights in the village and
also look after the dog, if necessary.

They unpacked, bathed, and dressed for dinner - a true picture of domesticity. They were both hungry after the long drive
and they looked forward to a good meal and a quiet, restful
evening.

Instead of dining at the hotel dining room, they decided to
walk into the village and try one of the many quaint Gaststubes
that unfailingly served excellent Austrian food. They were not
disappointed. The Gaststube they selected was a typical village restaurant, with paneled walls and thick wooden tables
and chairs. The menu was typically Austrian. The wine, food
and service were excellent and even Dachsie, whom they had
brought along, behaved. The diners at the next table had their
pet German Shepherd with them. It is common in Austria to
take pets into restaurants. The small dachshund, obviously real-
izing that discretion is the better part of valor, was on his best
behavior. Smart dog, Kurt thought. After an evening of light
conversation, good wine and food and a leisurely walk through
the village surrendering to a woman's prerogative of window
shopping, they returned to their room and decided to call it a
day and retire.

They made love only once that evening, then, both naked, they cuddled up together and drifted off to sleep. It had been a strenuous and tiring day.

They awoke simultaneously the next morning as the early morning sun streamed through the window. Sonya pulled up close to Kurt, put her arm around his chest and gently kissed him. "Do you think what we are doing is wrong?" she asked. "I just feel like I'm a part of you and nothing could possibly be wrong."

"Nothing is wrong between us," Kurt answered. "If there is such a thing as a paradise, it has to be right now. I wish we could be like this forever." He kissed her softly on the forehead, the tip of her nose and lightly on the lips.

They dozed off together for a few minutes but were awakened by Dachsie's rustling. Kurt called for the houseman who soon arrived and took out the tail-wagging dog on a leash.

They both then bathed and dressed. Since it was a sunny and already warm day, they decided to have breakfast on the patio overlooking the lake. It was only about nine a.m. but so far it had been a busy day.

"Let's take a walk along the south side of the lake after breakfast," Sonya said, sounding like an excited young girl eager to take in all the tourist attractions. "The houseman told me we should see Maria Worth. That's the village right over there," she said pointing down the lake. "There's a church there that's a shrine to the Blessed Virgin. According to legend she appeared there two hundred years ago and is supposed to return some day. There are supposed to have been many miracles for people who visited the shrine."

After a typical continental breakfast, they returned to their room and changed into more casual clothes and shoes for the long walk ahead. The blue jean fashion had caught on in the Soviet Union and Sonya could have been another Brooke Shields on Soviet television with the way she filled out her Calvin Klein jeans.

"Tsk, tsk," he chided her. "How do you representatives of the proletarian masses justify wearing designer jeans? But I'm glad that you do." Kurt could see the imprint of her bikini panties showing through the form-fitting jeans. A pink cashmere pullover added to the picture that would humble a New York fashion model.

"You know, we could take that walk this afternoon," he said as he put his arms around her and started kissing her on the neck.

"We're going to go now," she laughed breaking his hold. "We have to go as soon as possible to pray for your sins." She picked up a windbreaker with one hand and hurried to the door.

Kurt attached the leash to the happily barking Dachsie and meekly followed her out the door. The walk along the lake to Maria Worth was a delight for all three. The little brown dog, unleashed, ran ahead and at one time jumped into the cold April water after an unsuspecting swan that was swimming too close to the shore. When the swam refused to be intimidated and started furiously flapping its wings at Dachsie, the dog made a hasty retreat back to his protectors on the shore.

Kurt and Sonya were like two young childhood sweethearts, laughing, holding hands, teasing each other, racing and, above all, avoiding any serious conversation. They were a young, happy couple, deeply in love, that one would see anywhere in the world.

Whenever Sonya was happy or sad, she would sing. She had a low, sultry voice and Kurt really believed that she could have made a living in the West singing torch songs in nightclubs. She would often sing Russian love songs to Kurt but her favorites were American classics, especially Cole Porter and George Gershwin. When she was in a mellow, romantic mood she would softly sing Gershwin's 'The Man I Love' to Kurt. It was her favorite. Her songs would reflect her moods. On the walk along the lake she was obviously very happy because all of her songs were happy. She was quite familiar with American music. "Do you know almost all of your country music tells a sad story?" she once asked him. He began to listen to the words after that and she was right. She had obviously been listening to American broadcasts because on the walk along the lake she sang some of the most current hits, some that even Kurt had not yet heard. She even liked American rock music, much to Kurt's dismay, as he would try to change stations when she found it on the radio in the car.

Soon they came to the little village of Maria Worth. It was a beautifully kept little village which old buildings from the past as well as new small hotels and pensions that were designed not to clash with the old Austrian architecture. The village was built on a peninsula jutting out into the lake and at the tip of the peninsula on a hill stood the village church that Sonya had been told about. The winding path led up the hill and around to the front of the church which faced out to the lake. On each side of the path were gravestones of the village parishioners, some dating back over two hundred years.

Kurt hooked the leash back on the dog and tied it around a fence post in front of the church. Sonya had gone in ahead of him. She had a light scarf, that she brought along, over her head. He could see her dip her finger in the holy water fountain at the inner church entrance and make the sign of the cross, touching her right shoulder before her left as is customary in the Eastern church. He followed her and the two of them walked up the center aisle and knelt at the altar at the far end. He could see her lips silently praying as she looked up to the elevated cross on the ornate altar.

This certainly is not what one would picture a Soviet KGB agent doing, he thought momentarily to himself. She turned her head up and looked at Kurt and he could swear he saw tears beginning to well in her eyes. Without a word she grasped his hand and led him around the side. There she asked him for a coin which she deposited in the box next to the candle altar in front of a statue of the Blessed Virgin. She lit a candle and knelt in silence for a few minutes, stood up and led Kurt out of the church.

They walked back through the town, naturally looking into every shop window, and in the direction from which they came. They were both hungry from the walk and since it was already noontime, they decided to have a small lunch at a Gasthaus on the edge of town. What they had intended to be a snack turned out to be a full meal for both. Kurt could not resist all the temptations that appeared on the "Speisekarte" and ended up duplicating Sonya and ordering soup, Wienerschnitzel, salad and even dessert. He was like a small boy in a candy shop. He had a silent dining partner in Dachsie under the table, feeding him small pieces of the delicious veal and even beer in his cupped hand. Sonya pretended to disapprove but on one occasion, Kurt caught her also feeding the small dog a piece of her entrée.

After the delicious meal, and two more large glasses each of the strong Karnten beer they left and walked back toward Velden. The effects of the beer made them giddy and talkative. Even Dachsie had more than he should have because he staggered down the path. When they reached Velden, they went directly to their room at the Schloss and went to bed. All three were soon sound asleep.

They awoke around supper time and debated on whether to have a quiet meal in the hotel or "go out on the town".

"Let's go to the casino tonight," Kurt suggested. "We'll only have one or two nights more before we start having some visitors, probably your people." Kurt was quite aware of the Austrian system of keeping track of all individuals traveling or residing in the country. It was a necessity in a country such as Austria which is land borne and surrounded by six other countries, some not particularly friendly. Austria was a natural pathway for refugees from the Community countries bordering it and as a so-called "neutral" country, was a conduit for people legitimately leaving those countries, not to mention terrorists, spies, and even business people. As a result, there were strict regulations which required all hotels to report the names of their guests to a central police station within twenty four hours. If a traveler stayed at a private residence, the host was also required by law to report the visit. All this is entered into a computer network maintained in Vienna. Naturally the KGB has penetrated this network. Although Kurt was traveling under a pseudonym, the KGB was well aware of Sonya's various names. She was, in fact, traveling under her own name this time. Kurt gave them at least another day to pinpoint them. He, of course, did make his daily telephone contact to his own people. He was not due back in Vienna for four more days.

Sonya, who loved gambling, quickly agreed to the casino suggestion and after a quiet dinner in the hotel dining room, they
walked the short distance to the casino.

Kurt preferred the European casinos to the more gaudy
American ones in Las Vegas or Atlantic City. It was much more
serious and sedate in Europe and did not have all the flashing
lights, row after row of slot machines and general carnival atmosphere, although he did notice on his last trip to Monte Carlo
that the American atmosphere was being introduced. The slots
were bringing in the small gamblers who had not frequented the
casinos in the past.

The casino in Velden was still "unspoiled". He and Sonya
were checked at the front entrance. This, too, was a computerized organization now and the "sharpies" were all listed and
quickly identified. They passed the check and entered the casino.
Other than the sounds of the whirling roulette wheels, the roll of
dice, and quiet conversation, it was very quiet there. Being only
April, the pre-season, and also the middle of the week, the room
was only half filled so Kurt and Sonya did not have to contend
with bustling crowds.

Sonya was impulsive and wanted to win quickly and that is
usually fatal as far as beating the tables. What money she had
allocated to herself to gamble, she quickly lost. Kurt had to re-
strain her from "one more try" more than several times.

With Kurt, gambling was a serious business. In the first hour
he made a minor profit on the baccarat table and he then moved
to the roulette wheel. For one hour, in spite of Sonya's growing
impatience, he only studied the wheel, entering the results in
his little pocket computer. Each wheel has its own characteristics and these characteristics can be identified after many runs.
Casinos are aware of this and periodically "overhaul" the wheels.
After one hour, Kurt had analyzed the one wheel and two hours
after that, with a now excited Sonya, had won enough to cover
the whole week's expenses and then some.

"Why didn't you warn me first?" Sonya asked. He staked her
a small amount and in a short time, following his suggestion, she
had recouped her previous losses. By that time it was midnight

and Kurt had to almost drag a protesting Sonya out of the casino and back in the direction of the hotel.

"I'm really saving you from yourself," Kurt said. "You Commies aren't supposed to like gambling. It's supposed to be one of the sins of capitalism," he added, teasing her.

"You must teach me that system," she replied greedily. "I have to supplement my income somehow. We don't have the big salaries that you capitalist spies have." She hooked her arm around his and leaned her head on his shoulder as they were walking back to the hotel.

Many times they engaged in this repartee, sometimes seriously but usually in light humor. Capitalist and communist to them were only words and neither took the description of themselves seriously.

Sonya was really no Communist in the sense that she was ideologically motivated. She never would defect to the West, although she had many opportunities and in spite of the fact that Kurt, whom she loved, had often suggested it. "I am not Communist," she had tried to explain to him. "I am Russian. You have to be Russian to understand it. It is in our soul and whatever economic system governs our country, we always have it. Many of our people who have gone to the West do come back because of the void they always feel in leaving the mother country. You can see it in the music of the composers or in the works of our artists or even in the choreography of our dancers who have defected. They miss their homeland and long for it until the day they die. America is a young country and in time, if the world survives, will have a tradition of its own and a truly nationalistic entity of its own. Then you, too, will experience what we Russians do." Sonya also knew that Kurt understood her feelings and that he, too, had those feelings toward his own country. Neither would ever defect to the other side and they would only joke about it. They only hoped that professionally their paths would not cross. If they ever did again it would be a real strain on those loyalties.

It was well after midnight when they reached their room. They went right to bed, made love, and were soon sound asleep in each other's arms.

The next day, Thursday, was again idyllic. They slept late, had breakfast, took a walk around the other side of the lake, enjoyed the sun on the outside patio and discussed a wide range of subjects. They completely enjoyed each other's company. Nothing was too banal to discuss nor too complicated. She would correct his attempts at speaking Russian and he would correct her near perfect English.

The next day, Friday, as predicted, other "guests" showed up. The Austrian computer system and KGB efficiency proved itself. Kurt and Sonya considered moving off for the next two days but both decided against it.

"It's so beautiful here," she said, "and they won't bother us. We'll just spend more time in our room and more time making love."

And they did. Kurt thought that they must have set some kind of record. "I wonder if we should contact that Guinness Book of Records," he said.

Sunday came around too soon. They checked out of Schloss Velden after an early breakfast and headed back to Vienna.

"There's only one car following us," Kurt said, looking into the rear view mirror. "Let's lose them." He soon did.

At Volkermarkt, instead of taking the northeastern route directly toward Graz, he took the southeastern direction which, for a while, skirted the Yugoslavian border and then pointed directly north but bypassing Graz. It was through a mountainous area but it avoided the heavily traveled main route. His "tail" undoubtedly assumed he took the main route and although shorter, it was longer in time. They arrived in Vienna in mid afternoon and, Kurt was certain, at least an hour or two before the other car.

"You might as well take me directly home," Sonya suggested. "My people know, of course, where I've been all week. I'll tell them I have you on the verge of defection. That might take off some of the heat. I suppose even Nicholai knows by now but so be it."

"I'll be leaving Vienna in the early part of the week," Kurt told her sadly. He actually did feel sad about saying goodbye to her again. He had a premonition that he might never see her again, at least not under the same circumstances. Sonya, in her own way, had high moral standards. If she married Nicholai, he knew she would be faithful to him as long as they were married.

Kurt, in his last telephone contact, had learned that Ursula Gross was due in Vienna that very evening. He decided to try to make contact as soon as possible, probably the same evening. He could then get about his assignment Monday or Tuesday at the latest. From his briefing in Washington, he was aware that the water level at Lunersee would be at its very lowest by the coming Friday, by an ironic coincidence, the anniversary of the day that the Kisten had been buried forty five years previously.

"You have to let me demonstrate my culinary genius before you leave," Sonya said, trying to sound cheerful. "Can you come tomorrow night? I know you can't tell me when and where you are going, but I sense it is very soon. Please, one more night, Kurt," she almost pleaded.

"Of course, let's make it tomorrow night. Unfortunately, I can't see you tonight," he answered. It was actually the first night that he would not spend with her since they met the previous Sunday. Although he was still with her, suddenly a feeling of loneliness overwhelmed him.

He drove the Mercedes directly in front of her apartment building. The houseman, seeing them arrive, hurried out to the car to help with her bags and with Dachsie.

"We'll say goodbye now," she said as she kissed him, turned and went quickly into the building. He started to call after her. She had not said what time he should be there the following day, but he hesitated. It would give him an excuse to call her that evening if even only for a few minutes. As he drove off in the direction of his hotel, he wondered how many observers there had been waiting for them.

XX

A Trip to Hell

Within a few minutes, he had pulled up in front of the Astoria. There was no doorman, but the gray-haired tail was standing off to the side of the entrance. Kurt was tempted to call over to him and ask him to carry his luggage in. He'd probably do it, Kurt thought to himself. The area directly in front of the entrance was a "no parking" zone but Kurt had decided to turn the Mercedes in so he left it there, took his valve pack and suitcase and walked into the hotel.

He checked in at the desk and was given the key to the same room he had had before. "There is a letter for you," the desk clerk told him.

"Thank you," Kurt answered, taking the sealed large envelope which he correctly assumed were the press credentials that he had requested through Max at their last meeting. He turned in the keys for the rental car and, followed by the porter with his luggage, went up to his room.

He had learned from his telephone contact that the Dresden Symphony Orchestra was due in from Prague at the Hauptbahnhoff, the main railroad station, at seven p.m. There was always a contingent of reporters that greeted such a famous group when they arrived in Vienna so Kurt thought that would be the best time to make initial contact with Ushie.

Since he only planned on remaining in Vienna for two more nights, Kurt did not unpack completely. He opened his luggage and took out just what he thought he would need for the relatively short time he'd be there.

Reporters in Austria are not as casual as American reporters so Kurt selected a conservative business suit, a white shirt, and a tie. He checked through his press credentials. They're perfect, he thought. Our I.D. people certainly know their business.

By the time he bathed, shaved, and dressed, it was almost six p.m. and it was time to go to the railroad station to contact Ushie. He had to allow himself some extra time to lose his tail again. It's getting sort of annoying to have to go through this, he thought. Maybe I should have changed hotels but that would only have presented other problems.

It was impossible for the gray-haired man to check the front entrance and back exits so Kurt, on foot, had no difficulty this time in leaving the hotel unnoticed. He walked over to the Hotel Sacher entrance and hailed a taxi and after the taxi had driven for a block, gave directions to the Hauptbahnhoff. The taxi reached the station at about six thirty so Kurt had time for a snack at the Imbiss Stube inside the terminal. It also gave him time to survey the people waiting for the train bringing not only the East German orchestra, but an assortment of business people, tourists, and students. Other than those who were from Western countries, one could assume that the others were "political reliables" whose Communist leaders did not think it was a one way trip. Kurt spotted a group of what he was sure were reporters and mixed into their group. There were enough newspapers in Vienna and in the cities in the vicinity of Vienna that not all reporters knew each other. In fact, in their efforts to "outscoop" each other, rival reporters avoided making friends with each other.

It was said that a person could set his watch by the efficient Austrian trains and today was no exception. The train from Prague was due at 7:04 p.m. and it arrived exactly at that time. It was not difficult to spot the Dresden Orchestra. They stayed in a group at the urging of their security escorts and there was, of course, the real giveaway, they all, when possible, carried their own instruments. No one would trust their precious musical instruments to even an efficient Austrian Trager.

The reporters moved in on the famous orchestra, interviewing on the walk, whomever they felt were the most famous. Most of the Austrian music reporters did know who was who so Kurt just followed their example until he spotted Ushie.

Ushie was, indeed, a grown woman now. She was no longer the shy teenage adolescent that Kurt knew from the past. Even in her conservative traveling clothes and a complete lack of makeup, Kurt saw a beautiful young woman who would turn any man's heads. He knew by the flash of her eyes that she recognized him as he approached her, paper and pencil in hand and asked her some inane questions about the orchestra. Walking along beside her, and with the noise of all the other people and the incoming and outgoing trains, Kurt was able to make plans for meeting.

"Tonight will be impossible," she quietly said to him. "There are too many security people with us tonight. We are allowed out for a short shopping trip tomorrow. I'm sure I can slip away and meet you. Just tell me where."

"A public place would be best," he said. If she were followed, especially by a pro, it would be dangerous, he thought. She would never be able to shake them and a public place would be more inconspicuous.

"We'll meet at Demel's at twelve noon," he said. She nodded in acknowledgement and continued on with her group. Kurt approached a musician who looked important and "interviewed" him too and then left the group and took a taxi back to the center of town.

He asked the taxi driver to take him to the Hotel Sacher. When they arrived there, he paid the driver and went into the main lobby. There were four telephone booths in the main lobby and Kurt picked the one on the end. He had to find a hotel for Ushie tomorrow. If she were going to defect, tomorrow was probably the best time. After he met her at Demel's, the most famous coffee house in Vienna, he could slip away with her and set her up for a short time in a hotel room until he could arrange for transportation and proper documentation to get her out of the country. The Company would get her out as soon as he could stash her somewhere safely.

Through experience, Kurt learned that the best place is the busiest place, where there is a lot of traffic and where one could be lost in a crowd. A person is too conspicuous in a quiet, half empty hotel. He tried the Hotel Am Stephansplatz and was lucky, hitting it the first time. They had one room left for tomorrow and Kurt reserved it in a second pseudonym that he had. He did not want the computer in the Central Polizei Praesidium to come up with the same name twice in hotel reservations. It might arouse undue suspicion. He did have documentation to back up both names as well as his own real name if necessary. The second call was to Sonya. She answered the call on the first ring. Although she sounded happy to hear his voice, she also seemed distant. They confirmed the time for the following day for seven p.m. The third call was to his telephone contact to get Max's number. He learned that Max had changed hotels to the Hotel Bristol which was actually nearby. Shira, whoever he was, was also there. Kurt then placed a call for Max at the Bristol but was told he was not in. He left a message that he would call the following day.

It was only nine p.m. and Kurt had accomplished all he had planned. He missed Sonya. After spending the last seven nights with her, he felt very lonely being by himself. Must be like withdrawal symptoms, he thought. He walked back to the Astoria. The snack at the bahnhof was not enough so he had a quiet dinner by himself at the hotel dining room and retired early. Tomorrow will be a busy day, he thought.

He awoke early the next morning after a very restless night. He dressed quickly, slipped out of the hotel and found a public telephone booth and called Max at the Bristol. He gave Max the number of the telephone he was on and waited for Max to find another telephone to call him back. In about five minutes, he called. Kurt mentioned that he was to meet Ushie later at Demel's and had a room at the Hotel Am Stephansplatz reserved for her. He would have the information about Lunersee by that evening. He suggested leaving Vienna early the next morning. Time, now, was becoming a critical factor. Max said that he would have a car and would pick Kurt up around six a.m. at his hotel. He would have Shira with him.

"Is the guy getting in your hair?" Kurt asked.

Max grumbled about being stuck with all the unpleasant jobs while Kurt was on a wild fling in the country so Kurt quickly changed the subject. "See you tomorrow at six," he said and hung up. He slipped back into the hotel through the back entrance, had breakfast, went to his room and studied some Austrian maps that he had gotten in the lobby. At about eleven a.m. he walked out the main entrance and was almost disappointed not to see his gray-haired follower. In fact, he did not see anyone following him. He almost felt neglected.

He arrived at Demel's purposely early at about eleven thirty. Demel's is a world renowned Austrian coffee shop and boasts of the finest coffee and pastries in Vienna and, really the world. They do live on their reputation and Kurt, who is a discerning pastry gourmet, has never been disappointed there. Demel's is always busy and especially as noontime approaches. He had to wait for about fifteen minutes and was finally given a table for two in the rear of the shop. It is customary in Austria to join strangers if there is an empty chair in a crowded restaurant or café and as the room filled, Kurt, several times, had to tell some poor customer looking for a seat that he was expecting someone. At noon, as she had promised, Ushie walked in the door. By that time, Kurt had the only unoccupied chair left at his table and it was natural for her to ask for and be seated with him, ostensibly a stranger.

She could hardly contain her happiness at seeing him again when she sat across from him at the table. This time she was dressed for the occasion and Kurt was pleased to see what a stunningly beautiful woman she had become. Not that he was overly surprised, however. As a young teenage, she had shown all the potential to develop into a voluptuous, beautiful woman. Her hair was blonde and she kept it long and parted in the middle. As she turned her head, she would always have to brush with her hand the long silken hair that would cover her eye. Her eyes were deep blue, like her mother's, he remembered. Her mother, too, had been a beautiful woman. Her wide mouth and full lips revealed her large, beautiful teeth when she smiled. Her figure compared to Sonya's and to Kurt that meant perfection.

"My, you have grown up," Kurt said. "You are a lovely woman."

"I still have a terrible crush on you, Kurt," she said. "You told me that you would wait for me to grow up, if you remember. Are you married or can I accept your proposal to a shy little girl many years ago?" she asked in mock seriousness. "You know, Mother and Father always expected you to marry me some day. I think that is one of the real reasons that they want you to find everything in the mountains. Father wouldn't trust my own brothers," she added, now being very serious.

"By the way," he asked, how is your family?"

She went through her whole family updating Kurt's knowledge on each of them.

Kurt did not want to prolong the conversation at that time in fear of arousing the suspicions of anyone who was following her. He did, in fact, sense that she had been followed and this special sense that he had developed through the years in his profession was usually accurate.

"Are you ready to make the break today?" he asked her.

"The sooner the better," she replied. "Just tell me what to do."

"We'll talk more when I get you safely in a private room," he said. "What I want you to do now is remain here for about thirty minutes after I leave. Have some more coffee. Then go to St. Stephan's Cathedral and walk up to the choir loft. I'll meet you there in exactly forty minutes. All tourists go there, even those from the DDR, so it will look natural."

Kurt did not relish the idea of using a Catholic church for operational work but in Catholic Austria, it was the most practical. After paying the waitress, Kurt got up from the table, bowed his head to Ushie as any Austrian gentleman would do, and walked out the front door. He immediately walked over to a department store on Kartner Strasse and made some purchases.

He arrived at the cathedral before Ushie and was waiting in the choir loft when she arrived as instructed exactly forty minutes later.

"Here," he said, unwrapping the package that he had bought. "Put these on." He had bought a scarf, a raincoat, and some flat-heeled shoes. He could only guess the size and fortunately he was close. She tied her long blonde hair in a knot and tied the scarf around it. Kurt also had bought a pair of wire rimmed sunglasses which she put on.

They walked together down the steps through the whole length of the church toward one of the two back exits. The church was full with tourists but they could move through the crowd. Kurt did detect two men who seemed to be searching for someone.

They walked out the back and along the side street of the church back out toward the front. The Hotel Am Stephansplatz was exactly across the street from the main entrance of the church. In a matter of seconds they were in the lobby of the hotel. Kurt, looking out the front window, was sure that they had made it without being detected.

Kurt checked into the hotel assuring the desk clerk that his bag, having been misplaced at the air terminal, would soon follow. This not uncommon occurrence, even in efficient Austria, did not seem unusual and the desk clerk told him his room number and handed him the key. Since he had no luggage, he assured the porter he could find the room himself. Making sure that Ushie had heard the room number, Kurt took the elevator and went up to his room. Ushie followed a short time afterward.

They quickly got down to business. Ushie had a photographic memory and that was one of the several reasons that Willi entrusted her with the information. Helping her to defect and have a life in the West was the primary reason, of course. Kurt did not like to think what would be Willi's fate when this was all over. It was quite a sacrifice for his daughter. Willi always finds a way to survive, Kurt thought. It anyone can survive this, it is certainly him.

Rather than risk any loss in translation, Ushie, with her eyes closed, began to recite in German the exact description of where the containers were buried, that her father had written for her. After she had memorized it, he had destroyed it. Kurt wrote as Ushie talked.

"Die Sache stimmt, soweit sie Dir mitgeteilt wurde. Die Ortlichkeit; es ist der Lunersee in der Schesaplana, An der, der Douglashutte gegenuberliegenden Seeseite fuhrt ein Pfad ent-lang, an dessen rechter Seite (also bergwarts) ein weithin si-chtbarergrosserer Felssich aus dem ubrigen Schutt und den Almiviesen erhebt. Drei Schritte vor (?) diesem Felsblock nur soll sich der Schacht bifinden."

She then opened her eyes and drew a map that she had also committed to memory. She summarized on the map what she had previously described.

"Von der Alm fuhrt ein Weg zum Bach. In der Halfte dieses Weges, funf Meter vom Weg, ist ein Fels, vor dem Felsen ein Schacht."

She then described to Kurt what was buried there, but that Kurt already knew from his briefing in Washington.

To make sure that nothing was omitted, they went over what Kurt had written and reviewed the map.

Kurt then outlined to her his plan for getting her out of Vienna and eventually to America.

"I will come by shortly after six a.m. tomorrow," he said. "Two of my people will be with me. We'll pick you up and take you to a safehouse in Salzburg. We will, of course, be going on to Lunersee. The Company will take care of you in Salzburg. You will be given documentation and be taken to Munich and from there to America."

"I would like to go with you to Lunersee. Maybe I could help," Ushie said.

"I wish we could take you but it's too dangerous," he replied. "The KGB has been watching you. It's best to get you out of the country as soon as possible. They know what we're after but all that they know is that it's in the Vorarlberg area. They haven't narrowed it down to Lunersee, I hope, so there is a good chance that they are watching the area. We would be jeopardizing your safety and the mission if we took you along."

"Are you going to stay here with me tonight?" she asked, smiling at Kurt.

"Your parents are still old fashioned," he answered. "Old Willi would get after me with a shotgun if I did," he laughed. "You are perfectly safe here. Before I leave, I'll order some food and bring it to the room. I do have an important meeting tonight," he added.

"Well, I guess I will still be able to wear white at our wedding," she said, feigning disappointment. "You are going to marry me, you know. I decided that a long time ago."

Kurt smiled and kissed her lightly on the cheek. He thought she really meant it and she did.

It was soon late afternoon and Kurt had to leave. He first went down to the dining room of the hotel and had a tray of food prepared for Ushie. He did not want her to leave the room at all for the rest of the day. She had no luggage and all her clothing was left behind in her own hotel room. By now the word was out that she would not be returning and undoubtedly a search was underway. He felt confident, however, that no one had observed her going into the hotel so he felt she would be safe until he came for her early the next morning. She would get new clothing and whatever she needed when they reached Salzburg. Before he left, he drew the curtain and instructed her to keep it that way. It was a quiet room in the back part of the hotel and faced a blank wall across a narrow alley but Kurt still felt that she should not advertise her presence there. He also double-checked the door locks and instructed her to keep the door locked and bolted. Also, she was not to answer the phone under any circumstances. As he turned to leave, she quickly put her arms around him and kissed him. It was not the kiss of a little girl or a family friend. He found himself returning the kiss. He almost had to tear himself away and he really did not want to. He looked forward to seeing her again the next day.

"Don't forget. Six a.m. tomorrow. I'll come to the room for you," he said as he left, hearing the door being locked behind him.

It was only about six blocks to the Astoria and this time he walked in the front entrance waving to the gray-haired man still reading a newspaper. The second "observer," the one he had seen outside Sonya's apartment house, was also there this time. From the way they acted, Kurt did not think that they were working together. They seem to be scowling at each other, Kurt noted.

By the time he bathed, shaved and dressed, it was time to keep his dinner invitation at Sonya's apartment. He was happy and also sad; happy, of course, to see her, and sad because it would be saying goodbye again. It was always difficult to say goodbye to someone you love and he had to admit that he loved Sonya, more than he had any woman before, even more than he had loved Jackie.

He went out the front entrance, waved to the two newspaper readers and walked up to a flower stand at the corner. He looked for gardenias but, finding none, he bought ten long-stem white roses. They're the next best thing, he thought. With his now double shadow, he walked down to the Ring, turned left and was at Sonya's apartment at exactly seven p.m.

She greeted him at the door even before he knocked. "Exactly at seven," she said as she lightly kissed him and invited him in.

She thanked him for the flowers and took them into the kitchen to find a vase. She had closed the kitchen door and when she opened it, Dachsie darted out and ran up to Kurt wagging his tail in happiness.

"Dachsie stays in the kitchen tonight," she said, coming back into the living-dining room with the roses in a water-filled vase. "You have been really spoiling him, giving him food at the table and, worse yet, wine. I swear, you have made him into an alcoholic," she mockingly scolded Kurt.

Sonya had obviously made special preparations for the evening. Kurt could smell his favorite dish, a lamb roast. Lamb, or Hammelfleish, was relatively inexpensive in Austria with beef and veal the most expensive. The Austrians did not consider it the specialty that Americans or people from the Eastern countries do. It was the favorite of both Sonya and Kurt and tonight had to be something special.

Kurt made himself a vodka martini from the small bar that Sonya had set up and he prepared a straight vodka drink for her. They toasted each other and then sat on the divan together making small talk. Although they tried to act happy, they both found they had to force it and there was an air of sadness in the room.

After a second martini he began to relax. Alcohol temporarily cures a lot of problems, he thought, and the worst part is that depression usually followed euphoria. It's a cyclical thing. He was determined, however, to be euphoric this evening, their last night together.

Sonya was running in and out of the kitchen and eventually had brought all the food to the table. She put Dachsie in the kitchen and closed the door and then lit the two candles on the dining table.

Kurt opened a bottle of Pinot Noir, their favorite red wine and filled her glass and his.

"Well, my lord and master of the house, at least for one night," she added. "You have to carve tonight as is the custom in your own country. In Russia the woman has to do all the work but tonight is your night." She had placed a large serving fork and a carving knife on the table next to the large lamb roast.

The meal was excellent and Kurt had a second helping of everything, even the Baklava dessert that she served. "I never realized that you were such an excellent cook," Kurt said. "In all the years that we have known each other and all the time we've spent together, this is the first time you have cooked for me."

"See, I would make a good housewife," she replied. "Why don't you come back to Russia with me? We could be happy together."

He did not really have to answer her. They both knew that it could never be. He could never defect to the East and she could never desert her homeland. It was a dead end for them and they both knew it.

The momentary silence was broken by Sonya. She picked up Kurt's now empty wine glass and hers and took them to her bar where she filled them both. She gave his to him and kissed him, and taking him by the hand, led him to her bedroom. They looked out the wide open window marveling at the beautiful city.

"Make love to me, now," she said, this time in English, not in Russian as she usually did when she wanted to make love.

Kurt emptied his wine glass in one swallow and quickly undressed. Sonya was already undressed waiting for him with her arms outstretched. He kissed her passionately and soon they were making love, almost violently as if it were going to be the last time.

Kurt kissed her gently on the cheek and thought he detected a salty taste. He noticed tears on her cheeks as she lay there saying nothing. As he lay back staring at the ceiling, he could feel his heart pounding and he felt extremely drowsy. He sat up in bed and suddenly felt very disoriented and his head began to pound. He began to perspire profusely and he looked over to Sonya to tell her how he felt. She had gotten up and had put a robe around her shoulders. He could see in her eyes that she was aware of what was happening.

"Kurt," she said in a very detached voice. Even her voice did not sound like the Sonya he knew. "You must tell me about your mission in Vorarlberg. I know you met Ursula Gross today and that is why you were planning on leaving tomorrow. We have to have what is buried there. It's not just the gold but what else is buried there. If you don't tell me, you are going to die. I have the antidote, but you must tell me before I can give it to you. Please, Kurt," she suddenly pleaded. "Please tell me."

It had to be the wine, Kurt thought to himself as he struggled to get out of bed. And that's why, for the first time, she kept the dog in the other room. She knew I would give him some.

Kurt, through years of physical conditioning, was much stronger by comparison than most men his size and age. He managed to stand up and stagger toward the dining room, as even in his confusion he knew where the telephone was. Through some superhuman effort, he managed to reach the telephone and tried to speak into it.

Sonya, in the meantime, had run to the front door, unlocked it and opened it, crying out, "Yuri, Yuri!"

The big fat man rushed into the apartment and headed for Kurt. All that's missing, Kurt thought, in his confused mind, is the fat, dark dachshund that had helped set up the chance meeting at the promenade the week before.

As the fat man rushed at him, Kurt reflexly grabbed the carving knife that was still on the dining room table near the telephone.

"Never go straight in, it might hit the sternum or a rib and break, and never go in too low. You might hit their guts and they don't die right away. Come in low under the rib cage and then up." These were the instructions from his operational training that were pounded into his subconscious as Kurt swung the carving knife in an uppercut motion and plunged it into the fat man. The blade did not even feel as if it had met any resistance as it found the fat man's heart. Other than a gurgling sound, the fat man did not even make a sound as he slid slowly to the floor with the knife handle still protruding from his belly. He was dead before he got to the floor, his mouth and eyes wide open.

Kurt turned toward Sonya who had run back into the bedroom. She was naked. The robe that she had over her shoulders fell off as she ran into the room. As he staggered into the room, he could see her pulling out the drawer on the nightstand next to the bed. She took out a small black revolver and brought it up to point at Kurt. As if it were a conditioned reflex, Kurt lunged at her, striking at her with his right clenched fist. It caught her square on the tip of her jaw and sent her flying backwards. She did not even hit the window still as the force of the blow threw her through the wide open window into space. She seemed to grab out to Kurt as she plummeted ten stories to the ground below. He did not even hear her screams. She must have been unconscious from the blow, he wanted to think afterward.

He somehow managed to get to the telephone which was lying on the floor off the cradle and buzzing loudly. He asked the operator for the Bristol Hotel. In his confusion, he could not remember his contact number. By some good fortune, he quickly was given the hotel and he was immediately connected to Max's room. He vaguely remembered telling Max that he was at Sonya's and that he had been poisoned. That was the last thing that he remembered until he woke up the next morning in what looked like a hospital room.

There were three hazy figures standing before his hospital bed when he first opened his eyes. As his mind cleared and he could focus his eyes, he saw first a tall man in a long white coat, Max and Susan Smith. "Susan?" was his first word. "What in hell are you doing here? Where am I?"

"It's not Susan, it's Shira. The Smith part is right. My name is Shira Smith and you are in a private room at the University Klinik. I'll explain it all later."

"You've had quite an evening," Max spoke up. "If you had not called me when you did, you'd be in a box now."

Kurt started to remember the events of the previous evening.

"You are really quite lucky," Max continued. "You got a good dose of Ricin. If it had happened six months ago, we couldn't have saved you. Now, thanks to our lab people, we have the antitoxin and we were able to completely neutralize it. You should be ready to get up soon. When we first found you and brought you here, we had to slap a pacemaker on you. People that die of Ricin poisoning develop an arrhythmia," he explained, sounding like the physician that he was. "You just started to fibrillate when we got to you."

Kurt knew Ricin well. It was one of the favorites of the KGB and had been used by them against two Bulgarians who had defected to the West. They had refined it to the point that just a minute amount of it, an amount that they had inserted in a small, hollowed-out B-B, was fatal to one man in London and would have been fatal to another in Paris if he had not been given medical care in time. Alerted to this, Company scientists had developed an antitoxin, Ricin being a toxin that was derived from the very poisonous castor bean.

"Fortunately I got to you, even before they found your girlfriend," Max said. "This is Professor Hans Haid. He's one of our people here at the University Klinik. I got you here myself and Dr. Haid treated you in time."

The Company had people such as Haid around the world. He was an Austrian but like many of the others who had received all or part of their medical training in America, he had been recruited by The Company. Many of these people actually owed their positions in their own countries to The Company. Kurt was quite thankful that Haid was there.

"My God, poor Sonya," Kurt said as the events of the night before began to recur to him.

"Poor Sonya! For Christ's sake, she tried to kill you. Don't feel sorry for her. She deserved it," Max blurted out. "You know, I find it quite amusing," he continued. "When you two were making love, and it was obvious from the way I first found you that that is what you were doing, it actually helped speed up the action of the Ricin in you. She was a real cool cookie, believe me. She was literally fucking you to death."

"I just remembered," Kurt suddenly said, sitting up in the bed. "What time is it?" he asked. "Ushie. We were supposed to pick her up at six this morning."

The three did not answer. There was a long silence.

Max finally spoke. "I don't' think we have to worry about the time. Dr Haid," he continued looking up at the Austrian professor to explain further.

"I'll get a wheelchair," the Austrian said. "I want to take you to Gerichtliche Medizin. I'd like to do it now, if you can make it, before the criminal police arrive."

"Not Ushie?" Kurt asked. He knew that Gerichtliche Medizin was forensic medicine and where homicide victims were sent for examination.

He got up from the bed, put on a hospital robe and, surprisingly, found he was strong enough to walk. They followed Dr.

Haid who led them to what was the morgue in the adjoining building.

Kurt was hoping that there had been some terrible mistake but as Max explained what had happened, he had a sickening feeling that it was Ushie even before they got there.

"She was found in the room that you got for her in the Hotel Am Stephansplatz," Max explained. "The maid found her. She had knocked on the door and when there was no answer, she opened it to turn back the covers the way they do here in Austria. I never knew her but I assume it was her. It's not a pretty sight."

They were admitted to the morgue examining room by an attendant and they saw a sheet-covered figure on the examining table.

Haid pulled back the sheet and Kurt, who was not unfamiliar with death, almost became sick. It was Ushie. She was grinning from ear to ear.

"It was strychnine," the Professor started speaking, sounding like he was giving a lecture to his students. "Strychnine poisoning results in a generalized heightened muscle reflex. The slightest stimulus, such as the clapping of the hands, or even light, causes a violent response of muscle contraction. The body," he continued pointing at Ushie, "becomes arched in hyperextension, what we call opisthotonus, so that only the crown of the head and heels of the victim may be touching the ground. The jaw is rigidly clamped and the strong contraction of the facial muscles produces what you see here, that hideous grin. It's called risus sardonicus. Strychnine is a poison of choice for interrogations. It can be controlled, if given in injections. You can see," he said, pointing out needle marks on her arm, "that is what happened. Whoever did it was also a sadist. He gave her much more than he had to. In fact, my guess is that she died before she could be interrogated."

"That's enough," Kurt said feeling nauseous and turning away. If his stomach had not been pumped from the night before, he probably would have vomited. Shira was already vomiting in the next room. They covered Ushie and left the room.

"Poor Ushie. Poor Sonya," Kurt muttered. If he knew how to cry, he would have. That was an emotion that had died in him. Inwardly he was suffering a thousand deaths.

"We should leave town as soon as possible," Max suggested. I've check you out of your hotel and have your luggage in my car outside. This has been listed as a suicide but the Austrian police will figure this out pretty soon and I'm sure the KGB does not think to highly of you at this point."

"The sooner the better," Kurt answered.

In less than an hour, the three of them, Kurt and Shira, with Max behind the wheel of the large Peugeot that he had rented, were on the autobahn heading west. No one spoke. It was not the time to make light conversation. Max finally broke the silence by turning on the radio.

Viennese newsmen are no different from their American counterparts and sensationalism is a part of their business. The first sounds on the radio were a news broadcast announcing the "suicide" of a young, beautiful woman who had been found nude on a side street off Schubertring. According to the broadcaster, the young woman, who had been despondent, according to friends who had been interviewed, jumped from the tenth floor window of her apartment, taking her pet dachshund with her.

Kurt turned off the radio.

"Looks like the KGB is starting the cover-up", Shira said.

"I don't remember killing Dachsie," Kurt said looking at Max. "Why would I do that?"

Max did not say anything. No one did as the car sped on in the direction of Vorarlberg and Lunersee.

XXI

THE TUNNEL

"I suppose that you would like some explanation about Washington, D.C.," Shira said, breaking a long silence as the Peugeot sped by Linz on the autobahn heading for the West German border.

"Not particularly," Kurt replied, still staring out of the window as the Austrian countryside whizzed by.

Except for especially dangerous stretches of the superhighway, there was no automobile speed limit. Even if there had been, Max, who Kurt often accused of having a death wish, would have pressed the high speed car to its limit. He maintained the speed at one hundred sixty kilometers or about one hundred miles per hour.

"I love the way this baby holds the road," he said, trying to change the subject of conversation. He knew what emotional turmoil Kurt was going through and he also knew that the events in Washington would only compound it at this particular time.

Shira apparently understood and she too became silent. She knew it was an inopportune time to discuss anything controversial but she felt that she had to at least try to bring up the subject. It would have to wait until Kurt was ready. She did not enjoy the deception in Washington, especially after she had met him. She had known almost every detail of his life at the time she had "arranged" to meet him on the flight from Texas. The Company had planned the meeting and, in fact, had arranged through their airline contact to have her listed as a part time flight attendant. She had actually made several flights to maintain that cover and other than one executive of the airline, no one knew her true situation. Because of the extreme sensitivity of the operation that Kurt was being assigned, The Company wanted an evaluation of Kurt, especially in view of his known relationship with Sonya. That was Shira's specialty - evaluating personnel for particularly dangerous missions. Not that Kurt was ever considered not capable. He had certainly proven himself many times before but because of the "burning out factor" that many such agents as Kurt experience after years of such hazardous duty, they felt the need to evaluate him. Some seemed to love the violence. Those like Max seemed to thrive on the type of life that such agents lived. More sensitive ones like Kurt were closely observed and if there were any indications of cracking, they were brought "in from the cold" and given prolonged headquarters assignments. Kurt had passed her "test" and that was why he was on the assignment. But Shira was now worried about Kurt. Not that she was afraid he was on the verge of cracking but because now she saw signs in Kurt that he probably would never be able to crack anymore. He had built up such a wall within himself that his emotions might never again surface as they should in normal people. In their brief encounter in Washington, she had seen a warm, emotional Kurt, one who had survived many painful and traumatic experiences. She had been deeply moved and became emotionally involved with Kurt. It had never happened to her before. In that brief time with him she began to fall in love with him. Now she was seeing a different man in Kurt. She feared that the violent events of the last few hours might have had a permanent effect on him. He was now a man drained of all feelings and emotions. A person with no emotions is a sociopath and that worried her. She was not sent to Austria to continue evaluating Kurt but primarily because it would help give him cover. A man and woman traveling together raised less suspicion than two men traveling together, especially in a tourist country such as Austria. Max was supposed to be more in the background while she and Kurt were supposed to appear to be a husband and wife on a vacation in the Austrian Alps. She was even given documentation to back that up. She had welcomed the assignment, one which was concocted after she and Kurt had gotten along so famously in Washington. In fact, she had subtly suggested it herself when she had given her evaluation report on Kurt. A week in Austria with him seemed a wonderful idea and it would give her the opportunity to make amends for the deception. But things were not working out the way she had planned. When she arrived in Vienna she found that Kurt was with Sonya. She actually felt jealous of Sonya but there was little she could do at the time other than let that romance run its course. Right now she did not know whether to hate Sonya for trying to kill Kurt or feel sorry for her because of her violent death. And then there was also beautiful Ushie. She knew that tragic ending had also terribly affected Kurt. It was all a big mess. She was beginning to wish that she had never become involved with The Company. When she had graduated from Smith (that was one of the true things that she had told Kurt), she continued on to get her Ph.D. in Human Factors Psychology at Columbia. That part she did not tell Kurt. Her specialty was in personality assessment and human potential evaluation, a perfect background for her position with The Company. She had always welcomed a challenge and she craved excitement but this was something she had never envisioned. It was a cruel, violent and tragic world she was seeing. It was not what one sees in the movies or reads in paperback novels.

As they approached Salzburg on the autobahn, it was near noon.

"Do you two want to stop for lunch?" Max asked.

"Let's keep going," Kurt answered, before Shira could speak. "There's a U. S. military snack bar at Chiemsee before we get to the Rosenheim cutoff. We can grab a quick snack there. If we stop here in Salzburg, we'll lose a couple of hours and we have a long way to go. We should try to get to the mountains tonight."

Kurt especially did not want to stop in Salzburg. That was where he was supposed to take Ushie. She was going to stay there for a few days in a safehouse until it was time to smuggle her out of Austria and eventually to America. Kurt was still in a state of shock over seeing the violent way Ushie had died. Why did the KGB have to kill her? He asked himself. It did not make sense. They usually did not do anything like that unless there was no alternative. It could not have been because of what happened to Sonya. The time element did not allow for that.

Poor, poor Ushie, he kept repeating to himself. She never really got to live. He thought maybe she was really in love with him and that made it even worse for him. She might still be alive if she had not felt that way and had not come to the West to be with him, as she said she had.

They continued on and soon came to the Austria-West Germany border. There is a part of Germany that juts down into Austria. It would be possible to avoid crossing into Germany and to remain in Austria; however, it would take much longer to do this by car. The autobahn continued on into Germany in the direction of Munich. At Rosenheim, halfway between Salzburg and Munich, was a turnoff where a branch autobahn headed back into western Austria. There was a risk of detection by crossing borders but since time was important, Kurt and Max felt that it was worth the risk. Kurt was now using his alternate identification, not the one he used in Vienna. Shira, being along as his wife, added to the credibility of his cover.

The crossover into Germany was without incident. United States passports generally are hardly even looked at in these busy checkpoints and this time was no exception. Soon they arrived at the U. S. military hotel at Chiemsee where they had lunch and quickly moved on. In a short time they were at the Germany-Austria checkpoint going back into Austria. Again there was no problem with the border guards who just waved them on at the sight of the passports.

Kurt did not say anything but there was something that disturbed him. On the Austrian side of the border, parked in a black Mercedes was a familiar face. Although Kurt did not place it immediately, he knew he had seen it before. Searching his memory, he remembered it as being one of the observers outside Sonya's apartment house. The face has seen me too, Kurt thought.

Max soon had the Peugeot up to one hundred sixty kilometers and Kurt noticed in the rear view mirror that the Mercedes was not following. Either he didn't spot us or he's calling ahead to someone else, Kurt thought. He still did not tell the others what he had seen.

They were soon in Innsbruck where they stopped briefly at a "Kaufhof," a department store on the main street, Maria Theresa Strasse. Department stores were relatively new to Austria, even provincial towns like Innsbruck. The Austrians attempted to preserve their old country image by delaying the invasion of these commercial enterprises and maintain small, independent shops but slowly gave up to the inevitability of progress. This Kaufhof was not in Innsbruck on Kurt's last visit there but this time he was thankful. They were able to purchase all they needed in the one shop rather than spend a good part of the day going from one shop to another. They purchased the necessary clothing and shoes for their "mountain climbing" visit, collapsible picks and shovels, and knapsacks, or Rucksacks as they are called in Austria.

In less than an hour they were back on the autobahn. It splits at Innsbruck, one part continuing on through the Brenner Pass into Italy, the other part heading, for the next fifty miles, toward the Arlberg Pass, ending near the town of Imst. From that point it reverts to the old alpine road that winds up through the Arlberg Pass.

"This is the same road that Mueller and the others took over forty five years ago," Shira said. She, too, had been briefed on the mission before she arrived in Austria.

"It's like reliving history. I can just picture them driving in their military trucks with all that gold. We're going to save a lot of time, though," Max added. "According to the map, there is now an eight and a half mile long tunnel. It starts just before we get to St. Anton. In winter time the snow gets pretty deep up there in the mountains so the tunnel makes it much easier. Thanks to it, we should make Bludenz or even Brand by suppertime."

Kurt was still quiet. Except for answering necessary questions about the trip, he did not enter into any of the conversation. The other two thought he was still brooding and they did not try to push him. They both carried on an animated conversation between themselves. They were traveling through one of the most beautiful, scenic areas of Europe and it was difficult not to comment on it.

Kurt was not brooding, however. He was worried and concerned about the "face" back at the border. He also knew that the KGB just does not do nothing when one of their best agents is killed, especially one that is the daughter of their Chief of Operations. Kurt could sense danger and that sense was not desensitized by his ordeal in the previous twenty four hours.

They reached Landeck and stopped briefly for gasoline and then continued on up into the mountains approaching St. Anton.

"If we had time I would certainly like to visit the Gasthof where they stayed back in 1945," Shira said. "I'll bet that it's still there and probably run by the same family."

Just before they reached St. Anton, an access road to the tunnel veered off to the left, the main road continuing on into the village of St. Anton. Before the tunnel entrance was a toll booth manned by a toll collector and an Austrian gendarme (an Austrian state policeman).

As Max pulled up to the toll booth, Kurt got out of the Peugeot. "Give me the key to the trunk," he said. "I've got to get something out." He went to the rear of the car, opened the trunk, and took out his valve pack. He slammed the trunk lid closed and put the valve pack in the front seat of the car with him.

"How long is the tunnel?" he asked the gendarme as Max was paying the toll.

"It's fourteen kilometers and ends in Langer," the gendarme answered as he waved them on.

"That wasn't cheap," Max said as he drove into the tunnel entrance. "It cost about seven dollars. I supposed it's worth it in the winter just to avoid all the ice and snow but this time of year the road is pretty good. I suppose that's why there's no other traffic in the tunnel, just us rich Americans."

"It is a beautifully constructed tunnel," Shira said. "It must have taken years to build."

Kurt still did not say anything. He reached down into the side vent of his valve pack and took out his 32 automatic. He attached the silencer to the nose of the gun, checked the clip, pulled back the receiver and put it in his lap, covering it with the opened road map that he had been reading.

The continued on through the tunnel and after about five miles, they spotted a flashing red light in the lane ahead. It was a gendarme patrol car and there were two uniformed gendarmes signaling with their hands for them to stop.

"Must be an accident ahead," Shira said.

"There's probably only one other car in the whole damn tunnel and it has to have an accident," Max replied, as he pulled up and stopped a few meters from the police car.

The two gendarmes approached the Peugeot, one on each side, as both Max and Kurt opened the car windows on their sides.

As the gendarmes simultaneously reached the car and bent to look into it, Kurt moved quickly.

Light travels quicker than sound. Often the fire blast from a gun can be seen before it is heard when fired at a distance. Even at this short distance, two small holes could be seen, one in each forehead of the gendarmes as Kurt first shot the one at his window, and with a swishing movement, the one at Max's window, before there was a realization of any noise. Both with surprised looks still on their faces, were dead before they even started to fall. It was almost a trademark for Kurt to shoot his targets directly between the eyes. It was quick, final, and painless. Even in killing he tried to be humane.

"What the hell are you doing?" Max shouted. "You can't go around killing Austrian police. We're going to be in real trouble now. The toll wasn't that expensive."

Shira was too stunned to even speak.

"You'll probably find the Austrian police dead in the bushes out near the entrance to the tunnel. These two and those two at the toll booth aren't Austrians. Austrian gendarmes don't carry Makarov P51s," he said pointing at the two guns that the "gendarmes" had apparently been carrying in one hand hidden behind their backs. "They carry the standard Walther P7. That's strictly KGB. Also they wear their uniforms a lot neater than these two." Kurt had never seen an Austrian policeman whose uniform did not look neat and tailored. "Those are probably the uniforms of the police they shot. Also that 'gendarme' at the toll booth spoke German with a Russian accent. I've known enough to spot that accent."

They quickly examined the bodies of the two gendarmes and Kurt's suspicions were confirmed by the identification that they found. They were KGB.

"We'd better get the hell out of here," Kurt said. "We're awfully vulnerable here in the tunnel and some other car might come along. Let's put their bodies back in their car. It might give us a little more time."

They dragged the two bodies back to the police car, opened the trunk and stuffed them in. Kurt picked up the police hats that the gendarmes had been wearing and handed one to Max. "We're going to have to go back to the toll booth and take those two out also," he said. "It'll give us a couple of days. Otherwise they'll be after us in hours. By the time the Austrian police and the KGB figure out what happened we can be in Switzerland with the goodies. Shira, you can start earning your keep," he added. "You follow us in the Peugeot. Max and I will drive back to the toll booth in the police car. Just give us a couple of minutes ahead of you."

"You drive the police car," he said to Max. "And wear the hat so they'll think at first that we're their boys coming back."

Max and Kurt got into the police car, turned it around in the two-lane tunnel and headed back toward the entrance with Shira following discreetly behind in the Peugeot. As the police car, with Max driving, emerged from the tunnel, the "toll booth operator" and the "gendarme", seeing it, waved and walked toward the approaching car.

"Why should you have all the fun?" Max said, as he jammed his foot on the accelerator, aiming the now speeding car at the two surprised KGB men. It hit them both at the same time, sending them flying up over the hood and roof of the police car. As Max screeched the car to a halt, Kurt jumped out and quickly emptied his automatic into the still breathing men lying on the pavement.

Kurt looked around to see if there had been any witnesses but there were none. Fortunately, since it was the off season, there was little, if any traffic in the expensive tunnel. The commuter traffic had taken the main route through St. Anton.

Max and Kurt dragged the two bodies into the toll booth and closed and locked the door just as Shira was driving up in the Peugeot. It had all taken no more than one minute. Max and Kurt quickly jumped into the car and with Shira still driving, headed toward St. Anton. "Didn't even dent the car," Max laughed.

"Well, you really did want to drive through St. Anton, didn't you?" Kurt asked trying to calm an excited Shira. "Don't ever say that things are dull around Max and me. I guess they didn't tell you about the scenic tour that we provide."

Shira recovered quickly from the shock of the violence she had just witnessed. She felt unusually calm and clear headed. "I've never seen anyone killed before," she said. "And it's strange, it doesn't bother me at all. Maybe I'll have a delayed reaction."

"Well, we'll let you handle the next one," Max replied. "Maybe there's hope for you yet in this business. I'd rather have you for a partner than old Kurt here. You're much prettier than he is."

Curiously the whole incident seemed to make them more talkative as they continued on in the direction of Bludenz. Even Kurt, who had been quiet and morose on the early part of the trip, joined in the light conversation. Probably a post-adrenaline euphoria, Shira, the analyst, later thought to herself looking back on the whole incident.

XXII

BURSERBERG

They reached Bludenz as the sun began to disappear over the mountain chain to the west. They did not even stop in the city but immediately headed south on the narrow, twisting road which took them up into the mountains in the direction of Brand.

"We have about ten kilometers to go to get to Brand," Kurt said. "There aren't many of the tourist hotels open since this is the off season. I hope we can find one since we'll have to stop and prepare for the climb up to Lunersee. The cable car up there won't be operating yet."

Ten kilometers is a relatively short distance. However, because of the narrow, curving road, constantly upward, from slight at times to steep, it was almost a half an hour before they saw Brand off in the distance. A short distance before Brand was an even smaller village called Burserberg, which had only one distinction, a new hotel, Hotel Taleu, and it was open for business.

"That looks like a nice place," Shira spoke up. "And I see that they're advertising a Hallenbad and Sauna. I certainly would welcome a relaxing sauna after what we went through today."

"I guess it's as good as any," Kurt replied. "And it might be better to stay here rather than in Brand. Every hotel in Brand has been in the same family for generations. I'm sure many of the people remember the Luckners and it would be better not to even take the slightest chance with our interests. A new hotel like this couldn't have any association with the past."

Shira drove up and parked the car directly in front of the hotel entrance. Kurt went into the hotel and registered for two rooms, one for himself, and Shira as husband and wife and the other for Max.

It's funny how things work out, he thought to himself as he was registering. Last week I would have jumped at the opportunity of checking into a hotel with someone named Susan. Now I don't give a damn. The last thing that interests me now is another romance. The still fresh memory of Sonya and Ushie pained him as the thoughts of the previous day flashed through his mind. Maybe it was all a bad dream and I'll wake up and find it's not true, he thought to himself.

"We had our choice of rooms," he announced to the other two who were waiting in the car. "There's hardly anyone else staying here."

The Diener, or porter, came out to the car to get their bags. Max and Kurt unloaded the trunk themselves and handed the bags to the Diener who had brought out a small cart. They left the large suitcase, which contained the detector and their other operational equipment, in the trunk. "It'll be safer and more convenient to leave it there," Kurt said as he slammed the trunk lid shut and checked it to make sure it was locked. He then drove the car around to the back of the hotel and parked it where it would be less noticeable from the road and joined Shira and Max who were waiting for him in the lobby.

They were shown to their rooms by the Diener. They were on the third floor, the top floor with a balcony facing the Brand Valley. Max was given a room on one end of the hall and Kurt and Shira, a room on the other end.

Kurt tipped the Diener who had taken them to his room first. The Diener was not Austrian and it was immediately obvious to Kurt who, having native fluency, detected any foreign accent. Kurt could also differentiate between the various German dialects. He could tell from what part of Germany or Austria some-one came or even if someone had come from some of the Eastern European countries where there were large German-speaking colonies. This Diener was none of these. He was a foreigner and although he spoke good German, his swarthy appearance and accent identified him as either Turkish or Arabic. This concerned Kurt somewhat, especially in view of the briefing in Washington about a possible PLO complication. There were, however, many such people working in Germany and Austria who had left their native countries for the higher earnings available in these more prosperous countries. Both Kurt and Shira felt uneasy at the ar-rangement. It was a large room with two single beds that were individually made up but were pushed together. Being a new hotel, it had a private bath, a luxury not found in many of the older continental hotels. The furniture was heavy pine, blend-ing with the pine paneled walls. The floors were a beautifully finished parquet with several plush oriental-type rugs scattered throughout the room.

The view from the large balcony was breathtaking in its beauty. From the balcony it was possible to see the Brandner Valley winding down to the city of Bludenz below and to the right it was possible to see the village of Brand and beyond to the mountains topped by snow and the glacier that fed the Lunersee, the lake near the top that was their final destination.

Neither Kurt nor Shira spoke at first. They were just staring out at the beautiful sight which was slowly disappearing as dark-ness set in. Each was lost for the moment in private thoughts.

They were brought back to reality by Max knocking at the door. "I don't' want to disturb you two newlyweds," he said through the door, "but it's dinner time. "I'll wait for you at the bar."

"I feel crummy after that long trip," Kurt said. "I'd better shower and shave but I'll play the gentleman. You can use the bathroom first."

"No, you go first," Shira answered. "I'm going to exercise a woman's prerogative and take a hot bath. It will take me longer.

You can wait for me in the bar or have dinner with Max if you can't wait."

Kurt did not answer but unpacked what he needed and went into the bathroom.

He would have preferred a shower but it was a typical Austrian bathroom with a tub and a hand shower that looked like a telephone. He filled the tub, climbed in, quickly washed and then rinsed himself with the shower. That, and a quick shave, took no more than about fifteen minutes. He changed into clean underclothes in the bathroom and put on a pair of slacks before he re-entered the bedroom.

It was an awkward situation for both. They felt like strangers to each other.

Shira was hanging up some of her clothes as he entered.

"Don't unpack everything," he said. "I don't know how long we'll be here. Probably not more than a couple of nights."

She nodded and without a word sent into the bathroom and closed the door. He could hear her filling the tub and doing whatever women do in bathrooms.

He dressed quickly, putting on a turtleneck sweater and a sport coat. He checked his automatic and slipped it into the inside pocket of his sport coat. Through the closed door he told Shira he and Max would wait for her in the bar. He left the room, checking to make sure the door automatically locked behind him, walked down two flights to the ground floor, and joined Max who was sitting alone at the bar.

"I'm already on my second drink," Max said as Kurt sat on a bar stool next to him. "Here, live dangerously and have one of these Austrian cigarettes."

Kurt, forgetting for the moment that he had given up smoking, instinctively took a cigarette and accepted Max's offer of a light.

"Phooey," he said, blowing out the smoke that he had already inhaled and dubbing the cigarette out in the ashtray. "It takes like shit! I never realized how bad cigarettes tasted until I quit. Are you trying to get me hooked again? What kind of doctor are you, anyway?"

"Whiskey on ice," he said to the bartender in English who came to him for his order.

Kurt would have ordered his favorite, a vodka martini, but few bartenders in Europe made them right. Ordering whiskey was really ordering Scotch in Europe. American whiskey or bourbon was something a person had to specifically order. Scotch was his second preference.

The bar looked like a typical American lounge bar, something that was becoming more popular in Europe and Kurt was somewhat surprised to see it here in this tiny Austrian village. It was a horseshoe-shaped bar with a mahogany top and leather padding on the sides. The back bar was mahogany with glass mirrors which reflected the large selection of bottles of almost all imaginable imported and domestic brands of drinks, including Kurt's favorite Scotch, Glen Livet. When he saw that, h e asked the bartender for it rather than one that he had just started to pour. The rest of the lounge was very attractive and comfortable looking with padded booths next to the walls and cushioned chairs at all the tables. With the soft, indirect lighting in the room, it looked like a plush Washington lounge bar.

"Where is the blushing bride?" Max asked. "You know we should have arranged to have her be married to me. I don't think that you're going to be good company for her on this trip," he added, trying to make light conversation.

"I really wouldn't care," Kurt answered. Sonya and Ushie were constantly on his mind. Shira was only a necessary evil to him at this time. She was one of the two women who had deceived him and he vowed that it would never happen to him again. "We really had no choice in the matter. All our identification was made out that way. Anyway, those pricks back at Headquarters think that I am the one who is flipping out. She's supposed to bird dog me, not you. You're the normal one by their standards. They hired you knowing that you're crazy. That's what they want. She'll join us here at the bar as soon as she's dressed."

"I get fed up with Headquarters too," Max said, suddenly getting serious. He hesitated as the bartender served Kurt's Scotch and walked away. "They never do appreciate what we go through. I wonder sometimes if anyone in the whole country gives a shit. Not that I want to be a big hero but I get pissed off sometimes at the bad press we always get. I can't remember ever reading anything good about us in the *Washington Post* or *New York Times*. Sometimes I begin to wonder if my values are right. I should have gone into private practice instead of coming to The Company. Is it all worth it?"

"Christ, listen to me. I'm beginning to sound morose like you. Tell you what. Let's get sloshed tonight and get our minds off anything controversial. I don't think I'm going to get laid tonight anyway," he added looking around the nearly deserted lounge for potential pick ups. "This is obviously not the peak of the tourist season."

Kurt was somewhat taken back by Max's uncharacteristic emotional comments. Max had always given the impression of being totally cool emotionally. He had always seemed to make light of any situation no matter what it was, the events of that day being an example.

Well, it shows that he is human, Kurt thought to himself.

Kurt could see Shira approaching and he motioned to the bartender. "Two more of the same," he said, knowing Shira's favorite drink after that jone evening in Washington. "I must admit after spending the day with you two characters, I could certainly use a drink," she said as a greeting.

Kurt offered his stool to her and moved over one allowing her to sit between Max and him. "We could sit at a table if you would prefer," he said.

"No, this will be fine," she answered.

She sat on the bar stool and crossed her legs, causing her knee length skirt to rise revealing her long, shapely legs. For the short time she had spent getting dressed and getting prepared for the evening she had done a magnificent job. She was wearing a dark brown turtleneck cashmere sweater, a finely tailored beige jacket and skirt, and high heeled shoes. Her coal black hair was pulled back in a ponytail and held by a gold band. She was the beautiful woman again that had caught Kurt's attention on that flight from Texas that seemed like a lifetime ago. But then she has the

natural beauty that really doesn't require any special prepara-
tion to exhibit, Kurt thought, momentarily forgetting everything
that had happened the previous day.

"Kurt and I have decided to get sloshed tonight and then go
skinny dipping in the sauna and pool afterward," Max said to
her. "And we'll let you join us since you're one of our buddies
now."

"Don't tempt me," she laughed. "A sauna would feel good, but
I'll just watch."

"He's an exhibitionist," Kurt chimed in, joining the light conversation. "Don't promise him that."

"But that's only fun when I have my raincoat," Max said. "It's
the shock effect that turns us perverts on. You should know that,
Doctor Psychologist," he said to Shira. "Besides, I am really more
interested in a ménage a trois. That's probably what everyone
thinks of us since we travel together."

"This conversation is getting raunchy," Kurt said. "Let's have
dinner now."

"Surprisingly after what we went through today, I'm very hungry," Shira answered. "I'm more than ready."

"See, you're getting as bad as us," Max said.

"We'll be back after dinner," Kurt said to the bartender as they
walked toward the Speise Saal, the dining room which adjoined
the lounge. The bartender must be related to the Diener, Kurt
thought. They look and even sound somewhat alike.

The dinner was excellent as it usually is in Austrian countryside restaurants. All three found that they were quite hungry
and they ordered full meals, not disappointed by any of the entrees. Kurt and Shira even exchanged some of the entrée that
they had ordered. There were several tables filled in the moder-
ate sized dining room. Some were probably guests in the hotel
who took advantage of the off season rates to visit this beautiful
part of Austria and others were probably people from Bludenz in
the valley below. Kurt doubted if any of them were townspeople
from Brand since they only dined out, if at all, on weekends.

As is the custom in Austrian restaurants, the Besitzer, or manager or owner of the restaurant, visited each table, introduced

himself, and asked if everything was in order. He was a typical looking man from the area, probably in his sixties or early seventies, Kurt thought, with gray hair, who actually looked older than he probably was. These mountain people who live in the high purified air atmosphere and who spend much of their spare time skiing and mountain climbing have tanned, leathery faces, prematurely aged skin because of the harmful effects of the ultraviolet rays at that elevation not being filtered out of the polluted air of civilization.

Max, exercising his own inimitable wit, dubbed him "Pruneface" after the Dick Tracy character of the comic pages.

"Do you notice all those lines in his face?" Max, now the doctor, added. "Those are the skin's natural lines, called Langer's Lines. We all have them but you don't notice them unless you look at the skin under a microscope or a strong magnifying glass. They become noticeable only after years of exposure to the sun. Lifeguards, for example, who are always in the sun, have prematurely aged skin. That's probably what happened to Pruneface here. He spends too much time outside and not enough here tending to his hotel."

"I wonder if he knew the Luckners," Shira said. "He's old enough o have been here at that time. It's certainly tempting to ask him, although that, of course, is impossible."

They finished their dinner and returned to the lounge for an after dinner drink.

This time they took a table off to the side where there was more privacy than on the now half filled bar.

After they had sat down, Kurt noticed that the bartender, who was also waiting on the tables on this probably less busy night, was serving two men in a booth on the far side of the room. One of the men, the older of the two, was the gray-haired "tail" whom he had seen in Vienna. The "tail" had seen him too.

XXIII

"Getting Sloshed"

"We have a problem," Kurt announced to the other two. "Do you remember, Max, that I told you in Vienna that I had picked up a tail outside of the Astoria? He's sitting over there on the other side of the room with another guy whom I don't recognize."

Max and Shira both looked over and saw the gray-haired man that Kurt had described.

"We'll have to take care of that problem soon," Kurt said. "Time is too critical now and we can't afford to play games. This is Tuesday and we have to be on top of that mountain by Thursday night. Friday is the seventeenth and that's when we have the time window, as far as the water level at the dam is concerned."

"Tonight?" Max asked.

"I think it would be better if we did it tomorrow sometime. Probably at night. We don't know where they're staying yet. They have to stay somewhere because they're obviously not local. Maybe here." Kurt was the professional again. He reacted instinctively to any of these unexpected situations. He was cool, clear-headed, and the killer that he was trained and conditioned to be.

"If we take them out tomorrow night, we'll be long gone by the time they're found."

"Do you think they're KGB?" Shira asked.

"Could be that I doubt it," Kurt answered. "The KGB wouldn't take a chance on being seen and they would probably blast us at the first opportunity after what we did. Also I don't think that they've had the time to regroup and they are probably getting some heat from Austrian Security after what they did to the gendarmes. I think that we have a couple more days as far as the KGB is concerned. We had better be through by then because, believe me, they'll come." Kurt knew quite well what was probably going through the minds of Bohdan Krymko and Nicholai.

"Well, that narrows it down to just the Nazis, Israelis, and the PLO," Max commented. "Speaking of the PLO, did you notice our porter and the bartender? Even I can tell that they're not local yokels. And if they're not Arabs, I'll kiss Shira's ass. In fact, I'll do that even if they are Arabs," he added, patting her on the leg.

"I'm beginning to think that I should have listened to Daddy and married that nice, dull internist years ago," she said. "But, on second thought, after meeting Max maybe it's better that I didn't marry a doctor. Here we killed four people today, we're talking about two more tomorrow just as if we were casually planning a business merger or something. I don't think that this is what Mother visualized for me when she sent me to finishing school one summer. And you know the odd thing about it all. I don't know if I'm just numb but I feel strangely excited about all this. We're even making jokes about it."

"Never try self analysis," Max said. "Doctor, never treat thyself. I think that's how the warning goes. I really think that you should come to my room tonight for analysis. I have a couch there and I'd like to probe into the inner recesses of your mind."

"That's not what he wants to probe," warned Kurt. "And as far as making jokes over our business," he continued being more serious, "we all do that, I think, as a defense mechanism. It's not fun, what we do. It's something that has to be done and if we let it get to us, we won't last long."

"Christ sake, we're all trying to be analysts," Max laughed. "C'mon, let's do some serious drinking."

Other than one after dinner drink of Hennessey VSOP Cognac, Kurt did not order any more drinks for himself. He wanted to keep a clear head in case of any possible imminent danger and for what might present itself the next day. A hangover is not a good thing for coping with unexpected situations. He also wanted to observe the two on the other side of the room and see if they were staying in the same hotel. It was evident that they were, as Kurt saw them finish their drinks and then leave and walk up the stairs to one of the rooms.

Shira and Max were not so cautious. Shira, possibly because she was subconsciously trying to blot out the events of the day and the apprehension of what was in store for them the next day, and Max, just because he wanted to follow his own suggestion and get "sloshed," ordered cognac after cognac. They were both pleasant drunks. Max got more witty and more amorous after each drink and Shira got more giddy, laughing at even Max's not-so-funny jokes. When she reached the point where she had difficulty keeping her eyes focused and speaking with a slur, and, more importantly, becoming more vulnerable to Max's amorous advances, Kurt decided they should call it a day.

"Come, dear. It's time for us to go to bed," he announced as he firmly helped her stand up and led her from the room. Before Max could protest, Kurt had hustled Shira out of the room and led her up the stairs to their room. "You son of a bitch," were the last words he heard from Max.

Shira could hardly walk and Kurt had to support her the whole way up to their room. When they reached the door to the room, her knees finally buckled and Kurt had to catch her to keep her from falling. Holding her up with one arm, he unlocked and opened the door with the other, then lifted her up and carried her into the room.

"Jush like getting married and carrying me across the threshold," she slurred as he carried her over to the bed and gently laid her down. He went back and closed and locked the door and then opened the door to the balcony to let in the cool, refreshing mountain air.

He looked over at Shira who was completely passed out by this time. He went over to her suitcase, searched through it, and picked out the sheerest nightgown she had. He chuckled to himself as he completely undressed her and then, somehow, managed to dress her in the filmy nightgown. He pulled back the covers of his bed and put her in it and covered her up. After changing into pajamas, he crawled into her bed, turned out the light and was soon sound asleep.

He was awakened early by the sound of a barnyard rooster crowing somewhere in the nearby village and by the first rays of sunlight coming into the room through the opened balcony door. He looked over and saw that Shira was beginning to stir. Quickly he jumped out of bed and hurriedly made it up to appear as if it had never been slept in. He then went into the bathroom, closed the door and turned the water on in the tub, filling it to its limit. He could hear Shira groaning in the next room. Opening the bathroom door slightly, he called out to her, "The tub is filled, dear. Would you like to get in it with me?" He was answered only by another groan.

He got into the hot, steaming tub and started to wash himself, singing a bawdy fraternity song that he had learned in his college days. He leisurely finished bathing, shaved, brushed his teeth, and walked back into the bedroom whistling another song.

By that time, Shira was sitting in the bed with the blanket pulled up to her neck, her eyes wide open and with a shocked look on her face. Before she could say anything, Kurt spoke up. "There is one thing I didn't ask you last night. Are you on the pill? You know, you really shouldn't drink so much. I never thought that you would act the way you did," he added, looking dismayed.

"What happened last night?" she finally spoke up. "I don't' remember a thing and my head feels like it's going to burst. And what am I doing in your bed?" she asked looking over at her own made-up bed.

"You insisted," Kurt answered. "You kept saying you wanted to comfort me and that's the last thing I wanted last night. You took advantage of my situation," he said with a hurt look on his face.

"Go away and let me die," she said. "I've never had that much to drink before and I certainly never acted like that before. Don't even tell me what happened last night. I'm afraid to find out. You must think I'm terrible." With that she pulled the blanket up over her face and let out another long groan.

Kurt picked out a pair of warm slacks, and a wool sport shirt and quickly dressed. He put on his heavy mountain shoes that he had bought in Innsbruck and picked up his warm down parka. Walking over to the still totally covered Shira, he lifted the blanket from her head, bent over and gently kissing her on her forehead, whispered, "You were terrific last night."

Before she could say anything, he headed for the door saying, "I'm going to find Max and go out and check the car. I'll meet you in the dining room in half an hour. Dress warmly and wear your climbing shoes. We have a lot to do today." He unlocked the door and walked out, closing the door behind him.

Max, an early riser even after a hard night of drinking, was leaving his room at the other end of the hallway as Kurt was walking down the hall toward the stairs which were halfway between their two rooms.

"Let's check the car first thing," Kurt said to Max. "I want to make sure that we have everything we need. By the way, did you find out which room our tail is staying in?"

"The second floor in the front," Max answered pointing to the room as they reached the second floor walking down the stairs together. "They probably took the front in order to watch the cars coming and going. We won't be able to drive away without being seen. They can see a good distance both ways. By the way, where is the blushing bride? You know, old buddy, you're a real prick. You deprived her of a real educational experience last night by snatching her away from me."

"You're all bad," Kurt laughed.

They walked out to the Peugeot which had been parked behind the building, in an area that could be seen from the balconies of their rooms. From the little pieces of tape that they had left in inconspicuous places on the car it was obvious that no one had tampered with it. They opened the trunk and checked the large suitcase with the operational equipment.

"Metal detector, walkie talkies, radar unit, four sticks dynamite, plastic explosive, fuses, detonator caps, wires, two 38 revolvers, ammunition for 32 and 38s, and rope, military rations, for us at Lunersee," Max ticked off the inventory. "All the things we need are here."

The knapsacks and shovels that they bought in Innsbruck were also there. "We don't want to take them up to our room," Kurt said. "We don't' want to tip anyone off that we might be going up the mountain. We'll pack what we'll need for Lunersee sometime later in the car. We take only what we absolutely need up there," he added, looking off in the distance at the mountain which they would have to climb.

They closed the trunk of the car, checked to make sure everything was locked, and went back into the hotel and into the dining room.

There was only one other table occupied in the dining room and that was by an elderly couple who appeared to be Germans. They picked a table on the opposite side of the room from the Germans and away from the large picture windows that looked out over the valley below. Those were usually the tables that were the first filled and they preferred to be more isolated where they could carry on a conversation without being overheard. They were hardly seated when Shira walked into the dining room, nervously looking around the room until she spotted them. She walked over to the table and sat down across from Max and Kurt. "Have you ordered breakfast?" she asked in a weak voice.

"Not yet," Kurt answered. "We just arrived ourselves." He waved to the young waitress who was on the other side of the room to come and take their order. The waitress brought three "Speisekartes" which included the breakfast fare.

"I only want black coffee and some rolls," Shira said.

Max echoed her request.

"Also, drei mal Fruhstuck, Kaffee," Kurt told the waitress, ordering the same a the other two.

The waitress scurried off to get their order. In spite of her night of drinking and hurried dressing, Shira looked her usual beautiful self. She was dressed in a high neck ski sweater, ski pants which did nothing to hide her perfectly formed thighs and long legs, and hiking shoes. She had had little time to go through the time-consuming procedure of applying makeup, so she apparently had not used any. She doesn't need any, Kurt thought to himself. After last night's bender and with an obvious hangover, she is still beautiful.

The waitress quickly served their breakfast - coffee in a porcelain coffee pitcher, fresh cream in a small server, and freshly baked semmelen, still warm from the bakery which must have been in the village of Brand nearby, and the usual fresh country sweet butter and marmalade.

Shira was not very hungry, but she welcomed the strong black coffee, drinking it without any cream or sugar.

"I never had that much to drink before," she repeated twice. "I should have known better than to trust you two," she said, not even looking at the grinning Kurt.

"I'm sure that this cad took advantage of you in your helpless condition," Max said to her sympathetically. "You must let me protect you from him in the future."

"We have a lot to do today so I hope that you two have clear heads," Kurt said turning the conversation to a more serious vein. "We should drive over to the base of the mountain and the "Talstation" where the cable cars are. They're not working, of course, but we'll take care of that later ourselves. There's a complete electric shutdown at the station and for the whole Lunersee area on top. I hope that our briefing in Washington was correct. There is supposed to be an emergency generator up at the top in the Douglas Hutte. According to the pictures we were shown, the cable car station at the top is connected to the Douglas Hutte and the emergency generator up there can be used to run the cable car. We'll need that because we sure as hell can't carry everything back down the mountains when we dig it up. That is

IF we dig it up. With the detector and with the map and description that I got from Ursula Gross, we should be able to hit it on the first try."

"Exactly where is it buried?" Max interrupted.

"Once we get up to the Douglas Hutte, I'll show you both," Kurt answered. "There is also a small truck in a garage up at the Hutte. It was carried up there in parts and reassembled. There's a storage bunker where there is supposed to be enough fuel for the generator and the truck. We'll need the truck to haul the containers back to the cable car station. They'll be too heavy to carry since it's about a half a mile but the path is wide enough for the small truck. We'll take everything down in the cable car and load it into the Peugeot. Now we'll be going up the mountain tomorrow afternoon. It should take about three hours to get up there. There's a narrow zigzag path but it's dangerous and we have to make it before it's dark. We'll carry only what we need for one night and, of course, the operational equipment that we need. We'll spend the night in the Hutte. You're the expert, Max, on opening locks so you'll have to open the stations, at the bottom and at the top, the Douglas Hutte and the POL bunkers to get the fuel. We'll find and dig it out early Friday morning and if everything goes well, we should be bringing it down by around noontime. After that, everything, if you'll pardon the pun, should be downhill. We're going to take everything to Bregenz and The Company has arranged to take it into Germany from there to the States. We have a few loose ends that we have to take care of first. In fact, speaking of the devil, here comes our first problem," he added, noticing the gray-haired tail from Vienna and his companion walking into the dining room.

XXIV

NEGOTIATIONS

The gray-haired tail saw them as he entered the room, hesitated for a moment, and, followed by his companion, approached their table.

"I think it's time that I introduced myself, Mr. Hoffman and Mr. Mitchell," he said in fluent English.

Kurt thought that he detected an Eastern European accent.

"I am sorry that I do not know the name of the young lady here." Looking around the room first to see if anyone was within hearing range, he continued. "I am Aryeh Avrim. My friend's name here is Shimon Shifrin. We are both from Mossad. I have the uneasy feeling that you might have been making plans for us so I thought it was time to meet. May we sit down?"

"Of course," Kurt answered, pointing to the one empty chair.

Avrim sat down and his companion moved a chair from an adjoining table and sat down next to him. His companion, Shifrin, was a tall, burly, dark, curly-haired man in about his mid thirties. He had a wide scar on one side of his neck that ran from under his ear to the under part of his chin. He could be best described as looking like a tough professional football player who had just taken an early retirement. Kurt could not tell if he was intelligent or not, or even if he could speak or understand English since he did not say one word.

Avrim continued. "We have some interests but not entirely in common. Maybe we can cooperate and help each other. We can negotiate on some of the points. First, we know why you are here. That was why I was waiting for you in Vienna. We knew the KGB was waiting for you and I knew that by following Fraulein Krymko I would eventually find you. You did lose me once in Vienna. I must admit that you were quite good at it. I thought I was better than that. After that, I let you see me but my friend, Shifrin here, was my backup. I fooled you on that one."

"Touche'," Kurt replied.

Avrim continued. "I was deeply sorry about Fraulein Krymko. I am sure you did what you had to do. I believe I understand how you felt toward her. I was also sorry to hear about Fraulein Gross. That was tragic. I only learned of that yesterday. You certainly did leave your calling cards on the route here. I must say that I abhor violence but, again, I am sure that you did what you had to do. The KGB would have killed you for certain. After Vienna you are not too popular with them. Finding you here was simple. There are only two hotels open here in the off season. We tried the other one first and then this one. But back to business. I said that our interests are not entirely in common. Let me explain. We know about the gold and other valuables and we also know about the plans and the specifications for the directed energy weapon. We also know about the Lunersee locale and about the water level. Of course, we don't know exactly where it is all buried. Our priorities are different than yours. Our first priority is Mueller and Konzett, especially Mueller. He was one of those whom we never caught. We got Eichmann and many others but never Mueller. Someday we will also get Mengele who is now in Paraguay, but that is another problem. The people of Israel will never rest until the Butcher of Dachau Mueller is in our hands. Your first priority is probably the weapon plans. As long as it is in American hands, we will feel safe. Thirdly, however, is the gold and other valuables. There are many Jewish lives that are associated with that and it becomes a matter of principle. That we will negotiate."

Kurt, Max, and Shira were quiet and just listened. Kurt, the spokesman, finally spoke up. He was angry. "First, Mr. Avrim, if that is really your name, we are not in any position to negotiate at all. That is something that is up to our superiors. That is the route you should have taken since you knew about this from the beginning. We had heard that you knew about it. This is a hell of a time to try to join the team. Secondly, what have you got to negotiate? We don't need you and, in fact, you would probably only get in the way. Tell me why we need you and tell me why we shouldn't just take you both out."

"As I told you," Avrim replied, "I abhor violence but my friend, Shifrin here unfortunately thrives on it. Unfortunately, that is, for others. Sadly, it is a way of life these days. We would much prefer to cooperate with you than to fight. Fighting might, as you Americans say, blow the whole deal. Also our respective governments are friends. They would frown on our squabbling with each other. As a gesture of our eagerness to join the team, as you put it, we would be more than happy to take care of those two PLO people whom I am sure you have already noticed. They are really not here in our best interests. They are well known terrorists and high up in the PLO hierarchy. I am curious in how they came here. But we are disturbing you at your breakfast. Shifrin and I will leave you to enjoy. Please stop by our room this evening and let us know your decision. I am sure you already know the room number."

Avrim and Shifrin both got up and moved to a table in front of the window and signaled to the waitress to order breakfast.

"I'll say it before you two do," Shira was the first to speak. "Those bastards!"

"I agree with you," Kurt replied. "But you've got to admire them. They are real pros. We've got to think this out ourselves," he continued. "We sure as hell can't place a long distance call to Headquarters to get permission to negotiate. On the other hand, we don't have the authority to make any concessions to them, and tempting as it might be with those two, we can't very well do them in. Avrim was right. It could blow the whole deal. I think our most immediate concern is our two PLO types. From what we were told at the briefing, they are cooperating with the Nazis and they don't need any maps. Mueller and Konzett, who must be around here, know where the stuff is buried and they'll all make their move on Friday when the water level is lowered."

"Well, we can't very well just sit around here with our fingers up our ass and wait to meet on top of that mountain on Friday," Max said.

Kurt winced at the vulgarity used in Shira's presence. In spite of the fact of what she had been exposed to in the past few days, his boyhood conditioned aversion to profanity before women still prevailed. He would rather kill someone in front of her than use a four-letter word. "You're absolutely right," he answered. "We're going to have to take care of them before we get up in the mountains. You can be sure if they suspect us they are making similar plans. By the way, I haven't seen either of them this morning. I wonder where they are."

"I saw them drive off toward Brand on a motorcycle when I came downstairs," Shira answered. "It's Wednesday. Maybe it's their day off."

"They seem to have the run of the place," Kurt said. "I even saw the Diener using that hot whirlpool by the sauna yesterday evening. He's more like a guest than a porter."

"Those camel drivers are probably just trying to keep warm up here in this cool weather," Max laughed. "They probably never even saw snow before they came here. Maybe we should try to cook them in that sauna. I'm sure that they would prefer that to freezing. It would be the humanitarian thing to do."

"Enough chit chat," said Kurt, getting up from the table. "Let's get in the car and drive around and get the lay of the land. I'd like to check out the Talstation. I'll meet you two by the car. I'm going back to the room and check my 'bible'. I'd suggest that you get your 38 out of the trunk too, Max. We may run into those Arabs out there somewhere."

Kurt went to the room as the other two went directly to the car. He unlocked and opened his suitcase and took out his hollowed-out bible where he had put his 32 star automatic. He did not attach the silencer to it this time since it did increase the length of the weapon. Without it, it fit nicely in the inside pocked of his down parka.

He joined Max and Shira who were waiting in the car for him and with Max driving, they drove off toward the nearby village of Brand.

Being the off season, Brand was very quiet. There were a few villagers to be seen walking in the streets. There was one hotel, about the size of the Hotel Taleu, open; however, there did not seem to be much traffic in the vicinity. As they drove through the village, there was actually only one main street, they had to come to a complete stop at one time while a herd of cows slowly walked down the middle of the street. A farm boy with his German Shepherd dog was guiding the herd through the town probably heading toward the pastures in the mountains skirting the valley, probably to spend the summer there and to return only in the fall.

"I can just picture a young Franz Luckner doing that many years ago," Shira said pensively, looking out the side window of the car. "What a tragic life he had. I wonder which of these houses he lived in. I'm sure it's still here. I've never been here before but I feel that I know the place."

Kurt experienced the same feeling. He also felt that he knew the entire Lunersee area, probably the result of the thorough briefing that he had received and because of hours studying maps and pictures of the area.

They passed through the village and after one kilometer more, they approached the Talstation that led up to Lunersee. There was a gravel parking lot adjoining the station that was large enough to accommodate the cars of tourists that would start arriving in about another month. Rather than park there, where one car would be obvious to anyone in the vicinity, Max pulled up and parked behind the station near a wooded area.

The station was completely deserted and from the lack of tire tracks it was obvious there had been little, if any, traffic there since the station closed the previous fall. There were some foot tracks and there was one motorcycle track that looked fresh. It led off to the ascending path to the east into a pine forest.

They walked around the station looking through the windows. "Let's look inside," Kurt said.

It took Max, who was a real pro at it, no longer than it would with a key, to open the heavy entrance door with a little adjustable tool that he carried with him.

"That looked just like they do it in the movies," Shira said, following Max and Kurt into the cold, clammy entrance hall.

There was another inside door, locked from the inside by a sliding bolt that led to a platform where two cable cars were sitting beside each other on two parallel tracks and attached to two parallel cables extending out an open passage and up the mountain. By following the two cables it was possible to see them lead to the Bergstation, at the top of the mountain. The cable cars also were locked but again, no match to the curious Max.

After looking around the station and making mental notes of all the rooms and exits, they left, relocking the door which they had entered.

From the station the zigzag path that led up the mountain also began.

"This station wasn't here in 1945," Kurt said, "but the path has to be the same one that they took at that time. Those things never change. There were probably some small avalanches through the years but that couldn't change the formation of the mountain too much. You two stay here. I'll climb up the path a little way to see what kind of shape it's in."

While Max and Shira waited by the station, Kurt walked quickly up the ascending narrow path. At the base of the mountain there were some pine trees but no more than a couple of hundred yards up, the trees thinned out being replaced by small scrub pines and rocks and boulders. The higher the path was, the smaller were the bushes and from the station, Max and Shira could see Kurt winding up the mountain.

Kurt was about a quarter of a mile above the timber line when he stopped to rest and then to head back down to his companions below. Sitting on a large boulder he looked down the mountainside. He could see Max and Shira, who were only specks standing next to the station below. From that point they could also see the villages of Brand and Burserberg. He was just moving off the boulder on which he was sitting when he heard the whizzing followed by the thud of lead hitting the boulder at the exact spot where he had been sitting. This was followed by another, the heat of which he could almost feel going past his ear, both followed by the sound of the two shots echoing from somewhere in the valley below. Kurt dove behind the boulder hearing nothing else other than the sound of the fluttering of birds who had been disturbed by the unusual sound. After a short time Kurt thought he heard the sound of a motorcycle far off in the valley below.

Kurt half ran back down the path. Going down was much easier than going up but, in a way, more dangerous because there was a tendency for everyone to be less cautious. In a short time he was down the mountain where he was greeted by Max and Shira.

"You were a sitting duck up there," were the first words Max said. "We could see you completely exposed most of the way up. The shots came from the woods over there," he added, pointing off to the right. "We heard a motorcycle go off too. I guess it's not too hard to figure out who it probably was."

"I heard it too," Kurt answered. "Sound really travels in these mountains. We learned one thing. We're too vulnerable when we're exposed up on that mountain. It'll be even worse up on the top. We're going to have to solve that problem as soon as possible. They got back into the car and drove back to the Hotel Taleu.

XXV

Solving a Problem

As they drove up to the hotel they looked at the parking lot in the front. There was no motorcycle there nor was there one in the back. They parked in the rear again. It was obvious that the Israelis and the PLO knew who and where they were but there was also the possibility that the KGB would recover from their setback and would be looking for them.

"There's no point in advertising our presence," Kurt said as they drove the car around to the back to park.

"You know," Max quipped, "Maybe we should call them and tell them. Maybe we can get them all at each other's throats. It's getting awfully crowded around here. Where do you suggest we start?"

The walk from the back parking lot bordered the huge plate glass floor to ceiling windows that made up the whole wall. Inside it was possible to see the Hallenbad where there was a small swimming pool and a smaller whirlpool bath that adjoined the men's and women's separate saunas.

"Well, well, look who we have here," Max said as they walked by the window. They could see the Diener and the bartender just coming out of the sauna and getting into the whirlpool. Other than the two, the Hallenbad was deserted. "I'll bet they stashed their motorcycle somewhere and ran into that sauna. Maybe I should complain to the management about the hired help using the facilities."

"We can't just go in there and blast them," Kurt said, "but we've got to do something fast. I don't want to have to depend on our friend, Shifrin to help us out. There is such a thing as professional pride."

Kurt was suddenly the professional again. "Come with me," he said to Shira in a commanding tone. "Max, we'll meet you later in the bar or in your room."

Shira almost had to run to keep up with Kurt as he took the steps two at a time up to their room on the third floor.

"C'mon, we haven't much time," he said to her as they entered the room. "Put on that bikini bathing suit of yours and hurry," he ordered as he went to his bag and took out an extension cord that he used sometimes with his electric razor. He used the electric razor often in Europe when there was no hot water available for his conventional razor. Without even asking permission, he started rifling through Shira's bag and took out the electric hair dryer that she had brought with her.

Sensing the time urgency by Kurt's orders, Shira forgot her modesty and quickly stripped and put on her brief string bikini.

"Now, here is what you have to do," he told her while he was packing two towels, the hair dryer and her toilette kit into the small airline travel bag that she had brought. "Go down to the pool and jump in. Swim around for a few minutes and then get out. Put your towel on the floor between the swimming pool and the whirlpool. Then plug in this long cord. There are a couple of light sockets nearby. Start drying your hair. When you see me walk in just lay the dryer on the floor on the towel. My guess is that like typical Arabs, when they see you in that bikini, they won't be in a hurry to leave. In fact, it won't hurt to show them a little flesh. I'll get my bathing suit on and join you in exactly ten minutes. Those whirlpools are timed to run continuously for thirty minutes. There's about twenty minutes more for it to run. Now run," he ordered, slapping her on her seat.

Shira acted automatically. Perhaps it was the authoritarian manner of Kurt but without even questioning anything, she was hurrying to participate in a killing. A few days ago, she would have never dreamed that she would be involved in and become a part of the carnage that occurred in such a short period of time.

As she entered the Hallenbad, she looked around. The two Arabs were still in the small whirlpool sitting on the submerged ledge obviously enjoying the hot, swirling water. One, the bartender, had his head back with his eyes closed and with the water up to his neck. The other, the Diener, seeing Shira casually walk in and take off her robe, nudged his companion.

She stretched out the bath towel between the two pools as Kurt had suggested. She made sure that as she bent over to spread the towel that both of them had a front view of the very brief and loose halter top failing to conceal her beautifully formed breasts. She smiled at them, said hello, and dove into the nearby pool. She swam two lengths of the short pool and climbed out, arranging again for a glimpse of what had obviously become the topic of their conversation. She took out the hair dryer and, with the extension cord, plugged it into an outlet in the base of the outside wall. She then sat down on the large bath towel, took a smaller towel out of her travel bag, dried her hair briefly in the towel, and then turned on the hot air dryer and started to blow dry her long, black hair. The two Arabs were obviously enjoying this unexpected show and were laughing and joking with each other in Arabic. As Kurt walked in on the opposite side of the room, the Diener saw him and nudged his friend. Shira could see that they were going to get out of the whirlpool. As the first reached up for the handrail to step out, Shira quickly threw the electric dryer into the whirlpool. Sparks, smoke, and steam shot from the submerged dryer and from the extension cord plug that had not been completely fastened to the dryer.

The two Arabs did not even shout as they thrashed around in the swirling pool. Kurt walked up to Shira who was still sitting on the towel looking at the grotesque sight with her eyes and mouth wide open as if hypnotized. He stood next to her and put his hand on her shoulder, neither saying anything. It seemed like hours, although it was only a couple of minutes when Kurt said, "They've cooked enough. We'd better leave." With that, he pulled the cord out of the wall plug as Shira quickly picked up her towels and the dryer and put them in her travel bag. Together they walked hurriedly out of the door and up the stairs to their room. The whirlpool switched off automatically and the water became calm and still with the two Arabs floating face down in the water.

Everything seemed strangely quiet when they returned to their room. Shira, without speaking, took off her wet bathing suit, again ignoring modesty. She went into the bathroom and started the water in the tub, filling it to its limit and got in, not even bothering to close the bathroom door. She soaked in the tub for a few minutes, shampooed her hair, rinsed herself off and got out and dried herself. She still had not spoken a word and Kurt did not attempt to begin a conversation. She came back into the bedroom, this time with a robe on, and took the hair blower out of the travel bag. She started to plug the socket into the wall, when she stopped herself and put the dryer in her bag. Instead, she dried her hair as best as she could with the towel, and then went out to the balcony and sat down on a balcony chair. She slowly combed her hair, letting the rays and warmth of the afternoon sun serve as a substitute dryer.

Staring out at the valley below, she finally broke the long silence as Kurt, who had changed clothes, joined her on the balcony.

"You know what is really strange about all this? I don't feel any remorse at all at this point. In fact, it was all strangely exhilarating. I had thought that people like you and Max were somewhat strange for doing things like that. I must admit that I was somewhat afraid of both of you and as a psychologist, I thought you both had psychopathic tendencies. Now I don't know what to believe. Maybe I'm psychopathic too. I'd like to think that I'm normal, that we are all normal. Maybe this is how normal people react to stressful situations. I suppose that's how soldiers react in battle. I'm just confused."

"I guess that you're one of us now," Kurt answered. "I have to admit that I'm glad that you were sent along. Not just for personal reasons but because you did a good job down there. We would have had a hard time taking out those two without you. They were real pros."

"Incidentally, we are going to have to act like everything is normal. We have a couple of hours until dinner so we'll just go to dinner as usual. You stay here while I find Max. I'll be back soon." With that he left the room and walked down the hall to Max's room at the end of the hall. He knocked and after getting no response, he walked down the stairs to look for Max in the bar.

There was a commotion as he reached the lobby with several people scurrying around. Max was talking with Pruneface, the owner, at the other end of the lobby. Seeing Kurt, he waved him over to join them.

"There has been a terrible accident," Pruneface said as Kurt approached and before Max could say anything. "There must have been a short in the electrical apparatus in our whirlpool and two of my employees have been electrocuted. The doctor here tried to help but it was too late."

Max was very solicitous and Kurt offered his deepest sympathies. "It must have had faulty wiring. Have you called the Polizei?"

"Yes, yes," he replied. "They will be coming from Bludenz tomorrow morning. There is not much they can do now." He hurried off to join some of the employees who were standing around in groups discussing the tragedy.

"Very well done," Max said when they were alone. "That is sort of the way that I would do it. I'm impressed."

"Shira deserves all the credit," Kurt responded explaining to Max what she had done.

"I think that we underestimated her," Max said. "We still have two more that need attention."

"We're going to have to hold back on that," Kurt replied. "We can't have bodies all over the hotel. That would be too suspicious. So far they still believe that this was an accident and by the time they find out otherwise, we'll be long gone. We'll have to take care of the other two up on the mountain if they give us any trouble. And let's face it, Mueller and Konzett must be around here somewhere. I have a feeling that we might meet them up there also. C'mon, let's have a drink in the bar. Then I want to go up and keep Shira company. She may need some moral support."

"Christ, you're even thinking about pussy at a time like this," Max laughed as they were walking into the bar. "Have you no compassion for the poor woman? What she really needs is a physician's care."

"As far as I'm concerned she's really just a member of the team," Kurt responded seriously. "We can't afford any emotional involvement until this is all over. The last thing that I want is another involvement," he added, his thoughts going back to Sonya and Ushie. With all the excitement, he was able to temporarily forget the tragic events. It hurt every time he thought about it and he did not believe that he would ever get over them. He loved them both and he never wanted to love another woman again.

The waitress was acting as the bartender and she seemed confused when Kurt ordered his vodka martini.

"Here, let me make it," Kurt said as he walked behind the bar and showed her how to properly mix it. Few non-American bartenders know how to properly prepare one and a converted waitress could only prove disastrous, he thought. He even poured Max's scotch on ice for the appreciative new barmaid. European bartenders were always stingy with ice and usually gave only one small ice cube.

"Thank you," Max said. "You've really missed your calling."

"I really used to be a bartender, years ago when I was in college. My parents owned a couple of bars and restaurants and I had to earn my keep by tending bar."

It was the first good martini that Kurt had had since he came to Europe so he nursed it slowly. After just one drink, he left Max in the bar.

"I think that I'll let you newlyweds have dinner alone tonight," Max said before Kurt had left. "I think I'll have dinner at the hotel in Brand. Who knows, maybe I'll spot Mueller and Konzett. They've got to be around here somewhere. I'll either meet you here in the bar after dinner or for breakfast tomorrow morning."

When Kurt returned to his room, Shira was curled up in her bed, sound asleep. She deserves the rest, he thought to himself as he softly walked through the room and out to the balcony where he sat down, watched the sun setting over the mountain and was lost in thought of the days in Velden with Sonya.

She slept deeply for over two hours and Kurt, after watching the sun go down and darkness envelop the valley, lay on h is own bed, not dozing, just trying to think of pleasant things in his past. It was his defense mechanism that forced him to think pleasant thoughts. The ability probably keeps me sane, he told himself.

Finally Shira stirred and then suddenly sat up in the darkened room.

Kurt, hearing her, turned on the bed lamp.

"I was startled for a second," she said. "I completely forgot where I was. What time is it? How long have I been asleep?"

"Just a couple of hours," he replied. "I thought you needed your rest. Are you hungry yet?"

"We never did have lunch," she answered. "I guess I am hungry in spite of what happened."

"Good," he replied. "We should probably make an appearance. It's about 7:30 so let's go on down. I think the dining room is open until nine."

They both hurriedly dressed and went downstairs. They looked into the bar for Max and, not seeing him, went directly to the dining room where they picked out a table by the window.

Kurt looked around the room. The dining room was about half full but he did not recognize anyone.

"I wonder where our Israeli friends are," Shira said.

"I haven't noticed them since our meeting this morning," Kurt replied. "They said that we should come to their room tonight and give them our decision but we won't. We'll just have to play it by ear and hope that they don't get in our way up in the mountains."

They found that they were both hungry and ordered full meals, again sharing their entrees and a liter of red South Tyrolean wine. After a leisurely meal, and looking unsuccessfully for Max in the bar, they returned to their room with another liter of wine and two glasses.

They changed into their night clothes, he in his pajamas and she in a long flannel nightgown and they sat out on the balcony talking and drinking the wine. They talked late into the night avoiding any discussion of their "business" and, especially, of the recent events. At one time she tried to discuss their meeting in Washington but he assured her he understood all and there was no necessity of resurrecting all that. Since there was no need to live a cover story anymore, they were much more frank with each other. He even admitted that he had not made love to her the night before. She pretended she was disappointed. They did not make love that evening either. Kurt was not sure that he could ever make love to a woman again. The last two that had loved him had tragic endings. Everything happens in threes, he told himself. He would not want it to happen again. It was too dangerous for someone to fall in love with him.

Kurt slept fitfully the first part of the night. He kept waking, thinking of the events of the previous few days and also of the events that lay ahead. He was a man who did not like loose ends and there were loose ends in the Israelis and the Nazis who surely, he thought, were out there somewhere. All meeting on the top of the mountain was not an event that he looked forward to. They were all pros but not all of them would come back off that mountain.

Shira woke in the middle of the night and, sensing that he was still awake and without saying a thing, came over to his bed and crawled in next to him.

She's the one who should be uptight, he thought to himself, after what she went through today.

He put his arm around her as she snuggled up close to him. Feeling her warm body next to his, he soon drifted off to sleep, not waking until the sunlight, coming up over the mountain, told him that the new day had arrived.

XXVI

LUNERSEE

They both woke at the same time and Shira jumped out of bed first and won the race to the bathroom. They did not plan on going up the mountain until mid afternoon so there was plenty of time. They dressed and packed their bags setting aside only the few items that they would need for the one night stay at Lunersee.

On the way down to the dining room for breakfast, Kurt knocked on Max's door and again found that he was not there. Arriving in the dining room they saw Max seated at a table next to the window talking to Pruneface. He walked off as Kurt and Shira approached.

"He's still shook up," Max said as they sat down at the table with him. "The Austrian police are due here any minute to investigate the accident. Pruneface is worried that they'll give him a hard time. Apparently they have had trouble with the whirlpool before and he's afraid that they'll accuse him of being negligent and his insurance won't cover him. The old crook wanted me, as a doctor, to help cover it up. I couldn't do it if I wanted to. He wasn't very happy when I told him we were leaving today and he even offered to cover the bill if we stayed longer."

"He's probably in hock up to his ears for this place," Kurt said. "It's relatively new and it's a well built hotel. It's got everything."

"I really love this place," Shira said. "In spite of what happened yesterday, I'd like to come back here someday. It's so beautiful and picturesque and romantic," she added smiling at Kurt.

"How did everything go with you last night?" Kurt asked.

"Well, I didn't get laid in the thriving metropolis of Brand, if that's what you are wondering," Max replied. "I did have dinner in a hotel in the town. It was just as quiet as this place. I didn't see anyone that remotely resembled Mueller or Konzett. I came back early and looked for you in the bar but I guess you two just can't stay out of bed. I didn't even see our Israeli friends. Did you do them in too, I hope?"

"We didn't see them either," Kurt answered. "I haven't seen them around here this morning either. They do concern me. I hope that they don't give us any trouble. If we have to, we'll just take them out and worry about explaining it to Headquarters later."

"We had better check out of here around noon. We can get some rolls and cold meat at the Lebensmittel in Brand and have a little "picnic" in the woods before we go up the mountain. Up there we'll have the c-rations that we packed."

"Let's get a couple bottles of wine and cognac," Max suggested.

"You can forget the cognac, as far as I'm concerned," Shira said. "Even the thought of it gives me a headache."

They ordered breakfast. This time, at Kurt's suggestion, they ordered what would be more like an American breakfast - juice, ham and eggs, rolls and coffee. "It might be the last hot meal we'll have for a day or two," he said. "I hope that the Austrian police don't take too much of your time, Max. Timing is a critical factor in our plans." Just as he had finished saying that, Pruneface came back into the dining room with an apprehensive look and approached the table and said to Max, "The police are here and would like to speak to you." Max followed him out. "It shouldn't take me long," he said. "I'll be packed and meet you in the lobby at noon," and he left the room.

They returned to the room, packed, and relaxed until noon. It feels like the lull before a storm, Kurt mused to himself.

They checked out of the hotel at noon and Max, as he had promised, was also packed and ready to leave.

"Any problems?" Kurt asked when Max brought his bag out of the car that Kurt had driven around from the back parking lot.

"Not at all. I really couldn't tell them much other than that I suspected it was an accident, probably caused by a short in the electrical pump in the whirlpool. They agreed and are going to send an engineer from the Kraftwerke in the valley to check it out. We'll be long gone by the time they figure it out. Anyway, let's get the hell out of here."

They got into the car after they had loaded their luggage and drove off in the direction of Brand and the mountains.

"Strange, I still haven't seen Avrim or Shifrin," Kurt said as they were driving into Brand.

"We'll probably see them on top of the mountain," Max replied. "We'll just let Shira take care of them," he laughed. "She's really experienced now."

They stopped briefly in Brand and bought their provisions for their lunch. Austrian Lebensmittels are similar to the old mom and pop grocery stores that were once commonplace in America. They contained a little bit of everything that would be needed. As Kurt ordered the fresh rolls and cold meat, Max, true to his previous threat, ordered a bottle of Weinbrand, an Austrian cognac, and three bottles of red wine.

Shira grimaced at the sight of the cognac.

"Believe me, you'll be glad I bought it when, later tonight, we're freezing on top of the mountain," he told her.

They got back into the car and drove to the base of the mountain where they parked the car in the same secluded area that they had the previous day. After packing the operational equipment in their knapsacks along with the necessities for the one day at Lunersee, they started their long, strenuous climb up the zigzag path that would lead them to their destination. They reached what they estimated was the halfway point in about two hours and stopped for their picnic. Under other circumstances, the climb would have been a pleasant experience, the kind tourists look forward to doing. The weather fortunately was clear and the sun kept them so warm that they took off their windbreakers.

"You can get a good sun tan up here," Kurt said. "The air is so clean and pure and there is absolutely no air pollution. In fact, if you're not careful, you can get a sunburn, even in April."

They sat on a large rock which jutted out over the path that they had just taken. They could see the whole valley below and on the treeless mountain side, they were also clearly in view to anyone down there. They ate their lunch and continued their climb.

Four and a half hours later they finally reached the top. It was the flattened ledge that was the end of the path and was the gateway to Lunersee.

The three of them, like all who made the climb before them, were awestruck by the beauty of the sight. The pictures that they were shown at the briefings and the postcards that they had purchased in the valley below could not do justice to the pure natural beauty of the area. The blue moon-shaped lake was as beautiful as the descriptions that they had heard and reflected, as a mirror, the white capped mountains; it seemed almost unreal in its magnificence.

Standing on the ledge, Shira was the first to speak, bringing them all back to reality and the seriousness of their mission. "This is probably the same sight that they saw years ago and where we are standing could very well be where young Luckner was shot. Somewhere buried down there is something that cost many lives."

"Party pooper," Max laughed. "Let's not be morbid. Let's move in," he added, walking toward the Douglas Hutte, the inn that was a few yards from the end of the path.

It was a relatively new building constructed in 1956. It was connected on one side by the Bergstation and on the other side by the dam that controlled the water level of the lake. The level, as was explained at the briefing in Washington, was regulated remotely at the Kraftwerke in the valley far below.

The locked door of the inn was no match for Max and they quickly moved in. There were several two-bed rooms and a few dormitory rooms that could accommodate up to ten people each. The dormitory rooms looks out over the valley below while the smaller rooms looked out over the lake. Shira and Kurt decided to share one room on the first level of the three-level building, while Max chose a dormitory room on the valley side.

In the stillness of the night, with the windows open he felt it would be possible to hear anyone coming up the path below.

They unrolled the mattresses that had been rolled up and left on each bed. Kurt found the closet where the blankets had been stored for the winter.

"Here, we'll need these tonight," he said as he handed three blankets to each of them. "There's plenty more of them if you want them. I'm afraid that we'll have to forgo sheets. I couldn't find any."

"Obviously not a first class joint," Max joked.

"Let's check out the generator and the truck," Kurt said. "They should be in working order. The Austrians are very efficient people and they wouldn't leave them if they weren't."

They quickly located the emergency generator which was on the ground level, one floor below. Kurt remembered that electricity to the whole facility was actually controlled by the power station in the valley below. The emergency generator was available in the event there was a true emergency and it was powerful enough to provide power for the Hutte as well as the two cable cars. The bunker which contained the diesel fuel for the generator and the small pickup truck, was built into the mountain about fifty meters away. There was an ample supply of the fuel. They found the truck in a garage in a utility area behind the station.

Both the generator and the truck started at the first attempt. So far everything was going along according to their plans. They also checked the metal detector and their other equipment and everything was in working order.

Max demonstrated to Shira the small radar unit they had brought. "This is actually a small remote polygraph," he explained. "What it does is beam out microwaves that create an electromagnetic field that can pick up heart rates and respiration of a person at a distance. It has the capability of working up to about one hundred yards and can even penetrate walls. I was told that it was developed by our tech people but was never used operationally. Even though the microwave level is very low and couldn't possibly hurt anyone, The Company was reluctant to use it as a polygraph. After all the congressional investigations that they went through, they were afraid to expose anyone to any type of radiation. You can just imagine how the *Washington Post* or *New York Times* would have liked to "expose The Company" in subjecting poor unsuspecting people to microwaves. For our purposes we can use it to see if there is anyone in the building or even approaching the building. It's like a radar scan for people. This particular one was designed to be battery operated so we can use it tomorrow when we're out there digging to make sure we're not being watched. Here, I'll demonstrate it for you in this building to make sure we're the only ones here."

He pulled out two antennas that recessed into the cigar box size apparatus and turned on the switch. A low humming noise came out of the box that remained steady as Max aimed the antennas in various directions. "If there was somebody out there it would pick up in intensity and then diminish as you passed by. That way you could pinpoint somebody out there. If we wanted to use it as a polygraph or a lie detector, we could have a printout on tape. But we won't need that. Here, you try it," he said, giving it to Shira. "You'll be operating it tomorrow when Kurt and I do the digging."

Shira tried it until she learned how to operate it. As she pointed it in the direction of Max and Kurt, the humming became high pitched. They also tried the two wristwatch size miniature walkie-talkies that they had brought and they also worked perfectly.

"It's getting dark outside," Kurt said. "We can't turn all the lights on. We don't want anyone to know that we're in here. We can cover the windows in one room with blankets but that's the only room that we'll use until we sack in for the night." He noticed that the electrically operated wall clock was now working, an indication that the generator below was functioning perfectly.

"I think it's time to get those cable cars up here before it gets too dark. We don't want to make it easy for anyone to come up here tonight and they sure as hell can't climb up here in the dark."

All three of them went to the Bergstation where Kurt, finding the control room, pulled the two switches that controlled the cable cars that were still in the Talstation below. There was a loud whining and grinding noise as the cable started to move.

In the distance they could see the two cable cars, parallel to each other, coming into view from the darkening valley below. They looked at first like two space ships skimming side by side up the mountain and as they approached the Bergstation the group could begin to make out their true identity with the panoramic windows.

"Oh, oh, get down," Kurt ordered the other two. "There's somebody in that car on the right."

Max and Shira obeyed and crouched down behind the concrete retaining wall that bordered the shaft that served as the entrance for the cars ascending up into the station. All three drew their weapons. Even Shira had been carrying one of the 38 revolvers that they had brought.

The cable cars gave the impression of picking up speed as they approached the station when actually the opposite was true. When they were about fifty yards away, it was possible to differentiate two figures standing in the one car looking up at them. Within seconds the cars entered the chutes and stopped at the platform no more than five feet from the half-concealed, crouched threesome. Avrim and Shifrin were standing, looking out the window at them, smiling. They were grinning from ear to ear and they were stiff and stone cold dead.

"Rinsus Sardonicus," Shira gasped. "Just like we saw back in Vienna. What does it mean?"

"KGB," Max replied. "It means that they're not far away."

"I thought we'd have more time," Kurt said dejectedly. "They know where we are and it can only complicate things for u tomorrow."

Kurt opened the door to the cable car and he and Max entered it and examined the two bodies.

"Stiff as boards," Max said. "No question that it's strychnine. That's why they're still standing. They just had to be propped up against the side. You can see they were held there by hooking their belts around the handrail. Someone down there is having a good laugh at our expense."

Shira was becoming an old pro at death. She was not sickened as she had been in Vienna when she had first seen Ursula Gross. "What are we going to do with the bodies?" she asked.

"Well, they're really not going anywhere," Kurt answered. "We might just as well leave them there to stand guard for us."

They closed the cable car door and returned to the Hutte.

They went directly to the one room that they had selected to spend the evening before they went to their bedrooms later in the evening. It was the room that served as the smaller of the two dining rooms when the inn was open. The windows were comparatively narrow because of the harsh weather that high in the mountains so it was easy to cover them with blankets in order not to reveal themselves with the light on.

"I think we can relax for a little while," Kurt said. "Our little gadget tells us that no one else is up here. At least no one living. Nobody's going to climb that mountain in the pitch dark, but we can be damn sure that at daybreak they'll be coming up."

"Could somebody be up here already but far enough away to be out of radar range?" Shira asked.

"That's a possibility," Kurt answered, "although I sort of doubt it. No one else knows about our radar so they wouldn't be hiding at a distance. They'd be hiding in the hundred other possible places nearby. We'll be careful, though, and booby trap all the doors in the building tonight. Now let's gather around a table and I'll show and explain the map to you two."

They sat at a table in the middle of the dining room and Kurt unfolded the map that he and Ushie had drawn in Vienna. He felt a pang of grief as he opened the map. It was the first time he had looked at it since Vienna. In his mind, he could picture Ushie's excited, beautiful face as she helped him prepare it.

"It's in German, the way it was described to me, but I'll translate it for you as I speak," Kurt said. "This is how it was explained to me," Kurt winced as he said this because they were Ushie's words translated into English. "The vicinity is Lunersee by the Scesaplana. From the Douglas Hutte runs a path along the lake on the right side, that is, in the direction of the mountain is a large boulder that projects out of a clear area at the base of the mountain. Three paces before this boulder, covered by rocks is a shaft where everything is buried. To be more explicit, the path runs along the lake. Halfway between the Douglas Hutte and a large brook at the far side of the lake is a cleared area. From this, on the mountain side of the path is a cleared area from which projects a large boulder. Five meters from the path, which is three paces from the large boulder is a shaft. IN the shaft are the five containers and the metal attache case."

Kurt showed them both the sketch that he and Ushie had made which depicted what had been written.

"We have to remember," Kurt added, "that the Douglas Hutte they describe is not where we now are. In 1945, it was out on that peninsula that juts out into the lake." He pointed to current pictures that showed the peninsula. It was too dark for them to see it outside at that time. "Normally," he continued, "the path that Ushie described is underwater as is the shaft where every-thing is buried. Now, because of the water level being lowered, it would be out of water. In fact, there is probably no old path left. What we'll do tomorrow is measure the distance from where the old Hutte was to the brook on the new path, which would have to parallel the old path. We'll then simply head down toward the lake and if the old map is right and our detector works, we should pick it up easily. We can drive that small truck on the new path, load it up and be on the cable car going down. If we start as soon as it begins to get light, we can do it all within three hours. We can pass those coming up the mountain. They should be halfway up by then. By the time they spot us and get back down, we can be loaded up in our car and well on our way. We have one other advantage. It gets lighter up here sooner than down there in the valley so we'll gain a half an hour there. The whole thing will be a race against time."

"It sounds like a real cliff hanger," Shira said. "Everything has to go right the first time."

"You've got to think positively," Max said. "Kurt and I have been in just as tight spots before. That's what makes it so much fun. Now that that is all over with, let's eat the banquet that we brought along and break out the wine and booze."

They unpacked their military rations and spread them out on the table.

"Those are electric stoves in the kitchen," Kurt said. "We can turn them on and heat up some of this canned food in the rations."

"Good idea," Max replied. "Shira can do the honors and heat up our food. She's a woman, she's supposed to do those things."

"Chauvinist," Shira answered accusingly as she picked up the cans of food and took them into the kitchen.

Considering the circumstances, they had a pleasant evening. They heated up pork and beans, ground beef in gravy, and corned beef hash that were in the rations. They tasted like a gourmet's delight to the very hungry trio.

The two bottles of red wine did not last long. Shira, however, declined the cognac, even in the cool mountain air. She just wrapped a blanket around her and watched the other two, especially Max, finish off that bottle.

"We had better hit the sack," Kurt finally said. "We've got to get up very early in the morning when it's still dark. Let's booby trap the doors before we turn in."

"Piss call first," Max, who was half drunk shouted. There was no water as yet turned on in the building so there were no toilet facilities. "If you're afraid to go out in the dark alone, I'll be glad to escort you," he said to Shira. "I'll even hold your hand."

"Pervert," she laughed. "I'll go first."

"Don't piss in the lake," he shouted after her. "You might fall in and it's pretty cold."

After she returned, Kurt and Max followed suit.

"I'll booby trap the doors," Kurt said to Max. "In your condition, you're liable to blow us all up."

"Be my guest," Max replied as he walked off unsteadily toward his dormitory room. "See you bright and early."

Kurt quickly set up three booby traps with the plastic explosive and dynamite on the three entrance doors. I hope to hell that Max doesn't forget and wander out in the middle of the night, he said to himself.

Accompanied by Shira, he then felt his way through the pitch dark hall until he found their bedroom. They went immediately to their beds, one on each side of the small room, and tried to sleep. Anticipating what lay ahead of them the next day made them both sleep fitfully throughout the night.

XXVII

THE REVELATION

It was still dark when they woke. Kurt, checking his watch with the small pen light, found that it was five a.m. What woke him from his twilight sleep was the sound of cow bells that echoed through the mountains from the valley below.

It's pitch dark down there, he said to himself, but the cows can tell the time.

It would be starting to get light in about an hour and they wanted to be heading out to the site by that time. Shira heard him getting up and she, too, sat up in her bed. They did not have to bother dressing because they had never undressed, sleeping in their warm outer clothing. Shira had even kept her warm down jacket on throughout the night.

"It's crazy," were her first words. "The first thing that I thought about right now was that idiotic commercial about a couple waking up worrying about bad breath. I was worried about not being able to brush my teeth because we don't have any water."

Kurt laughed. "I'll bet that you didn't even bring your Scope."

"It's probably more of a subconscious desire not to think about what's in store for us today," she said.

"Christ, how can you do self analysis so early in the morning?" he asked. "Let's go get with it," he said, shining his small flashlight around the room to gather up his belongings. He put what he found in his knapsack and helped Shira do the same. They could hear Max getting up as they walked by his room. "I'll meet you upstairs," Max called out to them as they passed by.

"I'd better disconnect the booby traps," Kurt said when they had arrived in the dining room. He quickly went to the three doors and returned with the explosives.

Shira had turned on the light in the room whose windows were still covered. "I'll try to make some coffee," she said. There was some instant coffee in the military rations and she went outside to the lake to get the water.

She soon had the water heated and had prepared three cups of black coffee by the time Max came into the room.

"Ah, you've realized your lot in life," he said. "I'll have ham and eggs and toast also."

"I'll heat up a can of something," she said, "and you'll have to be satisfied."

"You could very easily satisfy me if you really wanted to," Max laughed.

"even at a time like this you can think only about such things," she scolded him.

By the time they had finished their quickly prepared breakfast, the pitch darkness outside was becoming lighter and the image of the mountains and lake started becoming more clear.

They packed all their equipment and belongings in the knapsacks and by the time the sky was a dark gray, they were loaded in the small truck and driving down the path toward the landmarks that they first had to find.

When they had gotten to the point on the path that was on a direct line with the peninsula where the original Douglas Hutte had been, they checked the mileage on the speedometer of the truck. They then drove the length of the path until they reached the brook which was the second landmark.

"According to the map, it should be halfway between these two landmarks," Kurt said. He quickly turned the truck around and, checking the mileage, drove back to what was halfway between the two landmarks.

He stopped the truck at the halfway point. "It has to be on a line directly toward the lake," he said as they all got out of the truck. So far they had used no more than twenty minutes in their race against time.

Max quickly assembled the metal detector and, switching it on, headed directly down the rocky mountain side toward the crater overlooking Lunersee. Kurt and Shira, carrying the knapsacks, followed close behind.

The detector emitted a steady, low, audio tone as Max, slowly edging downward, swept the area before him covering a width of about six feet. On several occasions he had to circle around large boulders that were in the direct path. There was no parallel path below that had been the original path before the water level was raised.

When they had descended about three fourths of the way between the new path and the water level, the intensity of the audio tone suddenly increased.

"Bingo," Max shouted. "This has got to be it." He quickly swept the area above, below, and on either side coming back to the point of its greatest intensity.

"There's even a large boulder here above it," Kurt said. "This must be where it is." Looking up, he could see that they were really at the base of a huge mountain with a sheer, flat face starting just above where they had parked the truck, projecting into the sky at least another thousand feet.

"I can see why they picked this spot," he said. "That flat face of the mountain is a marker that would never change. We'd better start digging." They had now used up forty five minutes of their race. "They're probably starting up the mountain now," he said. "We've got no more than three hours. Shira, set up the radar and point it in the direction of the Hutte. Let us know if you hear anything."

He and Max then started digging and pulling rocks away. The soil around the rocks was soft after having been submerged in water for so long so digging was relatively easy. Also, since it had been under water, there was no vegetation with roots to complicate their excavation. They were both working furiously, almost to a point of frenzy. The anticipation of what they were seeking and the time element of the danger from the valley below spurred them on. Even Shira was caught up in the excitement and volunteered to help dig.

"Just watch that radar and keep your eyes open," Kurt ordered. "There's only room for two of us to work here anyway."

After about a half an hour more, they had dug a hole of about five feet and the intensity of the audio sound was reaching a high pitch. Kurt, using a pick at that time, struck something that gave out a metallic sound. He crawled down into the hole that they had dug and started digging into the soft soil with his bare hands. The sun, which had come over the crest of the mountain from the east, shined directly into the hole which was dug at about a forty five degree angle into the mountain side. Kurt reached down and pulled out the metallic object that he had unearthed. It was a pair of German binoculars, still in good condition.

"That's strange," Kurt exclaimed as he started digging further with the shovel. Max was standing there looking puzzled at the binoculars.

With the next shovel, he hit something hard again. Scraping away the dirt it was quite obvious what it was as Kurt pulled the white object out of the hole. It was a skull with a pair of thick glasses still sticking to it as if welded on.

Shira, who had been lured away from her lookout post by the fascination of the discovery almost shouted out. "Binoculars, thick eyeglasses, the skull that's been there for a long time. It's got to be Mueller. Who else could it be?" Behind the skeleton was the first box.

"Konzett must have killed him and stuffed him in with the Kisten," he said. "No wonder he seemed to drop off the face of the earth. He's been dead all these years. That means that we only have to worry about Konzett. He must be around here somewhere."

"He is," Max said in a strange sounding voice. He pulled his 38 revolver and without saying a word, fired it into the air.

"What in the hell are you doing?" Kurt asked, startled by Max's behavior.

"Just stay in that hole where you are," Max ordered, "and you, Shira, give me your gun and sit over there next to the hole by your boyfriend."

Shira handed him the 38 that she had been carrying in her pocket and moved over next to Kurt.

Kurt felt completely defenseless. He had left his automatic in the pocket of the jacket that he had taken off and laid nearby when he started digging.

"You'll see Karl Konzett in a few minutes. Here he comes," Max said, pointing off in the direction at a small figure that was approaching. "He spent the night up here out of range of our radar."

Shira was dumbfounded. "Max, you're a traitor. How could you do this?" she asked.

Kurt did not say a word. He just stared at Max, everything suddenly beginning to become clear to him in his mind.

"Kurt, you're a stupid asshole," Max said. "You and I could have split this. There's enough here for both of us for the rest of our lives. But you're too much of an idealist. I knew you would never buy the idea. Where do you think all this gold is going to go? It would probably have been put in a vault somewhere where everyone could argue about who it belonged to. And what the fuck would we get out of it? A measly pension if we would ever live long enough to collect it? Those bastards back at Headquarters get all the credit and all the promotions and what the shit do we get? Not a fucking thing."

Max was almost beginning to rave as he worked himself into a frenzy, wildly waving his 38 at Kurt and Shira. The small distant figure became larger as it approached them, interrupting Max's tirade.

"Let me introduce Karl Konzett," Max said as Pruneface walked up to them with a Luger automatic in his hand. "Herr Hoffman, Fraulein Smith," Pruneface said, "it's a pleasure to meet you under these circumstances."

"I thought you were sharper than you were," Max said. "I almost gave it away to you down there in the restaurant. Do you remember in the briefings we were told about Konzett here having a dueling scar? I told you about Langer's Lines and aging, but as you can see, one of those lines on his face does not match the others. It's running in the wrong direction. In fact, the lines hid the scar. I spotted it immediately and after you got rid of his two PLO cohorts, I became his partner. Isn't that right, Herr Konzett?"

"It is much better this way," Konzett said. "Those Arabs might have become a problem. I really didn't trust them once we would have found the Kisten."

"You're a fine one to talk about trust," Kurt said, pointing at the skull.

"I see that you have met Kommandant Mueller," he answered. "It really was an unfortunate necessity. As the Kommandant of Dachau he was, as you Americans say, hot. Like Eichmann, he was high on the list of war criminals and he probably would have been apprehended. We couldn't take a chance on that happening and possibly leading to these Kisten. You might say he died for the Fatherland. That reminds me, Herr Doktor," he continued, speaking to Max. "We will have a nice hole here, especially when we remove the Kisten. Don't you think your friends here should join Oberst Mueller?"

"No, that won't do," Max answered. "I've got to make it look like I was killed along with them and we have to leave something behind for someone to find. Let's all walk back to the Douglas Hutte. I'll explain what I have in mind. In fact, if I say so myself, it's pure genius. I'm sure you would appreciate that, Kurt."

Pointing the 38 at Kurt and Shira, he ordered them to walk in front of him back to the Hutte.

"I almost nailed you back in Washington," he said to Kurt as they were walking the short distance. "I would have been given the responsibility of the assignment rather than you. Why you all the time? Why have I always been your back up? I'm as good, no, better than you. You even get all the ass, like her here," Max was working up into a frenzy the more he talked.

"He's really a full blown paranoid," Shira whispered to Kurt as they were walking beside each other with Max and Konzett following.

"I was counting on your Russkie bitch to kill you back in Vienna," Max continued. "Actually it was lucky that she didn't. I couldn't squeeze anything out of your Kraut girlfriend, even with the strychnine."

"You killed Ushie," Kurt shouted wheeling around in rage.

"Stop or I'll shoot and kill her here," Max shouted back pointing his gun at Shira.

"Well, it wasn't the KGB that was using strychnine after all," Kurt said. "Then it was you who did in the Israelis too."

"I thought that that was clever, didn't you? I told them that you and I wanted to meet them in Brand. It was really quite simple. I must admit that I enjoyed that. They were really obnoxious. I like to think of them leaving this world smiling. I even enjoyed throwing your Russkie's dog out of the window. That was a nice touch, don't you think? Actually, the damn dog bit me when I went up to get you."

"You are sick, you son of a bitch," Kurt shouted at him. "I should have suspected you from the beginning. You always did get your kicks out of killing and it was obvious that someone enjoyed those killings."

"And I'm going to enjoy putting you two away. I think even you would appreciate my plan," he said as they reached the Hutte. "Walk on down to the room that you two stayed in last night." On the way down to the room, he stopped and took the electric clock off the wall and took it with him. When they reached the room, with Konzett holding the gun on the two prisoners, Max bound both Kurt's and Shira's hands and feet with rope they had been carrying. Pushing one of the beds over against the outside wall, he lifted Shira and Kurt up on to the bed, opening the door-like window so they could look out and see the whole length of the Lunersee. Then, using surgical tape that he brought with him, he bound them securely to the bed frame.

"Since you both spent so much effort trying to find the gold, the least I can do is let you witness me taking it," Max said, laughing. "See, if you look out that window, you will be able to see Herr Konzett and me load it on the truck and out of here. And to show how generous I am, I'm going to provide you with some company."

Leaving Konzett to watch Shira and Kurt, he went out of the room and returned in a few minutes dragging a still smiling, stiff Avrim.

"They say smiling is contagious," he said. "Maybe it will make you two smile to have such pleasant company." He took off his watch and some identification from his pockets and stuffed them in the dead Avrim's pocket. "The other Jew will join Mueller back in the hole," he laughed. "We'll come back and get him with the truck. Isn't that even more ironic?" he asked. "Mueller gassed all those Jews and now he's going to sleep with one in his grave."

Konzett laughed loudly. "Herr Doktor, you are really a man after my own heart."

"And now for the finale," Max laughed. "And to think, Kurt, you are the one who taught me how to make bombs." Taking the plastic explosives, dynamite sticks, and percussion caps out of the knapsack, he sat down at the table in the room. He took the back off of the electric clock that he brought down from the dining room. Connecting wires from the percussion caps to the plastic explosive and the clock, he quickly constructed a time bomb.

"Let's see now," he said, "I'll set it for two hours. That will give Herr Konzett and me plenty of time to load up and take the cable car down. The generator has enough fuel for at least another six hours so everything will work out fine. This whole place should go, including the dam next to this building. When they find all the pieces, they'll think I was with you. They'll never even look for me. Now you have to admit it is beautiful, don't you, Kurt?"

"You bastard!" Kurt sneered at him. "Those Kisten will be heavy. I hope you two rupture yourselves hauling it up to the truck."

"Ingenuity is always the answer," Max laughed. "We simply open the boxes and take up half at a time. Why do you always underestimate me? And the piece d-resistance. You can not only watch us, you can hear us. I'll turn on the walkie-talkie for you and describe how everything looks. I want you both to share in all the fun."

He looked at Shira and stared at her. "It is a pity that you'll be going to waste. You should have slept with me rather than him. I'm really much better and you'll never know what you missed. On the other hand..." He did not finish his sentence as he went over to Shira who was lying on the bed. He reached down and unbuttoned the top of her stretch ski pants and with one tug he pulled her pants along with her bikini panties down to her bound ankles. He pulled her ski sweater up and ripped off her bra. "I'd like to fuck you right in front of your lover here," he giggled nervously, perspiration breaking out on his forehead as he started to run his hands over her body.

"You pervert," Shira screamed, spitting directly into his face.

With a shocked look on his face, he reared back and slapped her across the face with the back of his hand.

"Herr Doktor," Konzett intervened, "we should not waste time." He was obviously eager to see the cache that he had not seen for forty five y ears.

Max walked over to the table and plugged in the electric clock bomb. "I'll be able to buy a lot better than you now." Without saying anything more, he turned on the walkie-talkie that was on the table and motioning for Konzett to follow, left, leaving Shira still lying there half naked.

From the bed where they were tied, Kurt and Shira could see the two walking back to the shaft where the containers were. All along the way Max kept speaking through the walkie-talkie, almost every other word being a vulgarity.

"He is really a full blown paranoid now," Shira said.

They both struggled with their bonds but could not even begin to loosen them.

"I hated to see what he was doing to you," Kurt said to Shira. "But as you can see, there's nothing I could do."

"I'm scared," Shira said, her lips beginning to tremble. "How are we ever going to get out of this?"

The clock had already shown a half an hour. Avrim was lying stiff on the other bed with his eyes wide open staring at them, still smiling.

Kurt, who was worried more than he had ever been before in tight situations, did not answer. He just struggled harder, trying to loosen the ropes. He was able to rip the tape loose that bound his legs to the bed frame but that was all.

Max's voice continued crackling over the wall. "Well, you love birds," he said for the first time, not using profanity, "we have all the Kisten out and I'll open the first and describe all the goodies to you. I know you'll appreciate my gesture."

Over the turned up walkie-talkie, they could hear the clang of metal against metal as someone obviously was forcing a metal box open. There were two other sounds - one, a gasp and the other, a split second loud noise as the communication was suddenly cut off.

From their position on the bed, looking out the window, they could see it, about a half mile away before they could hear it. The side of the mountain where Max and Konzett were, exploded, the peak of the mountain teetering toward the lake just as the sound wave reached the Hutte, slamming the open windows shut, shattering glass all over the room and shaking the whole building. A second loud rumbling could be heard as the mountain peak became an avalanche, sending thousands of tons of boulders and rocks tumbling down into the Lunersee.

Kurt and Shira, even though they were covered with the shattered glass from the broken windows, stared speechlessly as they watched the whole side of the mountain falling into the lake.

The lake seemed to rise in quick retaliation, creating what looked like a huge tidal wave aiming it directly at the dam and the Douglas Hutte where they were.

They watched helplessly as the giant wall of water moved toward them. In what seemed like an eternity but was really only seconds, the large wave enveloped the building sending the water gushing through the open window, knocking over furniture and hurtling the three bodies around the room.

As the crest of the wave passed the Hutte, the water receded as if sucked out of the building by a vacuum, the water level of the lake, although not returning to its original level, settling at the foundation. The major force of the water had apparently shot over the top of the dam.

Shira and Kurt looked at each other. Shira had been torn free from the bed and was lying against the inside wall next to the still smiling Avrim. In spite of the shattered glass and the force of the water, neither was injured, not even with minor cuts.

Kurt, who had also been ripped loose from the bed, was able to find a large piece of glass and, edging over to the side of Shira, cut loose the rope holding her hands. She quickly untied the ropes around her legs, dressed herself and untied Kurt.

"We don't even have to worry about the bomb," Kurt said. He noticed that the clock, which was still plugged in, was no longer working. "The water must have shorted out the generator." He pulled out the plug and quickly disassembled the still-intact bomb.

"Let's go up and check the damage," he said as they both hurried down the hall and up the stairs to the main entrance.

It was amazing how everything seemed almost normal. All the buildings had been constructed of solid rock and most had been boarded up for the severe weather that usually occurs during the winter time. With the exception of some of the unprotected windows being broken, everything seemed intact. The water level, with the mountain face now in it, had actually receded to the level it reaches at its highest in the fall.

There was, however, no more mountain side where the Kisten had been buried. It, along with Max, Konzett, the five Kisten and all the secrets that it contained, were all gone under tons of rocks and boulders.

"It had to have been Kommandant Mueller who did that," Kurt said to Shira, standing next to him with her arm around him as if asking for security after what they had been through. "No one ever knew what Mueller had put in that fifth Kisten, evidently not even Konzett. That was the biggest booby trap that I ever saw. I guess Mueller got his revenge after all these years. Now they're all buried down there together."

"I think that we had better get out of here," he added. "That blast has probably shaken up the whole part of this country and the Austrian border police will be all over the place soon. We'll have to walk down the mountain with the cable car knocked out."

They walked to the ledge that was the beginning of the path that led down the mountain side.

Kurt looked back at Lunersee, now calm and again beautiful. "All the people that died for that," he said, "many that I never knew, and some that I knew very well. It was all for nothing. I must admit that Max really pulled the wool over my eyes. I was so concerned about the KGB, the Nazis, the Israelis and the Austrians that I completely overlooked him. I should have known that he was as crazy as hell. It was always there but I didn't see it. And the most ironic thing is that The Company thought that I was the one flipping out. Isn't that why they sent you along? What did The Company want you to do if I had been the one to go off the deep end? Kill me?"

He looked questioningly at Shira.

She did not answer as she followed him down the steep mountain path.

XXVIII

TERMINATION

Gandria: One Month Later

Waiting for the inevitable, many thoughts raced through his mind. It all seemed so senseless now. All the killing that had happened just in the past month. Why did Ushie and Sonya have to die? For what? The hardliners would probably not survive because of Perestroika. Regardless of any political changes in the future, Sonya died to assure their survival if she were successful. What would the old man, the chief hardliner, her own father, think of all this? Revenge against her killer would help calm his conscience, if he had a conscience.

Kurt left the door to his hotel room unlocked. It wouldn't have made any difference to an old pro. He did turn off the lights after the prostitute had left. It had to appear that he was asleep. He just sat in the lounge chair reliving his whole life.

There was no elevator in the small hotel, just uncarpeted stairs which would creak when someone climbed or descended them. From the third floor, the top floor, where his room was, it was possible to hear anybody coming.

Just before midnight, his thoughts were interrupted by the sound of steps of someone coming up the stairs. It was slow and deliberate, as if someone didn't want to be heard. There were no other guests on the third floor so it had to be someone coming to find him. He could tell that there was only one person. The steps stopped outside his door. The handle on the door slowly moved and the door opened. Whoever was entering the room had also turned off the hallway lights to prevent his silhouette from being seen as he entered the room.

The light from the full moon, however, shining through the wide open window, clearly illuminated the room and the door to the hallway. Kurt reflexly picked up his automatic and pointed it at the figure of the person who had entered the room with his gun also raised. With the moonlight exposing the visitor, Kurt could see that it was a Makarov P51 being aimed at him and it was the old man who held the gun.

Even in the subdued light, Kurt could see the hate in the eyes of the old man being directed at him. There was no hate in Kurt's eyes, nor fear, but strangely also not a feeling of resignation.

There were the two men with their weapons raised and pointed at each other. Neither said a word. Two fingers started to squeeze two triggers at the same time, one deliberately, the other reflexly.

Because of the silencer, there was no loud report, just one barely heard thud as the assassin-designed hair trigger won the race. There was no pain at all because the hole directly between the eyes ended the torment and hate. Reflex self preservation reunited father and daughter.

SEQUEL - NICHOLAI